"One more thing," Sara said. "Just because I've hired you doesn't mean I'm going to...sleep with you."

Bull's-eye. Arrow straight through Liam's male ego. Just when he thought he was beginning to figure her out, she threw him another curve.

"What gave you the idea that I wanted to—" Then it hit him. *The kiss.* Of course. "I'm sorry if I acted inappropriately," he said, not meaning a word of it. "But as I remember, you kissed me, too."

Her full lips twitched as she studied him. "Well, now that our curiosity about each other has been satisfied, we should have no more problems sticking to business."

So she was only satisfying her curiosity, was she?

Dear Harlequin Intrigue Reader,

August marks a special month at Harlequin Intrigue as we commemorate our twentieth anniversary! Over the past two decades we've satisfied our devoted readers' diverse appetites with a vast smorgasbord of romantic suspense page-turners. Now, as we look forward to the future, we continue to stand by our promise to deliver thrilling mysteries penned by stellar authors.

As part of our celebration, our much-anticipated new promotion, ECLIPSE, takes flight. With one book planned per month, these stirring Gothic-inspired stories will sweep you into an entrancing landscape of danger, deceit…and desire. Leona Karr sets the stage for mind-bending mystery with debut title, *A Dangerous Inheritance*.

A high-risk undercover assignment turns treacherous when smoldering seduction turns to forbidden love, in *Bulletproof Billionaire* by Mallory Kane, the second installment of NEW ORLEANS CONFIDENTIAL. Then, peril closes in on two torn-apart lovers, in *Midnight Disclosures*—Rita Herron's latest book in her spine-tingling medical research series, NIGHTHAWK ISLAND.

Patricia Rosemoor proves that the fear of the unknown can be a real aphrodisiac in *On the List*—the fourth installment of CLUB UNDERCOVER. Code blue! Patients are mysteriously dropping like flies in Boston General Hospital, and it's a race against time to prevent the killer from striking again, in *Intensive Care* by Jessica Andersen.

To round off an unforgettable month, Jackie Manning returns to the lineup with *Sudden Alliance*—a woman-in-jeopardy tale fraught with nonstop action…and a lethal attraction!

Join in on the festivities by checking out all our selections this month!

Sincerely,

Denise O'Sullivan
Harlequin Intrigue Senior Editor

SUDDEN ALLIANCE
JACKIE MANNING

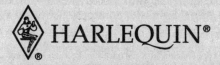

TORONTO • NEW YORK • LONDON
AMSTERDAM • PARIS • SYDNEY • HAMBURG
STOCKHOLM • ATHENS • TOKYO • MILAN • MADRID
PRAGUE • WARSAW • BUDAPEST • AUCKLAND

ISBN 0-373-22794-9

SUDDEN ALLIANCE

Copyright © 2004 by Jackie Manning

This edition published by arrangement with Harlequin Books S.A.

® and TM are trademarks of the publisher. Trademarks indicated with ® are registered in the United States Patent and Trademark Office, the Canadian Trade Marks Office and in other countries.

www.eHarlequin.com

Printed in U.S.A.

ABOUT THE AUTHOR

Jackie Manning wrote and published her first and last newspaper at the age of six. Her editorial career came to a screeching halt when her mother bought the first copy and realized that Jackie had exposed the family secrets. Undaunted, Jackie started making up stories, and she's been spinning tales ever since. Today, she lives with her husband, Tom (Bert), and their shih tzu, Emperor Foo Foo. Jackie loves to hear from her readers. You can e-mail her at jackie@jackiemanning.com or write to her at P.O. Box 1739, Waterville, ME 04903-1739.

Books by Jackie Manning

HARLEQUIN INTRIGUE
708—TOUGH AS NAILS
794—SUDDEN ALLIANCE

HARLEQUIN HISTORICALS
398—A WISH FOR NICHOLAS
454—SILVER HEARTS
562—TAMING THE DUKE

Previously published under the pseudonym Jackie Summers

HARLEQUIN HISTORICALS
260—EMBRACE THE DAWN

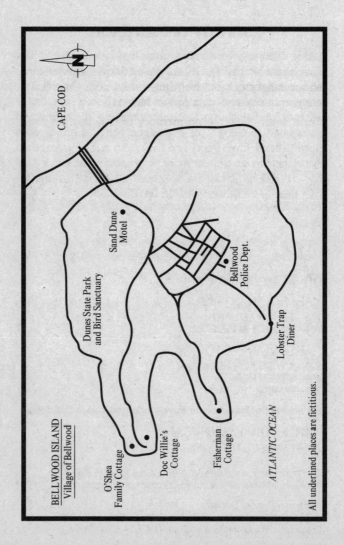

BELLWOOD ISLAND
Village of Bellwood

CAPE COD

N

Sand Dune
Motel

Dunes State Park
and Bird Sanctuary

Bellwood
Police Dept.

O'Shea
Family Cottage

Doc Willie's
Cottage

Fisherman
Cottage

Lobster Trap
Diner

ATLANTIC OCEAN

All underlined places are fictitious.

CAST OF CHARACTERS

Liam O'Shea—Ex-special forces, now a covert specialist for the TALON-6 Agency, knows everything about danger. But can his highly tuned skills keep the woman he loves from a pair of killers?

Sara Regis—She has no memory of her past. All she knows about her future is that somebody wants her dead.

Trent Sherburne—He wants political power, and he'll stop at nothing to get it.

Kitty Sherburne—Is she playing a game that's turning deadly?

Jeremy Regis—The brother Sara can't remember. Does he have a personal reason to keep a safe distance from her?

Al Ranelli and Francie Zarella—Bellwood Island police officers and childhood friends of Liam O'Shea.

The Ziegler Brothers—Hired hit men. Who paid these killers to hunt Sara down?

The Boss—Who is the man who wants Sara dead, and why?

This book is dedicated to Cheryl Shepard Rissman.
I love you, sis.

Special thanks to two of the dearest friends
anyone could have: Susanne MacDonald
and Karen Tukovits. I admire you both so much.
Thanks for your support and love.

And to my darling husband. I love you.

Chapter One

"Holy—" A jolt of adrenaline shot through Liam as he gripped the steering wheel. Was the fog playing tricks on him, or was that really a woman he saw, staggering along the side of the narrow road at almost four in the morning?

The woman froze like a terrified rabbit, her eyes wide with shock as she stared into the car's headlights. Her face contorted in horror, and when she screamed the sound was as piercing as if the hounds of hell were chasing her. A moment later, she swayed and collapsed to the ground.

Liam swerved the convertible to avoid hitting her, then downshifted into second. With a few deft motions, he spun the Alpha Romeo in a 180-degree turn, tires screeching in the early morning stillness.

The low beams of his car illuminated the sprawled figure lying on the sandy shoulder of the road. Leaping from the vehicle, he lunged toward where she had fallen.

Kneeling beside her, he cradled her head in his lap and brushed long strands of hair from her face. Probing gently, he found an egg-shaped lump near her temple. She moaned when his fingers gently touched the injury, her back arching in pain.

He felt for broken bones and was relieved that despite

numerous bloody scratches along her arms and legs—incredibly long and shapely legs—her wounds appeared to be mostly superficial. All except for that bump on the head. She might be suffering from a concussion.

Holding her carefully, he shrugged free of his windbreaker, then very gently cradled her again, slipping it around her shoulders. As he did so her eyes flew open—enormous green eyes, if the color wasn't a shadowy trick of the headlights.

Her oval face paled with terror. "No! No! No!" she screamed, fighting him with almost superhuman strength. Her fingers curled as if to scratch him.

Liam released her, afraid to further frighten her, and scooted back. "Hey, lady! I'm one of the good guys. I'm here to help." As she struggled to her feet, her long hair swung forward, and he saw bits of leaves and twigs embedded in it. The jeans she wore were ripped, and her yellow T-shirt looked as if she'd fought her way out of a bramble bush.

"What happened? Were you in an accident?"

He knew this isolated stretch of dunes, dubbed "lovers' lane," was a favorite with the local teenagers. But she looked much older. Twenty-five or so? Still, who could tell? Maybe her boyfriend had dumped her because her answer to Romeo was no. Or, Liam thought with a sickening twist in his gut, had she been raped?

"I'm not going to hurt you," he said gently, setting aside his fury at sick bastards who got their kicks from violating and abusing women. "I have a phone in my car. I'm going to call for help."

"No!" She screamed the word and stepped back, her hands shielding her eyes from the car's headlights.

"I want to help you. Are you hurt?" Liam asked, afraid to touch her. He feared she might be going into shock. "Are you alone? Can you tell me what happened?"

Instead of answering, she turned and bolted toward the dunes. But before she had taken three steps, she staggered, struggling for balance. Her arms flailed like a child learning how to ice-skate. Liam rushed to her side just before her knees buckled. He leaned her against his chest and, for a moment, she appeared too weak to protest. Her moist breath fanned his neck as she laid her head against the V of his open sport shirt. He sensed she was only resting long enough to regain her equilibrium, then she'd try to escape once more. Damn, he wished she'd let him help her.

Liam glanced along the deserted dunes that lined the road, hoping for some sign of a car, but all he saw was deepening shadows and fog. He knew that at this time of early morning, in early spring, the chance of someone coming along this stretch of summer cottages was practically nil.

He glanced down at the woman in his arms. "Look, miss," he said, noticing that she wasn't wearing a gold band or any kind of ring. Nor was there an indentation on her ring finger from a discarded wedding band. "My sister is a doctor. I'm on my way to see her at the family cottage, a few miles up the road. She can help you."

"No! Leave me alone." Her fists rapped his chest in a futile attempt to push him away. He winced inwardly, knowing her protests took every ounce of what little strength she had left.

"You're in no condition to be alone," he said, grasping her by the shoulders. "I grew up in these parts and I know that no one lives here this time of year. We're on a narrow peninsula with an isolated bird sanctuary on one side and the ocean on the other." His gaze took in her T-shirt and jeans. "You're not dressed for this weather, either."

She dragged air into her lungs and lifted her head, gazing blindly into his eyes. The whimpering sound she made at the back of her throat reminded him of a wounded puppy. Something twisted in his gut. She needed his protection, whether she wanted it or not. For a moment she quieted, and he was filled with hope that maybe she understood that he was trying to help her.

He put his arm around her as he led her toward his car. "There, that's not so bad, is it?" he said. She took several steps beside him, then suddenly jerked away again, as though his touch were deadly. Then she totally collapsed.

GRAVEL CRUNCHED ALONG the driveway as Liam's convertible pulled to a stop in front of the weathered clapboard cottage at the end of the peninsula. He honked the horn several times. Almost immediately, the porch lights sprang to life, and a blond woman poked her head around the screen door.

"Is that you, Liam?" Dr. Bridget O'Shea Thomas flung open the door and, when he called to her, she wrapped her chenille robe tightly around herself and ran down the steps. A collie lumbered beside her heels, barking a welcome. "Quiet, Bounder!" Bridget ordered, her feet beating a tattoo along the seashell-lined path. "With this fog I didn't expect you until morning," she said, "but…" She stopped when she saw Liam wasn't alone.

His sister sighed. "I wish you'd have told me before bringing a…" Her words trailed off when she saw the woman slumped against Liam's shoulder, in the front seat of the sports car, apparently asleep.

Liam turned off the ignition, pulled on the emergency brake and turned to the unconscious woman beside him. "Get a bed ready, Bridget. I found her alongside the road. She may be going into shock."

Bridget ordered the collie back to the porch. Then she dashed around the passenger side of the car and leaned over the woman. Her movements deft and professional, she lifted the woman's eyelids. "I'll call Willie," she said. "Luckily she drove down with me yesterday."

Liam should have known that Bridget would have brought Dr. Wilhelmina Prescott, the O'Shea family's long-time friend and summer neighbor since Liam and his sisters were babies.

"Carry her upstairs," Bridget ordered. "Put her in your room." The look she gave Liam was cautiously controlled, but he recognized the concern in his sister's eyes. Without another word, Bridget turned and made a beeline to the cottage.

Carrying the woman, Liam followed his sister up the porch steps. "Are David and the girls here with you?" he asked Bridget, knowing that her husband loved the old family cottage as much as his wife.

"No. Linda had basketball practice and Kathy had a swim meet. David is driving them later this morning."

When Liam approached the stairway, Bridget called out, "Watch your step. Kate waxed the floors yesterday and they're as slippery as an ice rink." Bridget stood on the first-floor landing and punched numbers into her cell phone.

Liam's boots clomped loudly on the polished oak steps as the familiar smells of furniture wax, mothballs and pine cleaning solution filled his nostrils. As he carried the slight body up the stairs, the woman's arms dangled lifelessly.

The collie was waiting on the landing, his tail thumping loudly on the floorboards. Then the dog raced excit-edly down the hall and whined outside Liam's closed bed-room door.

"Don't jump on the bed," Liam warned as he opened it.

The collie scampered inside and leaped on the bed. Liam scowled at the animal as he pressed the light switch with his elbow. The room sprang to life, and with it mem-ories of his boyhood summers. Army football pennants and posters of rock-and-roll icons shared wall space with mod-els of fighter jets and helicopters.

"Let me help you," Bridget said as she came up beside him, her medical bag in hand. "I called Willie," she added, folding back the red plaid bedspread on the dou-ble bed.

The injured woman groaned softly as Liam gently laid her down. Against the pristine white sheets, her scratches and cuts stood out like red flags along her arms and legs. Above her right temple, the goose-egg-size lump he'd felt earlier was visible now. Her fingernails were dirty, ripped and bleeding. She moaned, her head thrashing back and forth against the pillows.

"Did she have a purse or any ID?" Bridget asked, fum-bling inside her leather medical bag.

"Not that I could see in the car headlights," Liam said, reaching for the cell phone hooked to his belt. "As soon as it's light, I'll go back and check around."

Bridget inspected the woman's arms for needle tracks, then flicked back her eyelids, flashing a penlight on and off. "She's not on drugs, which was my first thought. Nor do I smell alcohol on her breath." She glanced up. "Who are you calling?"

"The police," he said as he made his way toward the

door. "Maybe she wandered from the scene of an accident. Or maybe there's a missing persons report out on her."

"Good idea. I want to get her cleaned up a bit before Willie gets here."

"Okay," Liam said, moving toward the door. "I'll be right outside if you need me." He stepped into the hall, shutting the door on his way out.

The receptionist at the Bellwood Island Police Department answered on the first ring. "Connect me to Detective Zarella," Liam said, unable to forget the fear in the woman's eyes. It had been a long time since he'd seen such terror. Not since Iraq and those fearful dark eyes of women searching for their loved ones among the war casualties. He blocked off the thought when Detective Frances Zarella answered.

"Francie, it's Liam. Were any accident reports filed today, or any missing persons reported in the past couple days?"

"Hmm. I don't hear from you in six months and I don't even rate a 'Hi, Francie, how ya been since I stole those ten bucks from you?'"

Liam smiled. "Don't be a sore loser, Francie. You lost that sawbuck fair and square. Next time, bet on a winning team."

He heard her warm laughter on the other end of the line. "Don't you know that it's an act of treason for a New Englander to bet on any team except the Red Sox?"

"That's not loyalty. That's stupidity." He grinned when he heard her swear.

"Hold on while I check."

The light teasing with Francie did little to distract Liam's thoughts from the mysterious woman lying in the next room.

"An eighty-two-year-old man wandered from the Bellwood Harbor Nursing Home last night," Francie said, coming back on the line. "But he was found several hours later. We had a report of a missing seven-year-old boy at 10:05 a.m. yesterday, but his mother called back to say he'd fallen asleep in the back seat of his grandfather's car. That's it, Liam." She hesitated. "Why, what's up?"

"Nothing," he said, surprising himself when he realized that he'd decided to wait until the woman regained consciousness before reporting the incident to the police. More surprising, he didn't know why. Maybe it was because she'd seemed so terrified. Until he knew who or what she was afraid of, he'd trust his instincts. "I'll stop in and say hi before I head back to the city. I promise."

"You'd better. Al will be wicked mad if you dare leave for the Big Apple before he has a chance to trade war stories with you."

"Well, I know better than to tick off your partner. Take care, Francie. And thanks."

He clicked off the phone and absently hooked it back onto his belt, his mind on the unconscious woman. Maybe she wasn't from this area of Cape Cod. The tourist season wouldn't be starting for another four weeks or more. Maybe she had been visiting one of the new year-round homes that had sprung up along the coast recently, and she'd taken a wrong turn. He hadn't seen her car, which brought him back to his first thought—that she'd been dropped off to fend for herself.

He strode back toward his room, determined to solve the mystery. When he knocked, he heard his sister say, "Come on in, Liam. I'm just about finished."

As Liam stepped inside, he was surprised to find the woman alert. She jerked her head up and glanced around the room.

"You're safe, dear," Bridget said in a gentle voice. She was sitting beside the bed. "You're with friends."

The woman's green eyes fixed on Liam. Her face had been washed, so the cuts and scratches stood out even more against her ivory complexion. Her hair had been smoothed back, and she was dressed in one of Bridget's flannel nightgowns.

Liam stepped to the fireplace mantel and leaned against it, wondering if she recognized him as the man who'd found her. Her stare held no sign of recognition.

"That's my brother, Liam," Bridget said, as if to remove the woman's confusion. "He's the man who found you on the road. I'm a doctor. A pediatrician. He brought you to our cottage because he knew you'd be safe here. I've called a neighbor who is an internist. I want her to have a look at you. Then I'd like to take you to the local hospital—"

"No!" The woman swung around and stared at Bridget. "I can't stay here!" She threw the cover back and struggled to sit up.

Bridget shot a worried look at Liam. "You're free to go, dear," she said, "but please let us help you." This woman was in no condition to leave on her own. "Can I call someone for you? It's four in the morning. Do you have a husband, a boyfriend, someone who is worried about you?"

The woman looked confused, then rubbed her head. "I—I don't know."

"You don't know?" Bridget repeated, then glanced worriedly at Liam again.

Liam knew from the bump on her head that she might be suffering from amnesia. He motioned to Bridget, then stepped back into the hall. A minute later, she met him outside the door.

"She's terrified of being confined and suffering extreme panic—symptomatic of hysterical amnesia. Did you find out anything at the police station?" she whispered.

"No. Nothing. Do you think she's been attacked?"

"I'll wait for Willie to take a look at her. Willie helped organize the local rape crisis center here on the island and will know how to approach her. The woman should be x-rayed, and checked by a trauma team at the E.R."

"Not without her permission. When I offered to take her to the hospital, I think she would have bolted off across the dunes if she hadn't collapsed first."

"Why don't you go downstairs and wait for Willie while I stay with our mystery guest?"

"Did you turn on the security alarm? You'll need to keep an eye on her," Liam said. "I've got a feeling she'll try to sneak off the minute your back is turned."

Bridget rubbed her forehead thoughtfully. "Okay, brother. I won't forget." She gave him a playful shove toward the stairs.

He remembered how reluctant Bridget had been when he'd first suggested that TALON-6, the security company in which he was a partner, install the latest bells-and-whistles surveillance system to protect the family's summer cottage. Regardless of his older sister's suspicions of high-tech gadgets, he knew she realized that the equipment he'd installed at the beach cottage was a good idea.

Several minutes later, Liam was pulling a set of sheets, a blanket and a pillow from the hall linen closet when he heard Bridget's light footfalls behind him. "I'll sleep on the living room couch," he said. "I'll keep an eye on the front door in case our houseguest decides to sneak out."

Bridget stood on tiptoe, reached up to pull out a hand-stitched quilt from the top shelf. "That might be a good idea." She shrugged. "She seems very agitated. Who knows what she might do?" She walked toward the stairs with Liam. "She's very lucky. With the darkness and the patchy fog, it's a wonder you saw her."

The coincidence wasn't lost on Liam, either. His sixth sense had been tingling ever since he'd spotted the woman. Something wasn't right.

Maybe he was just paranoid. He'd had very little sleep in the last twenty-four hours, and had been back in the country only since last night. No doubt what he'd been through was finally catching up with him.

Liam took the quilt without argument. "I'll send Willie upstairs as soon as she arrives."

"SO YOU'RE SAYING she wasn't raped?" Liam asked awhile later as he studied their neighbor. He'd known the gray-haired woman for as long as he could remember. Dressed in a faded flannel shirt, sleeves rolled up to her deeply tanned elbows, Dr. Wilhelmina Prescott returned his gaze over the top of her wire-rimmed glasses.

"That I'm sure of," Willie said, folding her stethoscope inside her black leather medical bag. "I can't tell you much more until she's x-rayed. She might have short-term memory loss from that bump on the head."

"Did she tell you what happened?"

Willie shook her head. "No, but I gave her something to relax her. After she's rested, I think she'll be more receptive." She leaned over to stroke the collie's head. "Keep an eye on her. Don't let her sleep too long. Bridget knows what to do, and she'll take the first watch."

Willie peered at Liam with a no-nonsense look in her

gray eyes. "Your sister said you drove up here from New York City in this fog."

"Now, Willie," he said lightly. "The highway was clear until I reached the island, and then there were only patches of it." When his answer failed to melt the censure in her flinty gaze, Liam added, "I just came off a mission in the Middle East and needed to finish debriefing. I left as soon as I could."

Willie's lips firmed into a tight line. "Bridget and your other sisters worry about you, Liam." She shook her head. "You're getting too old for living on the edge."

"Let me walk you to your cottage," Liam said, hoping to avoid the usual lecture. Dear Willie meant well, but ever since his Special Forces buddy and close friend, Master Sergeant Stewart Thomas, who was also Bridget's husband's brother, had been killed in a covert mission four years ago, Willie and his sisters had been clamoring for Liam to quit taking covert ops and find a less dangerous profession.

"It's time you settled down, got married. Your life is too risky, Liam. It's time you grew up."

Liam kissed Willie's leathery cheek. "Thanks for worrying about me, Will, but I'm fine."

"Don't think you can use your Irish charm on me," she said, but the smile in her eyes betrayed her words. "You'll be thirty-four in June. Time to get married. Settle down like your sisters."

"I'll marry you tomorrow, Willie, if you'll have me."

Her mouth curled and her eyes twinkled. "Ah, if I were forty years younger, I'd give you a run for your money."

Liam heard her chuckle as he helped her into her yellow hooded slicker. She was still grinning when she grabbed her medical bag.

"If anything changes, give me a holler."

"I will," he said, "and thanks for coming over so soon." His thoughts turned back to the woman lying upstairs. Thank God she hadn't been raped. Yet whatever had spooked her might have been as traumatic or worse. He followed Willie toward the porch steps, preparing to walk her to her cottage.

"Stay where you are," she said, pulling the hood over her short gray curls. "I've been making my way around these dunes since you were a twinkle in your ma's eye." She stomped down the porch steps, as agile as a woman half her age. "Get some sleep, Liam. You're still as handsome as sin, but you look as tired as I feel."

He chuckled softly. "'Night, Willie."

"Don't forget your niece's baptism is at one o'clock. Maureen will be sorely disappointed if you miss it." Willie's voice rang with spirit. "See you in church."

Liam nodded, then watched until the old woman disappeared behind the shoulder-high clumps of sea grass that sprouted from the shifting dunes between the O'Shea summer cottage and Willie's place at the end of the road.

He was about to shut off the porch light when Bridget's footfalls on the stairs caught his attention. He looked up to see her walking toward him, a pair of scuffed running shoes in her hand. "I laid a change of clean clothing out for her in her room. I think we're close to the same size." Bridget looked up. "Did Willie leave already?"

"Yeah," he said. "Think I should go after Willie to be sure she gets home okay?" he asked.

Bridget frowned, brushing past him. "Heaven forbid! She's like a mountain goat along the dunes." She laid the shoes on the welcome mat, inside the door. "Besides, you'd hurt her feelings. She'd think you decided she was getting old." Bridget straightened, bracing her hands at the small of her back as she studied him. "I'm so glad you're finally home." She moved toward him, then put her palm on his shoulder as if she needed to feel him to be sure he was really there. "Even if it's only for a few days."

He gave a deep sigh. "One day, I'm afraid, sis. I planned to head back to New York late tonight."

Bridget withdrew her hand and glared at him. "Damn it, Liam. David and the girls and all our sisters and their families will be here in a few hours." She swallowed, as though fighting back her temper. "You haven't been home in two years. And that was for Mom's funeral."

Liam knew the issue wasn't that he was away from the family, but that Bridget feared what had happened to Stewart would happen to him. He waited, giving his sister the time she needed to pull herself together.

"How's the patient?" he asked when she had quieted, purposely changing the subject.

"When I left her, she was asleep." Bridget leaned on the porch railing, gazing across the driveway at the silvery wisps of fog hovering among the shadowy pines. When she turned back to him, her eyes were thoughtful. "You've been bringing home strays ever since you were old enough to crawl. But you're going to have your hands full with this one, brother."

Surprised, he frowned at her. "What do you mean?"

Bridget pursed her lips. "I wonder what our mystery lady was running from?" One eyebrow lifted. "I hope you don't get involved, Liam. She's in a lot of trouble."

Liam completely agreed. Yet he didn't want his sister to worry. "There you go, conjuring up your Celtic dark side." He put his arm around her and gently guided her toward the stairs. "Get some rest while your patient sleeps. Wake me in a few hours and I'll take over."

Bridget shot him a look over her shoulder. "Don't think you can dismiss me this easily, Liam. For all we know, we may be harboring a fugitive. She might be putting us in danger."

"Or she's an innocent victim who needs our help."

Bridget blinked back a rush of sudden emotion. "The trouble with you, Liam, is you're attracted to danger. You always have been, even when you were little." Her voice was sharp and accusing. "Why can't you enjoy a normal job? Your friends Al and Francie love adventure, too. But they joined the police force. At least they can have a family life, live here on the island. No, my brother has to chase danger all over the globe—" Her voice broke and she turned away.

Liam knew that his teammate's death had affected all his sisters, but Bridget was the most sensitive. Her husband was Stewart's brother, after all. Yet Liam knew her anger would be piling up between them unless he faced this straight on. "Bridget, I'm not Stewart. You heard him say that when a bullet has your name on it, there's nothing you can do."

She snorted. "Do you really believe that? Do you think his wife and daughter believe that? I know you and your partners at TALON-6 have tried to make it up to Liz and Bailey. Paying for Bailey's education and looking out for her under everyone's watchful eye while she works as a receptionist for TALON-6 is very noble. But don't you think Bailey and her mother would rather have Stewart back in a heartbeat than—" Her eyes narrowed and she took a deep breath. "Dear God, I didn't want to get into this, but now that I have—" Bridget's eyes glittered with anger. "You know what I think? I think Stewart was a selfish bastard who never grew up. His place was with Liz and Bailey, not on a secret mission in some Colombian jungle fighting the—" Her anger gave way to tears, and she swiped at her eyes. "Damn it, Liam. You were right there with him. It might have been you when that rocket fired—"

He drew her into a hug. "Liz knew who Stewart was when she married him. She loved him anyway."

Bridget pulled away, then took a hankie from her sweater pocket and wiped her eyes. When her tears had stopped, he added, "I don't want you to worry, but I can't live your play-it-safe life just because you and the family want me to. If you can't accept me for who I am, sis, then I'm sorry. But I'm very good at what I do. I've been trained by the best our government has to offer. Since I've joined TALON-6, I can protect innocent people against the most inhuman situations."

She swallowed. "You're also a hopeless adrenaline junkie." She forced a weak smile. "Of course I'm proud of you, Liam." Her lips twisted. "I'm just so afraid for you."

He squeezed her hand. "Trust me."

Bridget shot him a look. "I better get back to our patient."

He sighed as he watched her climb the stairs. Damn, he loved her, but how could he expect his sisters to understand? Thank God he'd made the choice never to marry.

Most people didn't understand the covert operations so necessary in today's world. How could they? Most of the top-secret surveillance equipment he'd designed was unknown to the general public. Information technology was of prime importance to military power, and working for agencies like TALON-6 provided him the opportunity to do what he did best. But Stewart had understood.

Liam's stomach clenched like a fist as the memory of that Colombian night four years ago slammed into his brain. As though it were yesterday, he could still feel the sweat drip down his body, smell the rotting, fecund earth and hear the screeching of monkeys in the treetops as the TALON-6 team slipped silently through the dark, wet jungle toward the guerilla camp of the National Liberation Army, or ELN.

In record time, they'd wended their way past sleeping and half-drunken guards, to rescue the DEA agent held prisoner. Once they had cut the man loose from his cage, they'd carried him back, retracing their path through the mountains.

Like clockwork, the night op had gone successfully, according to plan. Too successfully, they'd soon discovered. As the team had crisscrossed the jungle on ancient footpaths, an ambush was waiting. Stewart, in rear guard position, his .308 Remington 700 sniper rifle held to his shoulder, had shuffle-stepped backward, waiting to draw a bead on the first ELN guerilla who showed himself. For an exceptionally large man—six foot five and two hundred eighty pounds of muscle—he'd moved deceptively fast.

Within three hundred yards of where their Blackhawk helicopter waited, a Russian B-40 rocket had sailed overhead and, with an earth-shattering blast, made a direct hit on the tree beside Stewart. Wood splinters and shrapnel had sliced the predawn air in a bloody dance of death. Moments earlier, Liam would have taken the hit.

He had made the first move, opening fire with a steady hail of bullets from his M-60. "We've got to get Stewart," he had screamed as strong arms dragged him aboard the copter.

"He's gone, Liam," the team officer, Mike Landis, had said."

"No, we've got to bring him back." Liam had turned to leap out of the open hatch just as the copter lifted and swerved, narrowly missing another rocket.

The explosion had lit up the ground, revealing scores of guerillas in camouflage fatigues swarming from the jungle. Gunfire had strafed the gray dawn as the Blackhawk pulled away from what was now a burning inferno.

Their mission had been successful. The TALON-6 team had rescued the DEA agent from ELN.

Liam closed his eyes. Four years. He'd thought he'd gotten past the haunting memories that were burned into his soul. Maybe he never would.

Was Stewart a junkie who'd needed an even higher dose of adrenaline to keep feeling good? Or had he taken on the dangerous jobs and fed off the danger to get the job done? And would a real adrenaline addict be able to tell the difference?

WHEN LIAM RETURNED to the living room awhile later, the collie was stretched out on the couch, ears pointed, claiming his territory. "Okay, Bounder. Get up. You're sleeping on the porch."

The dog studied him as Liam walked to the porch doorway and pointed to the stuffed rattan settee. The collie bounded playfully on the couch, as if enjoying the game.

Liam's gaze dropped to the scuffed running shoes lying on the mat. *Her shoes.* He picked up the right sneaker and examined it. A small pocket, fastened with Velcro, ran along the top of the padded tongue. He ripped open the fastener. There, inside, was a key with a tag. His curiosity rose a notch as he moved toward the living room light and peered at the tag. Sand Dune Motel, 26.

So the mystery lady was staying at the only motel open this time of year in Bellwood. He slid the key into his hip pocket as he strode toward the telephone directory in the hall desk drawer.

Chapter Two

She opened her eyes and stared at the white ceiling. Far off, birds were chirping. She turned her head toward the sound. Tie-back white curtains fluttered at the slightly opened window. The air felt cold and smelled of the sea. She tried to sit up, but when the pounding in her head got worse, she dropped back on the starched pillowcase.

Her hand flew to her forehead, and she was surprised to find a bandage covering a lump on her temple. Her legs ached and she noticed her hands were bandaged, too. Her heart hammered as panic exploded inside her.

Where was she? Why couldn't she remember how she'd gotten here? Worse, who was she? She raked her mind for answers but found nothing. She stared around the room for clues. Model airplanes hung from the ceiling. Posters of rock stars covered one wall. Black hockey skates and a West Point sports jacket hung from a peg.

What was she doing in a man's room? The ghostly image of a tall, dark-haired stranger shattered the cobwebs of her mind. He wasn't a ghost but a real man, the man who had rescued her in the fog. His voice had been low and gentle. *I want to help you.* Yes, she remembered his voice, deep yet kind. Was this his room?

Why couldn't she remember anything else? Had she driven here? She couldn't recall if she owned a car. Another wave of panic shook her and she forced herself to think, but her mind roared like a hollow drum. Uncertainty combated with instinct. Somehow she felt safe here, yet at the same time she knew she was in danger. Until she knew what was going on, how could she trust anyone? She had to get away. She had to run.

She bolted from the bed, almost tripping on the long nightgown she wore. Flannel. Nothing she recognized. On the top of the oak dresser were a pair of jeans, a yellow T-shirt and underwear, all neatly folded. Were they hers? If not, then whose? They didn't look familiar, but, then, nothing did.

Slowly, she forced her feet to move, not wanting to repeat the thunderbolt of pain through her skull. When her toes reached the hooked rug in the middle of the room, she noticed the mirror over the dresser. Carefully, she inched forward until she could see into the looking glass.

She gave a sharp intake of breath as she stared at herself. Beneath her bandaged forehead, wide green eyes gazed back at her. Long, tangled red hair hung down her shoulders. Despite her scratches and bruises, she didn't think she was seriously hurt, except for her pounding head. And the panic that she was a virtual stranger!

Who am I? I must have a name! "My name is…" Seconds ticked into minutes as she struggled to remember. She squeezed her eyes shut and forced herself to focus. Tears sprang to her eyes as she fought off the panic.

From nowhere came the sharp image of a flash of white light, with the sound of screaming…a woman's screams.

Danger exploded through her veins. She tasted the

metallic fear in her mouth as she remembered the feeling of terror. *Run! Run! Run for your life!*

She had to get away! Her fingers shook as she jerked the nightgown over her head. Her bandaged hands trembled as she tore into the pile of neatly folded clothing. The fresh smell of laundry soap rushed at her as she yanked the T-shirt over her head and dressed hurriedly in the jeans. Blessedly, they fit. When she'd finished, she pulled her hair back from her face and turned around, searching for her shoes. The sudden movement brought her stomach jumping into her throat. She grabbed on to the side of the dresser until the room stopped spinning. She had to get away before they—before they…what? Who was she afraid of?

Unable to find her shoes, she made her way barefoot to the door. Twisting the knob slowly, she quietly pulled it open and peered up and down the wallpapered corridor. The stairway was a few feet to the left. Listening, she heard nothing except the tick-tick of the grandfather clock at the end of the hallway.

Was she alone in the house? She couldn't take the chance of being seen. Somehow, she knew that much. She tiptoed toward the stairs. The smooth wood felt cold beneath her tender feet. As she crept downstairs, the third step creaked loudly. She paused, then glanced behind her.

When no one appeared, she continued until she reached the bottom step. Only then did she dare glance around. The living room was to the right; straight ahead was the front door, with a window through which she could see a screened porch and trees beyond the driveway. Her heart hammered in her chest as she tiptoed across the shiny oak floor toward the porch.

"Well, top o' the morning, Sara Elizabeth Regis."

Startled, she jumped as a tall, broad-shouldered man stepped out from the living room to block her path. *The man in the fog.* In daylight, he seemed large enough to fill the doorway. His thumbs were looped in the front pockets of his jeans, and he was naked from the waist up.

Fear shattered her insides as she stared at him. His face would be considered handsome except for those sapphire eyes that glinted dangerously. He was smiling, but his eyes didn't know it. His face was deeply tanned, as was all of his upper body. A black shadow of a beard covered his strong, sweeping jaw. When he folded his arms across his wide chest, his biceps bulged.

"Let me not forget my manners. I'm Liam O'Shea." He dangled a key in front of her. "Before I give you back your key, you and I are going for a little ride."

ARIEL ZIEGLER, known as Ziggy to the family, pulled the Cadillac into the no-parking zone in front of the Sand Dune Motel. Above the door marked Office a vacancy sign flashed on and off. He turned to his brother Vinny, who slouched beside him in the passenger seat. "Stay in the car," Ziggy muttered. "Leave this to me, see?"

Vinny swung his head up and glared at him. "An' why the hell should you go an' not me?"

Ziggy glanced at the rearview mirror and smiled widely, checking his teeth. Satisfied, he frowned back at his brother. "'Cause this job takes finesse."

"Finesse?" Vinny almost spat the word. "I got finesse!"

Ziggy ignored him as he tugged at the cuffs of his navy jacket and adjusted his gold cuff links. "Stay here with your trap shut and your eyes open. If you see her, come and warn me."

Vinny folded his arms and slumped farther down in the leather seat. "Hurry back. I'm hungry."

"You're always hungry." Ziggy slid from the driver's seat and slammed the car door. He glanced again along the row of nearly vacant motel units. Only six cars were in sight on this side of the building. Perfect. Slight chance anyone would be around to notice, just in case the redhead was still here. If she recognized him, he'd have to act fast and that might spell trouble.

He strolled leisurely up the paved walk toward the glassed entrance. When he saw his reflection in the window, he slicked his hair back with his hand.

The skinny young punk behind the registration desk looked up when Ziggy sauntered to the counter. He chuckled. Hell, this would be like taking a lollipop from a kid.

"Hi there," Ziggy said easily, placing his hand on the counter as he read the punk's name tag. Harold. Ziggy flashed his three-carat diamond pinkie ring directly in front of the kid. "Say, Harold. I wonder if you can help me." Before the youth could answer, Ziggy pressed on. "I found an expensive camera. Foreign job. The owner is a tall redhead." Ziggy gestured, the universal sign language for a well-built broad. "She's stacked, if you know what I mean. About twenty-five or so. She left the camera and case along the shore early today. I think she's stayin' here."

"Sorry, sir. That information is strictly confidential."

Ziggy clenched both fists on the counter. His forearm muscles bulged, straining the seams of his suit.

Harold's eyes bugged and he swallowed nervously. "Uh, what's the lady's name?"

Ziggy swallowed a laugh. "Well, that's the trouble, Harold. If I knew, I'd call her up myself. But while she was taking pictures of seagulls, I was, ah, watching her." He smiled for effect. "She has long, long legs and I've always been fond of redheads." He glanced around the alcove where the kid was standing, making sure they were alone. "I was hoping to leave my number, and when she realized that I'd found her camera equipment, well…" He winked, hoping the dumb kid got his drift. "I'm sure the lady would be most appreciative."

"I'd be happy to hold the camera for her here at the desk. If you'd like to include a note, I'll be sure she gets it."

Ziggy bit back a coarse oath. "Just tell me her name and room number, kid. I want to handle this myself."

Ziggy took another breath as the kid hesitated, deciding whether or not to tell him. Ziggy felt like punching the little creep in the puss. But instead, he pulled a roll of bills from his hip pocket and peeled a C-note from the top. "Here, Harold," he said, slapping the bill on the counter. "Take your girl out tonight on me." He winked again, then smiled when the clerk's eyes widened at the prospect of keeping the hundred-dollar bill.

Harold glanced around the empty reception area, then looked at the crisp bill. He snatched at the cash and slid it into his back pocket. "Just a minute, sir. I'll print out a copy of her registration form."

The clerk spun around and punched in some keys at the computer. Within a minute, the printer whirred as the report appeared from the top of the machine.

"Here you are, sir." The youth darted another glance around the empty lobby before he slid the copy across the counter to him.

Ziggy read her name and room number, then smiled. He pulled out a white card he had previously prepared. "Don't you forget to give this number to Sara before she checks out, you hear?" He couldn't quite keep his face straight as he handed the card to the clerk.

"Yes, sir."

Ziggy's smile faded and he suddenly glowered. "If she doesn't call me, I'll be back, and I'll collect every dollar from your hide. Understand?"

Harold's eyes widened, and damn if his skinny face didn't turn chalky white. Ziggy chuckled as he turned and made his way toward the glass entrance. "Have a nice day, kid!" he yelled over his shoulder before he pushed open the door.

Vinny was playing the car radio when Ziggy climbed back into the front seat. "Shut that off," he ordered, pulling out his cell phone.

"You're not the boss," Vinny muttered, his attention on the numbers that his brother was punching into the phone. Damn, why hadn't the boss given his phone number to him, too? Vinny scowled, but turned off the radio, more interested in listening to his older brother's conversation.

"Yeah. It's me," Ziggy said into the receiver. "I found her."

Vinny felt a rush of excitement. He was glad his brother had chosen him as his partner. But he couldn't let Ziggy know how much this job meant to him. Vinny needed a chance to show his big brother how clever he was. And this job was big. So big that it would sweep them into the big time. When this was over, he'd be known as Vincent Ziegler, not Ziggy Ziegler's little brother.

Ziggy's eyes glowed with satisfaction as he nodded. "Sure, boss. You got it." He looked at Vinny and smiled as he snapped the lid over the phone and slid it in his breast pocket. "We get to whack her."

Vinny took in a deep breath to cover his excitement. "How?"

Ziggy almost beamed. "Boss says he doesn't want to know." His smile widened, white teeth shining. "Still got those jack-in-the-boxes in the trunk from your last job?"

Vinny tried to act cool. "Yeah."

Ziggy nodded. "Then let's get to work." He glanced at the printout, then at the blue Ford Sedan parked at the end of a line of cars behind the motel. It took him only seconds to confirm the license number. "Come on, Vinny. Let's see how good you really are. I'll give you three minutes to wire that bomb under the hood."

"SARA REGIS? You're saying that's my name?" She felt a rush of hope.

Liam's dark blue eyes looked almost black when he shot her a sidelong glance from the driver's seat as the red convertible tore down the road. "You tell me," he said finally.

His answer confused her. Earlier, the man had seemed willing to help her. Now it seemed as if he didn't trust her.

"I—I don't know who I am. If you know anything about me, please tell me." She studied him, her hands fighting the long windblown strands of red hair that blew in her face. Finally she wrapped her hair into a thick rope, aware of his darting glances as she tucked the coil inside the neck of her T-shirt.

The way his eyes darkened as he watched her made her breath catch. Sara became aware that the T-shirt she wore seemed snug against the full rise of her breasts.

His hands tensed at the wheel, but he kept his voice even. "I called the motel where you're staying. It's down the road about five miles, in case you're wondering." He darted a glance at her, as if waiting for her reaction. When she gave none, he continued. "The desk clerk wouldn't tell me the occupant's name in unit 26, so I asked him to ring your room and he put me through to your voice mail. By that time it was a little after 6:00 a.m. I figured if someone was staying with you, they would have answered the phone. So I drove over and looked around."

"You went inside my room?"

His dark eyebrows lifted at her surprise. "So you remember staying there?"

She struggled to recall anything that might help her. "No, I—I don't." The words caught in her throat.

His large hands squeezed the steering wheel. "As I said, I looked around. Your bag was on the bed." He took his right hand from the wheel and slid it inside his jacket pocket, then pulled out a slim leather billfold and handed it to her. "See for yourself." He waited for her to flick open the wallet.

"Your driver's license says you're Sara Elizabeth Regis. The photo matches you—unless you have a twin sister."

Sara studied the photo ID. "It looks like me."

"The slacks and jacket I found hanging in the closet were size eight." His deep sapphire gaze raked over her again. "I'd say that was about right."

"Could you tell if someone else was staying in the room?"

His gaze remained on the road. "I'd say you were alone. The bed hadn't been disturbed."

Her mind tried to piece together the information. Her clothes? Would she recognize them even if they were hers? She glanced back at the driver's license. "Sara Elizabeth Regis," she read aloud, hoping the name would sound familiar. "One hundred ninety-six East Monroe Street, East Bennington, Massachusetts."

"East Bennington is the other side of Boston," he said. "About a four-hour drive from here."

"Four hours?" She glanced out the windshield, taking in his words. Her gaze drifted across the endless miles of sand dunes and patches of barberry thickets that stretched toward the sea. She searched for anything that might trigger a memory, but nothing looked familiar.

"If I'm from East Bennington, then what brought me here? It's too early for the tourist season. Why would I come all this way? Was I meeting someone?"

"Maybe if you try to think back to when I found you… Do you remember anything at all?"

"I remember you and the two kind women who took care of me. I remember a dog—a collie, I think." She looked at him. "Or did I dream it?"

His eyes were sympathetic. "No, you weren't dreaming. After I found you wandering along the coast road this morning, I brought you to our family cottage on the point. Bridget, my oldest sister, and Willie , the doctor next door, took care of you. My sister enjoys taking a week off from her practice in Boston to stay at the cottage while getting the place ready for the summer."

Sara couldn't help noticing how handsome Liam looked when he wasn't frowning. Unwelcome shivers of awareness made her arms tingle. "Your sister Bridget," she said, distracting herself from the inappropriate response she was having to this man beside her. "Does she have a family?"

"Her husband, David, and her kids will be coming later this morning, along with most of the O'Shea tribe. I have six sisters, all married. I was the only boy." He shot her a smile, and her stomach fluttered.

Was *he* married? He didn't have a gold band on his left

hand, but that didn't necessarily mean… She shook her head. "Does your family get together often?"

"We try. Today, almost all the clan will be congregating for the baptism of the newest member."

She liked the way his eyes warmed when he spoke of his family. What was the matter with her? She might be married or at least engaged. Why was she reacting like this?

"Do you have…children?" she asked.

His lips curved, crinkling the corners of his eyes. "No, much to my sisters' chagrin." His smile broadened. "Of course, they would like to see me marry first."

Something in the way he said that made her cheeks warm. "You and your sister have been very kind. I don't think I've thanked you properly. I'm very grateful it was you who found me."

"Try not to worry. Maybe once you see the motel and your things, your memory will come back."

The thought of leaving the safety of Liam's car and going into a strange place suddenly filled her with unexplained panic—at something unseen, yet so terrifying that she had to look away to keep Liam from noticing. She fought through the panic, but it was hopeless. Maybe if she concentrated on what she could remember…

Her gaze studied the corded muscles along Liam's tanned forearms as he gripped the wheel. An image of how he had looked earlier this morning when he'd practically jumped out at her, half-naked, flashed through her mind. He was definitely athletic, with incredibly broad shoulders, muscular biceps and forearms. The thick black hair covering his wide chest had trailed down to a V inside his jeans. She felt her cheeks blush at the thought. She turned her face away, hoping he wouldn't notice.

Dear God, but this man was attractive. Maybe she didn't have the right to look at any man like that. *Was* she married? Did she have a lover? Children? Her gaze flew to her own hand. No ring. No watch on either wrist. No jewelry of any kind. Nothing.

Her hands weren't callused. What did she do for a living? Was she good at what she did? Why would she think of such a thing?

Sara turned toward him. "Did you say the older woman who helped your sister take care of me was called Dr. Willie?" She shook her head. "It's all so fuzzy. Like a dream."

He nodded. "Dr. Wilhelmina Prescott. She's an internist who summers here on the island who still makes house calls. Dr. Willie is a legend around these parts." He raised his brows and glanced at her. "You weren't very cooperative. You refused to go to the hospital. Willie and my sister think you should be x-rayed, and I was hoping that later you'd let me take you to the E.R."

"No!" Gasping, she clutched the dashboard with one hand and the armrest with the other. Her eyes squeezed shut as she fought the white panic, like a snowstorm in her mind.

"Are you okay?" He pulled the car to the side of the road and parked, his eyes filled with genuine concern. "Take deep breaths. You're having a panic attack."

She struggled for control, gulping air. "I—I don't know what's wrong with me. All I know is that if I go to the hospital, something terrible will happen." Even to herself, she knew her reasoning wasn't making sense.

Liam put his strong arm around her shoulders. She leaned into his hard chest, fighting the overwhelming terror with his comforting embrace. Was she a fool to trust him? She didn't know. Yet something about him made her want to believe she could. Ignoring her pounding heart through willpower alone, she forced herself to focus on the man beside her.

She breathed in the clean scent of his aftershave. His black leather jacket was open, and against her cheek, the soft cotton fabric of his black T-shirt felt comforting. Blue-black stubble covered his strong jaw. A thin scar creased his chin left of the cleft. She stared at his firm, chiseled lips. Lips made for laughing, for teasing, for kissing.

She blinked free of the trance and pushed away. "I—I'm okay," she said, her voice a scratchy whisper.

His piercing blue gaze questioned her. "You're not okay. Let me take you to emergency."

"No!" Sara took in several deep gasps, aware of his arm still curled firmly about her shoulders. "Maybe later," she added, not wanting to appear hysterical. "First, let's go to the motel. Maybe if I see something familiar…" She held on to that hope as she stole another sidelong glance at him.

His arm uncurled from her shoulders, and he straightened, restarting the engine. The wind tousled his thick black hair as he pulled the convertible onto the road.

She drew a wisp of hair from her face and turned to stare out the windshield.

"The motel isn't much farther," he said finally. "Officially, we're on an island, Bellwood Island, which is connected to the mainland by a causeway. The island is surrounded by sand dunes, which makes a great tourist attraction. The town of Bellwood Harbor has a winter population of 260, swelling to 20,000 between the Fourth of July and Labor Day."

She glanced at the lobster boats bobbing in the harbor.

"Nothing seems familiar." She stared out the window, her head reeling in an effort to remember anything. Along Main Street, empty colonial homes and vacant boutiques lined both sides, silently waiting for their owners to return with the warm weather. Empty flower boxes hung from the storefront windows, waiting for summer's red geraniums, blue verbenas and white petunias to spill from the planters. An empty flagpole stood in the park square, and she could imagine Old Glory waving proudly as the Fourth of July parade streamed past.

So she knew about small New England towns, after all. Was her memory coming back? The idea filled her with excitement and dread. Dear God, why was everything so confusing?

Judging by the dashboard clock, it had taken them less than five minutes to drive through the village. Now more sand dunes stretched along both sides of the road. To the east, the Atlantic glistened, a blue horizon. When her eyes turned back to the road, an L-shaped single-story building appeared ahead. She stared blankly at the white block letters painted across the black slanted roof: SAND DUNE MOTEL.

Now maybe she'd find some answers.

"NOTHING LOOKS FAMILIAR?" Liam asked, relieved that his voice didn't betray the skepticism he was feeling. From what Willie had said, Sara hadn't suffered enough of a physical head trauma to produce complete amnesia. He found it hard to believe she couldn't remember *something*.

He jammed his fists into his pockets and studied her as she examined the slacks, cotton turtleneck and windbreaker hanging inside the closet.

"I obviously wasn't planning to stay long," she said finally, removing the jacket from the hanger and sliding her arm through the sleeve. So far, she'd said very little about what was going on inside that lovely head of hers.

Damn, but he couldn't figure her out. Was she for real, or was she putting on an Academy Award performance? Sara was hardly his idea of a covert operator, yet he couldn't rule it out.

Only last week, Interpol had notified the TALON-6 headquarters in New York City that a terrorist had been arrested in London and plea-bargained with them, offering information about a plan to steal the Land-Net 17, Liam's latest design for an electronic security net. Was Sara part of that plan? He thought of that silky red hair and those long, incredible legs. Hell, everyone including the local priest knew that Liam O'Shea had a weakness for tall, beautiful redheads.

Anything was possible. Until the schematics for his security net were safely in the hands of the Defense Department's Advanced Research Projects Agency, Liam knew he couldn't leave anything to chance. Especially a disarming redhead who looked as though she'd just stepped out of his most erotic dream.

He felt like a bastard for doubting her, yet he wouldn't put it past the terrorist mentality to think they could infiltrate TALON-6 with a woman like Sara. He'd made no secret of the fact that he was a self-proclaimed protector of alluring, downtrodden women. Especially a woman with sexy-as-sin looks combined with innocence and vulnerability. He was the first to admit it would be his favorite way to go down.

She turned toward him as she took a seat on the edge of the king-size bed. Her fingers sifted through the meager contents of a straw bag. She was truly stunning, he decided. Her hair hung down her back in a lustrous curtain of red. Long eyelashes swept her cheekbones as she studied the set of keys, the billfold and a tube of lipstick, as though she could piece together the framework of her life from these few articles.

What must it be like to lose a lifetime of personal memories? What was it like to feel mentally naked and completely vulnerable? He felt a tug of compassion for what she must be going through. Yet how could he possibly imagine the depth of her fear and panic?

Was there a special man in her life? Had the guy told her how very desirable she was? For a brief, insane moment, Liam wanted to be that man.

He swallowed against the surge of heated desire. He'd better get some sleep. He was becoming delusional. He shook away the thought and strode toward the window. Across the road he could see an expanse of sun-bleached sand, then cold gray sea for miles. A sailboat tilted back and forth in the breeze. For an odd moment, Liam was reminded of when he was six years old and had found a stray kitten after Labor Day along the sand dunes. Some bastard had abandoned the animal. His mom had let him keep it and he'd called it Tiger. He glanced back at Sara, whose head was bent over the assorted items in her hand. Would tender loving care heal her as it had his pet?

She must have sensed him watching her because she lifted her head and that megawatt green-eyed gaze fixed on him. He fought back the urge to pick her up and cradle her in his arms.

She wasn't a lost kitten. And until he received the results of the background check that he'd asked his

TALON-6 partner, Clete Lawton, to run, Liam needed to keep his emotional distance.

"If you're about through," he said, giving his watch a glance, "I think we should leave."

"Nothing looks familiar," she said, brushing her hair away from her face. "It's as if these things belong to someone else." She put the gold cap back on the tube of coral lipstick, then opened the billfold and stared again at the driver's license and her photo. She lifted her gaze to his, and if she was acting, he sure as hell admired her talent.

Still, she hadn't noticed one thing. He picked up her straw bag from where she'd left it on the bed and pulled out the picture of a man in his early thirties, standing in front of a palm tree. Liam had found the photo hidden in a side pocket in the lining of her bag when he'd gone through her possessions earlier that morning. At the time, he'd wondered if the photograph would trigger her memory. "Know who he is?" Liam asked her.

She stared at the photo, then shook her head. "No."

"Is he Gregory Urquhart?"

"I—I don't know. Should I?"

"Urquhart is listed as the person to contact in case of emergency." Liam lifted a brow as he showed her the ID card inside her wallet. "Think this is an emergency, Sara?" He couldn't quite hide the sarcasm from his voice.

Her lips opened slightly. "I don't know. Y-yes. Yes, it is."

Was Urquhart her ex-husband? Lover? Why else would she be hiding his photo? Was she running from him? Or to him?

Sara put her head in her hands. "Liam, I'm trying the best I can. I don't know why I came here. Was I passing through? Was I planning to meet someone?" She leaned over and reached for the phone on the bedside table. She glanced at Urquhart's telephone number, then lifted the receiver.

Liam stopped her. "If you're calling Urquhart from this phone, I don't think it's a good idea."

"Why not? He must know who I am."

"Okay, but let's not use this phone." Liam took the receiver from her fingers. "I've got a cell phone in my car. Why don't you pack your things, and if you want, I'll drive you back to the cottage? You can call Urquhart on the way. By the time we get there, my family will have left for church. The place will be quiet and you can rest."

She rose, picked up the set of car keys from the top of the dresser. "I obviously own a car. I'll follow you back to the cottage."

"Good idea." Liam slid the mirrored closet door open and pulled out a small floral piece of luggage that he'd seen when he first checked out her room. Opening it on the bed, he stood back.

She pulled a blue, long-sleeved T-shirt from a hanger and began folding it into the suitcase. "I feel like these are someone else's clothes and I'm stealing them," she said with a weak smile. When she looked away, a jab of sympathy charged through him and he had to physically stop himself from touching her.

"Don't worry, Sara," he said instead. "The answers will come when you're ready. Just relax." He picked up the photo of the smiling young man and slipped it inside her open bag.

"Can you guess why you might have come to Bellwood?" he asked as she finished packing.

"No." She gave a slight shrug as she closed the lid of the suitcase.

No? Not even a feeble attempt at a guess? He felt slightly irritated with himself. Should he have let her call Urquhart? Or would that have signaled her accomplice that she had made contact with Liam? He was beginning to doubt his own instincts. Was she playing him? Well, damn it, there was one way to find out, once and for all.

Something flickered in those pretty green irises when he came over and pulled her to him. His body brushed hers, and he felt her tremble when he wrapped his arms around her. She didn't resist when he pulled her closer. He found himself breathing in the scent of the sea in her hair.

Her breath caught; he felt her stiffen, but her eyelids fluttered shut. Morning sunlight slanted through the window, making a reddish halo of her hair. He could feel her heart hammering in her chest, or was it his own?

He was afraid that if he kissed her she might bolt out of the room, into her car and out of his life. That is, if she was innocent...

And if she wasn't? He took in a slow breath as he dragged the tip of his tongue along her full lower lip. Testing. Teasing. Taunting.

She didn't bolt. She didn't throw herself into his arms, either. Those ripe lips parted slightly, and he was lost.

He hadn't expected her mouth to be so warm, so sweet, so trusting. Kissing her was like slipping into a deep, delightful abyss. The kiss deepened, and the groan he heard vibrating low was his own.

This was no femme fatale. This was a flesh-and-blood woman. A beautiful, appealing woman who had stepped out of his fantasies and into his world. But at what cost? A woman like this could be more dangerous to a man than a thousand land mines.

He released her and stepped back, wanting to shake off the fog that had settled over his brain. What a foolish thing to do. He should say something. Instead, he made a helpless gesture with his hands.

Her green eyes were wide, confused. He made fists of his fingers to keep himself from pulling back a glistening red strand from her cheek. "I'll wait for you outside," he said, ignoring the underlying reason that he had to leave. If he didn't get out of that room, he'd take her into his arms again.

Chapter Three

"Thank you, Ms. Regis," said the desk clerk as he slid Sara's credit card through the machine. Liam couldn't help noticing the young man's appreciative glances at her from behind the counter as he finished preparing her checkout statement.

If Sara noticed, she gave no sign. Nor did she seem aware of her exceptional beauty. Yes, she was beautiful. Not in that flashy, glittery way he usually found attractive in women. But this woman had skin the color of clotted cream, and eyes as green as the first shamrock to greet the April sunshine.

Hell, when the rest of his family, especially his other sisters, arrived this morning, they would take one look at Sara Regis and think that he'd finally brought home "the one."

"Oh, we found your camera," the clerk said to Sara, almost as an afterthought.

She looked up from signing her credit card statement. "My camera?"

"Yeah. A man stopped in here a little more than an hour ago."

"Did this man have a name?" Liam asked.

"No, but he left his phone number." The clerk turned and

pulled a plain business card from the mail slot for room 26. "Feel free to use the house phone, Ms. Regis."

Liam reached for the card just as Sara did. "Thanks," he said, snatching it from the clerk's fingers." He looked at the youth. "Where's the camera?"

"The man didn't leave it." The clerk shrugged. "He wanted the lady to call him first."

The hair on the back of Liam's neck stood up. Something didn't sound right about this. He looked at Sara. "It will be quicker if you call from the car."

Her expression didn't give a hint of what she was thinking. "Okay." She looked back at the clerk. "Thank you."

When they were outside, she snatched the card from his hand. "I'm not helpless." Her green eyes glittered with agitation. "I'm perfectly capable of calling the number myself."

"I know you're not helpless," Liam said, "and I'm sorry if I gave that impression." He was overreacting, something he never did, but he couldn't ignore the possibility that this man who had her camera was connected with whatever had terrified her. Liam whipped out his cell phone and gave it to Sara. "Here, why don't you call the number? Maybe if you hear the man's voice, it will trigger your memory."

Sara bit her lip as she took the phone. "I hope so. Maybe he knows why I came here this weekend."

Liam's uneasiness increased as he watched her punch in the numbers. She acted calm, yet her shoulders stiffened, a mannerism he'd noticed before when she'd been overly tense.

She put the receiver to her ear. A few seconds later, her green eyes widened. "I don't understand." She repeated the number on the card. "A man left me this number to call. He said he had found my camera."

Her face paled as she listened to the conversation on the

other end of the line. Liam's senses went into full alert. "What's the matter?" he asked.

She handed him the phone without explanation. He grabbed it from her trembling fingers.

"Who is this?" he demanded, almost shouting into the mouthpiece.

"I already told the lady. This is the Bellwood Funeral Home."

"Did a man from there go to the Sand Dune Motel early this morning and say he'd found a camera?"

"Like I told the lady, no. What is this, some kind of joke?"

"Let me speak to the owner."

"You're speaking to the owner, and I have no time for games," he said indignantly, then hung up.

Liam clicked off the phone, then caught Sara's gaze. She shook her head, glancing at the business card in her hand. "I know I dialed correctly. The man verified the number written on the card." She tucked the card into her bag. "Maybe we should go there and question each employee?"

Liam didn't want to squelch her hopes, but the whole camera story sounded fishy. If someone had found a camera, why not leave it for her at the desk? Maybe Sara had a point. If they spoke to the other employees, someone might recognize her. "Good idea. Let's go," he said.

A few minutes later, after they had stowed Sara's bag in the trunk of Liam's sports car, they walked around the motel to the rear parking lot.

She held her fingers over her eyes, squinting into the bright sunlight. "Omigod. I have no idea which car is mine."

He looked at the cars parked in a row along the back of the building, then at the keys in her hand. "No problem. You have one of those new automatic ignition starters on your key ring. Just click the button, and whichever car starts is yours."

She pulled back her hair from her face as she studied the keys in her palm, then smiled at him. "You're a genius," she said, and pressed the starter button.

SARA FELT THE EXPLOSION before her brain processed what was happening. A force like a giant fist jerked her from the pavement and carried her toward the motel with the impact of a freight train. She felt herself cannon through the air and land with Liam, entwined in his strong embrace, against an evergreen hedge.

Heat burned her skin. Corrosive smoke filled her lungs. She choked on the acidic fumes as she peeked over his shoulder at what was left of her car.

The row of vehicles in which it had been parked now looked like a mound of burning, twisted metal, a smoking inferno. Although the explosion had occurred several seconds ago, plumes of black smoke, flying metal and debris still spiraled through the air.

"What happened?" she asked, her ears ringing.

Liam held her, frantically searching her face. "Are you hurt?" Pure terror edged his voice.

She glanced down at herself and realized her body was shaking uncontrollably. "My ears…I can barely hear you." Then she realized he might be hurt, too. "Liam?" she cried, her voice rising. "Are you okay?" She ran trembling fingers over his face, her heart hammering with fear.

"Yeah, I'm fine." He winced in pain as he moved beneath her, then shot her a crooked smile. "Really, I'm okay."

She stared at him warily. He was rubbing his shoulder. Black particles of soot clung to his skin, but he looked…incredibly wonderful. Her body sagged with relief, but she couldn't suppress the shudder that ran through her.

"We're both lucky," he said as he picked an evergreen needle from her hair. "We were far enough away from the explosion to keep from being burned, and the hedge broke our fall." He stood to help her to her feet, glancing over at the fire, which was burning out of control.

Several cleaning women in white uniforms hurried outside, screaming and shouting excitedly. Guests burst from their rooms, their yells adding to the din. A man, dressed only in striped pajama bottoms dashed barefoot from the door of his motel unit into the street.

"What could have happened?" Sara asked, unable to take her eyes from the blazing inferno.

"We'll know for sure once the police arrive and the bomb squad gives their report, but I think your car was wired."

She swung around to face him. "Wired? You mean someone wanted to blow up my car?" Her face froze as the possibility struck her.

Someone wanted to kill her. If she had turned on the ignition when she was sitting in the car, she'd be dead now.

Panic shot through her like a bolt of lightning. "I've got to get away," she cried, pulling out of Liam's grasp. She staggered a few steps before his large hands grabbed her shoulders.

Liam was reminded of when he'd first found her, lost and afraid and trying to run away from some unseen terror. He held her, wanting desperately to find a way to calm her. Finally she stopped struggling and looked up at him, her eyes wide with terror.

"If someone is trying to kill me, I'm endangering you, too. You could have been killed."

"Don't worry about me," he said. "Come on, let's go to my car. It's lucky I parked by the front door." As they made their way around the motel he smiled to himself. When was the last time a woman had cared about his safety? That is, a woman with whom he didn't share the same gene pool? He was surprised to find he liked the feeling.

As they neared the corner of the building, the desk clerk burst into view, nearly running into them. He stopped in his tracks when he saw the smoking inferno in the rear parking lot. His jaw dropped, then he turned to Liam and Sara. "My God, look at you! What the hell happened?"

Ignoring his question, Liam asked instead, "What did that man with the camera look like?"

The desk clerk shaded his eyes with a hand as he gazed at Liam. "He was almost as tall as you. Black, shiny hair, like Elvis Presley's." The clerk made a disapproving face. "Heavy in the shoulders and arms, like a wrestler. And he had a diamond ring the size of a doorknob."

Liam frowned. "Did he speak with the local accent?"

"No, more New Jersey or the Bronx. My sister's husband is from the Bronx and he talks like this guy did."

Now we're getting somewhere, Liam thought. "Anything else?"

"He had long arms. He lumbered when he walked, like he was skating almost." The clerk scratched his head. "I saw his car. Yeah, a classy set of wheels."

Liam looked up. "Did you get the license number?"

"Er, no. I was too busy looking at the Caddy. Black. Tinted glass. And the fanciest set of gold hubcaps I ever saw."

"Did he mention where I'd lost my camera?" Sara asked, her expression so trusting that Liam felt like a jerk for doubting her earlier.

The desk clerk thought for a moment. "He said you'd left the camera along the shore. You'd been photographing birds." The clerk scratched his head again. "Funny, now that I think of it, it was foggy when you left. Not a good morning for taking pictures."

She cocked her head. "Did you see me leave?" Her voice rose with excitement.

He shook his head. "I didn't see you leave. I was on duty when you checked in, don't you remember?" He didn't wait for her to answer. "You came back after seeing your room and asked if you had any messages. When I said no, you paced back and forth in front of the entrance, like you were expecting someone. You seemed to be in an awful hurry."

The howl of a police car sounded in the distance.

Liam put his arm around Sara's shoulder. "Come on, honey. Let's go wait for the police."

THE LOBSTER TRAP DINER was the best restaurant on Bellwood Island. It was also the only restaurant open this time of year.

"Two coffees," Liam called out to the fry cook as he followed Sara toward the back of the room. The place was deserted except for a middle-aged, gray-haired couple who were engrossed in reading the Sunday edition of the *Boston Globe,* which lay sprawled across the table of their booth.

Sara chose the rear booth, beside a window overlooking the ocean. He watched her gaze flick over the plastic-covered menu. Her skin looked translucent in the morning light reflected off the water. She held herself with a rigid stillness that he'd come to recognize. Considering what she'd just been through, she was holding up better than he expected.

After they had filed their statements with the police, she had cleaned up in the ladies' room, changing into the turtle-neck shirt and slacks that she'd brought from the motel. Now, sitting across from him, scanning the menu, Sara gave no hint that less than an hour ago she'd escaped death from a car bombing. But he knew that beneath that quiet surface she was as brittle as glass.

Maybe she's not as brittle as you think, O'Shea. Covert operators trained by military insurgent groups can be cold-blooded killers and appear as innocent as lambs. If Sara was what he thought she might be, she could know as much about and be as experienced with explosives as he was.

Yeah, well, maybe she was telling the truth. Maybe she was just what she seemed—an innocent victim who needed him.

Innocent? Maybe the car bomb had been staged to make her appear a victim. She might have clicked the ignition starter in plenty of time without his prompting. After all, the pieces had already been put into place: the desk clerk, the story about a man finding her camera, the phone call to the funeral home. What if the car explosion was only a ploy to gain Liam's trust?

Damn, he'd gotten so tangled up in Sara's bedroom eyes and long legs that he didn't know what to believe. He wanted to reach out and rub his thumb across the skin at the corners of her eyes, smoothing it. Instead, he balled his hands in his lap.

Brenda, the pretty, brown-haired waitress, interrupted his thoughts as she approached with two steaming mugs of black coffee. She gave Sara an assessing glance, then turned a beaming smile on Liam. "Been a long time since we've seen you, sweetheart," she said, placing the mugs on the tabletop between them. "Will you be staying in town for a while?"

"Hi, Brenda." Liam gave her a polite smile but didn't answer her question. He looked at Sara. "You must be hungry. How does the house special sound?"

Sara shrugged. "Fine."

Liam nodded to Brenda. "Make that two."

When she left, Liam picked up a spoon and stirred his coffee. "I think we need to talk about what happened," he said, noting that Sara's gaze remained on her mug.

She jerked her head up. "What do you want me to say? One minute I feel calm, yet when I look at my hands, they're shaking so badly I can't hold a spoon."

"Hey, anyone would feel like that considering what you've been through." *Get a grip, O'Shea,* he told himself harshly. Sara's innocence and vulnerability were having a critical effect on what passed for his brain. He had to find a way to put his doubts about her to rest.

He ran a finger along the rim of his cup, choosing his next words carefully. If she was a covert operator, he knew of a way to test her. "Well, for starters, I think you need my protection."

Her brow furrowed. "Protection?"

"I'm offering my professional services. This is what I do for a living."

"You said you worked for a security firm," she said, as though not convinced.

"I do. I also freelance." When she continued to look puzzled, he added, "I take on clients who are in trouble. In your case, I'll find out who put that bomb in your car and why. TALON-6, the security and surveillance agency I work for, will help cut through the police red tape. You'll have protection 24/7 while we get to the bottom of this. I'm offering you something I don't think you should refuse."

She took a deep breath as though considering. He expected her to act fearful and, with a bit of further encouragement from him, agree with open arms to his offer.

Instead, she studied him cautiously, as though he were a bug under a microscope. "What if I can't afford your rates? I might be unemployed for all I know."

"My rates are flexible. You can pay what and when you can." His smile, he hoped, was irresistible enough to get her to say yes.

He watched her consider his offer. Damn those green eyes and that yard of red hair. She was definitely his type, and that meant trouble. His vision of the perfect woman falling into his life, needing a protector. What a setup.

Sara slanted him a glance. "What if I hire you by the day?"

"By the day?" Where in the hell had she come up with that?

"Yes," she continued. "I was thinking that if we can't find the man who drives the Cadillac with the gold hubcaps, maybe the man whose name is on my ID card, Gregory Urquhart, can help us. I think we should call him."

Liam had no idea what to make of her. "Okay, and then what?"

"Let's take this one day at a time."

Damn, just when he thought he was beginning to figure her out, she threw him another curve. "Okay, you've got yourself a protector. For one day."

She smiled as though satisfied, then the smile faded. "One more thing." Her cheeks grew pink and she lowered her lashes. "Our relationship must remain professional." She shifted position and fiddled with her napkin. Finally her lashes rose and that green gaze shot straight through him. "Just because I've hired you doesn't mean that I'm going to…sleep with you."

Bull's-eye. Arrow straight through his male ego. "What gave you the idea that I wanted to—" Then it hit him. *The kiss.* Of course. "I'm sorry if I acted inappropriately," he said, not meaning a word of it. "But as I remember, you kissed me, too."

Her full lips twitched as she studied him. "Well, now that our curiosity about each other has been satisfied, we should have no more problems sticking to business."

So she was only satisfying her curiosity, was she?

He refused to acknowledge the sting of disappointment he felt. Well, he'd never begged a woman before, and he sure as hell wasn't going to start now.

Liam forced a smile. "No problem whatsoever."

She leaned back, her mouth curved into a tight smile of her own. "Then I accept your offer. But I feel guilty for taking you away from your family." She sat up suddenly. "What time is your niece's christening?"

"Not until one o'clock. Don't worry. I have plenty of time. Maybe you'll be able to lie down and rest while my family is in church."

"What about you?" Sara's voice softened with concern. "You must be exhausted."

"I'm fine," he said with a shrug. "Besides, I don't need a lot of sleep."

"I'm really sorry," Sara said, her voice soft as her gaze fell to his ripped jacket, the scratches on his hands and wrists. "You keep rubbing your shoulder. Are you sure you're all right?"

Before he could answer, Brenda returned, carrying two

plates filled with bacon, eggs, toast and fried potatoes. The appetizing aroma made his mouth water. After she left, he watched Sara stare at the mound of food in front of her.

"Is everything a blank, or can you remember if you like bacon and eggs?" Liam asked.

She smiled faintly. "A blank, I'm afraid. But this food looks delicious."

At this moment he believed her. If she was acting, then heaven help him, he was a goner.

"Should we call Gregory Urquhart?" she asked in between bites. Liam noticed that she had placed beside her plate the photo of the smiling man Liam had found inside the lining of her bag.

He pulled out his cell phone and set it in front of her. "No better time than the present."

She glanced at the phone, then back at him. "I'd rather you spoke to him. Do you mind?"

"Are you sure?" He couldn't keep the surprise out of his voice. "Maybe if you heard his voice—"

"I don't know why, but I'd rather you spoke to him first."

He shrugged, then took the ID card from her fingers. He recognized the area code as central Massachusetts. He punched in Urquhart's number, watching her as she stared out the window at the rolling breakers.

The connection went through and a woman answered on the second ring. When she called Urquhart to the phone, Liam heard children's laughter and a dog barking in the distance. Obviously Urquhart was a family man.

What if he was cheating on his wife with Sara? Was that why she wanted Liam to call? In case the wife answered, a man asking to speak to her husband wouldn't arouse suspicion.

"Urquhart," a baritone voice said a few seconds later.

Liam gave a brief nuts-and-bolts explanation of the situation. Urquhart gasped. "Sara's all right, isn't she?"

The guy sounded convincing, Liam noted. "Yeah, she's fine. A doctor checked her out, but she's having residual memory problems." He hoped he was making the situation sound light. Until Liam knew more, he trusted no one. If Sara was telling the truth and the car bomb explosion wasn't a trap for him, then she was in serious danger. The fewer people who knew how vulnerable she was, the better. Liam's suspicions of Urquhart were purely professional, he assured himself.

"How do I know you're who you say you are?" Urquhart demanded accusingly.

Liam frowned as he watched Sara sip her coffee. "Here, let the lady tell you." He held out the phone. Her lips tightened to a firm line and her hands clasped into fists. When he thought she would finally refuse, she reached for the phone with trembling fingers.

Chapter Four

"Hello?" Sara's voice was barely a whisper.

"Sara, are you all right?" She strained to remember anything familiar about Urquhart's voice, but failed. However, she felt relieved to hear the warmth and friendliness in his tone.

"What are you doing on the Cape?" Urquhart asked urgently. "You didn't say anything on Friday about going away for the weekend."

Disappointment wrenched her. She'd hoped he could tell her why she'd come to Bellwood Island. "Mr. Urquhart, I—I have a headache and I can't speak to you for very long. But I'd appreciate your cooperation—"

"Mr. Urquhart? Why all the formality, Sara?"

She struggled to remember his first name. "Gregory," she said finally. "In what capacity do you know me?"

"Dear God, Sara, what's going on?"

"Please, er, Gregory. Just answer my questions?"

She heard him take a deep breath. "Very well, Sara. You are good friends with my wife, Linda, and me. You teach freshman English and history at Smith Bordman Academy, the same private school at which I'm the administrator. Since your grandmother's passing, I've been like a father to you."

"My grandmother? What about my parents?"

"Oh my God, Sara." Now the voice was compassionate, as though he realized she indeed had a memory problem. "Your parents are dead. Your mother died in an auto accident when you were a child, then your father died some years later. You were raised by your grandmother, and lived with her until her fatal stroke a few months ago."

Sara tried to process the information, but it was all overwhelming. Then he asked, "Do you remember your brother? Jeremy?"

Sara felt a quick surge of hope. "I have a brother?"

"Yes. He's an engineer on some oil rig in South America. Venezuela, I think."

"Venezuela?" Her hopes fell. So far away.

After a long pause, Gregory said, "Sara, what's happened to you?"

"I'll be fine, really. Don't worry about me." She was hungry for more information, anything that would give her some sense of identity. "Do I have… Am I…married? Children?"

"You've never been married. And of course you don't have children." Urquhart's voice was hesitant, as if he was waiting for something. "Do you want me to come there, Sara?"

"Thank you, no. I'm with…" She glanced across the table at the intense expression in Liam's blue eyes. "I'm with friends," she said finally.

"Well, you know you can count on Linda and me. Remember that, Sara."

"Thank you." She felt overwhelmed with what she had learned, and yet she couldn't help feeling a sense of loss.

She'd hoped a large, warm family like Liam's would be waiting for her.

She averted her eyes from him when she asked the next question. "Am I engaged? Have a steady boyfriend?"

"No. Although it hasn't been that long since Daniel."

"Daniel?" She lingered over the name, hoping that the sound would bring back some happy memory, some warm thought, but it didn't.

"Well, I'm glad you forgot him. Good riddance, I say. He and Stephanie deserve each other." There was an uncomfortable pause.

Her boyfriend had left her and she couldn't feel anything? Or remember him? Still there was nothing inside but that same blank emptiness.

Who was Stephanie? Frustration boiled in Sara. Somewhere in the dark recesses of her mind, she must know. Why couldn't she remember?

"Do I have any other family?" she asked, bracing herself for more disappointment.

"No, my dear. Just Jeremy."

"By chance, do you have Jeremy's address?" she asked.

"Yes, I think I do. Hold on, I'll look it up."

"Thanks, Gregory." While she waited, she tried to ignore Liam's watchful gaze, but it was hopeless. She felt exposed, unsure what she would find, and although she couldn't understand why, she wanted this man sitting across from her to think well of her.

Maybe it had been that kiss. That heart-stopping, dizzying kiss. Her blood heated like a three-alarm fire beneath her skin, and she felt her cheeks flame just thinking about it.

What foolishness. Kiss or no kiss, she should be thinking about who'd put that bomb in her car, not about this devastatingly handsome man sitting across from her.

She took a deep breath and collected her thoughts. What kind of person was she? Was she honest and honorable? A good teacher? Liked by her peers? Sara would feel uncomfortable asking anyone such questions about herself.

Urquhart came back on the line and recited her brother's address.

"Is it possible for me to arrange some time off?" she asked next. "A week at least?"

"Well, under the circumstances…yes, of course. I'll arrange to have a sub come in for your classes beginning tomorrow. When do you think you'll return?"

"I'll call you." She said a brief goodbye and clicked off the phone, then gave Liam an account of everything that Gregory Urquhart had told her. "I feel as if I were in a play, talking about some make-believe character." She closed her eyes and tried to mentally connect to the woman Gregory Urquhart had described. But that woman's life seemed so strange. It was as if Sara's mind was a hollow shell and she'd never feel comfortable with who she was.

She blinked back hot tears, her hands clenching in frustration. "I—I'm sorry. If you'll excuse me…" She dashed for the rest room at the front of the building.

Feeling helpless, Liam watched her escape behind the ladies' room door. Damn, if only he knew he could trust her! Maybe his partner had learned something about Sara by now. It had been only a few hours since Liam had called Clete Lawton, his partner at the TALON-6 Agency, waking him out of a dead sleep. But Liam needed a background check on Sara Regis, the sooner the better.

He clicked open his cell phone and punched in Clete's

number. Moments later, he swore as he was automatically connected to his partner's voice mail.

"How are you coming with that report?" Liam asked. "Imperative I receive it stat." He hung up, then punched in the number of the Bellwood Island PD. As he waited, he noticed the photograph of the smiling man that Sara had placed beside her plate. Liam picked it up, his mind filled with questions. Was this Urquhart? If not, then who was it? Would he be waiting for Sara when she returned to her home in Massachusetts?

When the police department answered, Liam asked to speak to his friend Al, whom he had known since they were in kindergarten together.

Moments later, a feminine voice answered. "Detective Al Ranelli's desk, Detective Zarella speaking."

"Francie, it's Liam. Let me speak to Al."

"Sorry, he's on special assignment. Guess you're stuck with me."

"Where is he? I need a favor."

"Sorry, Al is in charge of security for the big political fund-raiser at the town hall. Trent Sherburne is running for senator. Most of the other officers are at the Sand Dune Motel. A car bomb went off. Can you believe it?"

Liam was glad that Francie hadn't yet read the reports on the bombing. If she knew he and Sara were eyewitnesses, she'd want his personal take on it. "Okay, Francie. Maybe you can help me."

"Not even a 'Hi, Francie. Sorry you're on duty while your partner, Al, get's all the cushy assignments? Sorry, Francie, that you missed my niece's baptism. Are you going to stop by later for cake and coffee?'"

Liam winced. "Okay, Francie, you made your point.

Sorry, but I'm tired and a little short on social niceties at present. And I am sorry that you're stuck holding down the fort while Al pulls the gravy-train jobs. But for old times' sake, I need a favor. Forgive me?"

He heard her long sigh on the other end of the line. "As I remember, you didn't have time for me in the old days. Why should now be any different than then?" After another exaggerated sigh, Francie finally asked, "What is it this time?"

He ignored her sarcasm. "Know of a local who owns a black Cadillac? Black-tinted windows? Gold hubcaps? A flashy job."

"Hmm. You know as well as I do that the locals are more pickup truck types, but I'll check around. Anything else?"

"Yeah. Ask Al and the guys to keep an eye out for a Caddy of that description. Then let me know where the owner is staying—that is, if he's here or on the mainland."

"I can do that. Say, when are you going to stop by the station and trade war stories? Al will be mad as hell if he doesn't see you before you leave."

"We'll see."

"Working a case?" Francie asked, curiosity in her voice.

"I don't remember saying that."

"What is it with you men? Can't give a straight yes or no if your lives depended on it." She chuckled.

"If you find out anything on that Caddy, give me a call. Here's my cell phone number."

After he had hung up, Liam picked up the check and put several bills on the table. Just then Brenda walked past. "Your latest conquest?" she asked, referring to Sara.

"You know I don't kiss and tell."

"Hmm. Think I might have a chance if I dyed my hair

red?" She tilted her hip and struck a comical pose as she pursed her lips into an exaggerated pout.

Liam chuckled, but before he could reply, a bloodcurdling scream reverberated off the knotty-pine walls and rafters.

Sara.

He dashed to the front of the restaurant, where she stood staring out the front window as though she'd seen a ghost. Her eyes were like saucers in her pale face. "It's him," she cried, pointing to the street.

"Who, Sara? Who?" Liam searched the area but didn't see any foot traffic, only a white van at a stoplight, an air horn mounted on the roof rack. He grabbed her by the shoulders and turned her toward him. "Sara, what is it?"

Too terrified to speak, she could only point back at the window. Again Liam scanned the street, focusing on the van waiting for the light to change. Covering the vehicle's side doors was an oversize head shot of senatorial candidate Trent Sherburne. The dark-haired, intelligent-looking man gazed out at his future constituents with a serious, yet caring expression.

"Sara, do you know Trent Sherburne?"

Her eyelids fluttered, then she pressed her face into his chest. "I'm not sure. I don't know how I know, but he's responsible for murdering someone. I just can't remember who."

"FOR HEAVEN'S SAKE, LIAM, what were you thinking? How could you go traipsing off with Sara after what she'd been through?" Bridget slanted an angry gaze at her brother as she stepped between them, taking charge of her patient. She led Sara from the front porch into the cottage. "You need to rest, dear. We'll be leaving soon for church. While we're gone, you'll have some quiet time for a nap. And I won't take no for an answer."

"I—I am feeling a bit tired." Sara glanced over her shoulder at Liam as Bridget guided her toward the staircase.

"Do what the doctor says," he advised as he leaned on the newel post and watched them climb the stairs.

"You'll feel like a new woman after a nap," Bridget said.

"Please, don't bother with me." Sara hesitated on the landing, her hand gripping the banister. "I feel guilty enough intruding on a family gathering."

"Guilty?" Bridget exclaimed. "You'll think no such thing. We're only glad to help."

Liam smiled to himself. After what Sara had been through today, she needed the tender loving care his oldest sister was noted for. He watched as Bridget finally persuaded Sara to rest, and he couldn't help wondering, again, who had rigged that car bomb, and what had Sara done to cause someone to want her dead.

BY THREE, most of the family and guests who attended the christening had already started for the long drive home. Those who still lingered at the family cottage would remain overnight and leave directly for work early the next morning, Liam knew. He had also planned to leave immediately for New York City, but now with Sara and the mystery of who was after her, he didn't want to leave her side.

From the porch, Liam glanced out at the familiar dunes where he and his siblings had played during their childhood summers spent at the cottage. The air was filled with children's laughter and shrieking, and the usual pandemonium of an O'Shea family gathering. If he closed his eyes, he could almost imagine that nothing had changed over the years, except now their parents' cottage was owned by him and his sisters and would serve another generation of O'Sheas for years to come. For a rolling stone, Liam felt grateful for at least this one shred of permanence in his life.

He glanced at his watch. If he was going to remain in Massachusetts, he had phone calls to make. As he stepped from the porch, two identical freckle-faced, red-haired nephews nearly knocked into him.

He chuckled as he followed the boys out into the sunlight. He waved to several of his brothers-in-law as they carried picnic tables and lawn chairs into the boathouse. Bounder barked after them. How in hell had Sara been able to rest with all the noise? He loved his family, but an O'Shea reunion was hardly peaceful and quiet.

He wandered along the beach to find a quiet spot to make some phone calls. He punched in his partner, Clete Lawton's number.

Clete answered on the first ring. After Liam brought him up to date on the car bombing and Sara's unusual reaction to the Trent Sherburne campaign poster, he added, "I need someone to work my back door, and I sure could use your expertise on explosives."

The usual teasing was gone from Liam's voice, and his partner immediately picked up on it. "I'm about finished with the paperwork from my last op, so I'm available. What can I do?" he asked earnestly.

"I'd like you to come to Bellwood Island and work with the police department's bomb squad. Any chance you could get fingerprints from the explosion?"

"If we can retrieve pieces of the bomb, maybe. Depending on what type of explosive was used. I'm willing to give it my best shot."

"Thanks, Clete. That's good enough for me. I also want a thorough report on both Sherburne and Sara." Liam thought a moment. "On the drive over here, she couldn't remember saying what she'd told me in the diner—that she thought Sherburne had murdered someone. It was as if she'd blocked out what little bit of memory resurfaced."

"I wonder if Brianna could help her?"

Brianna was a clinical psychologist who last year had married Michael Landis, CEO of TALON-6. "Hey, that's a great idea. Is Mike in the office today?"

"He and Brianna are in Maine, visiting her aunt Nora, but I can give you their number. Hold on, I've got it right here."

While he waited, Liam glanced toward the far side of the cottage where a number of his siblings and their husbands were getting ready for a game of softball.

When Clete came back on the line and gave him the number where Mike could be reached, the topic shifted back to Sara.

"I keep thinking about the Interpol warning that terrorists are planning to steal the Land-Net 17 schematics," Liam admitted. "I can't help wondering if Sara and her amnesia story are somehow involved."

"That's the Irish in you, bucko. You've always been the cynical one."

"Yeah, well, my hunches have saved my life more than once."

"Only teasing, Liam. Lighten up, will you? I trust your instincts any day. You're just doing your job, considering Sara a suspect until her background check clears her."

"I'd like you to run a check on Sara's brother." When Liam had finished giving the details, he added, "Check out the Smith Bordman Academy, and Gregory Urquhart, too. His name was listed as Sara's contact in case of an emergency."

"You got it. I'll call you as soon as I find out."

"I'LL NEED MORE information than what you're giving me, Liam," Dr. Brianna Kent-Landis said over the phone. "Hysterical amnesia is one of several types of memory loss. I couldn't begin to answer your questions without seeing your client."

Liam felt a twinge of disappointment. "Sara had a bump on the head, but Willie says that she didn't sustain enough physical trauma to cause loss of memory."

"An emotional shock can definitely render a person unable to recall their past," Brianna confirmed.

"How long could this type of amnesia last?" Liam inquired, trying to hold back his frustration.

"I have no idea, Liam. Even if I called Willie, I wouldn't be able to tell you anything without a complete psychological exam." Brianna sighed. "I'm sorry I can't give you the answers you want. If it will do any good, I'll be back in my office on Monday. Why not call me? If your client is willing to come to New York, I'll run some tests on her."

"Thanks, Brianna." He sighed in turn, thinking of Sara's extreme reluctance even to go to the hospital. "I'll ask her and let you know."

"Fine. But remember, amnesia isn't as it's portrayed in the movies. A person doesn't just get hit on the head and lose their memory, not without a lot of brain cells being destroyed. Usually a shocking incident will remain as memory, captured somewhere in the brain. With hysterical amnesia, the patient is unwilling to remember. Try as they might, their brain shuts off the horrific image in order to protect their conscious mind."

Liam started walking toward the cottage. He paused near the boathouse to get out of the way of several children running by. "Are you saying that Sara could recall her past if she wanted to?"

"If she remains traumatized, she may never remember. When she feels safe, free of the trauma that caused her to block the fearful event in the first place, she'll be in a better position to remember." Brianna paused. "As long as Sara remains terrified, she may never be able to face her fears."

Liam processed what the psychologist was telling him. "So she may never regain her memory," he said finally.

"There's always that possibility."

SARA WOKE UP TO THE SOUND of laughter. Children's laughter. She sat up, swung her legs off the bed and strode to the window. Pulling the crisp white curtains aside, she gazed out the spotless pane of glass to the apple tree below.

A dark-haired woman knelt beside a little girl whose tiny shoulders were heaving with sobs. When she turned, Sara saw that her ruffled pinafore dress was splotched with mud.

The girl swallowed her tears long enough to point a chubby finger accusingly at a boy sulking a few feet away. His dark blond hair was the exact shade as Bridget's.

Sara's lips twitched as she watched the scene unfold. Had she wanted children? Did she yearn to be married or was she satisfied with a career?

Amid the rowdy sounds of voices floating through the open window, Sara felt a jab of loneliness. *Yes, she wanted children. A girl and a boy with dark sapphire eyes. A house with a huge backyard filled with laughter, and a husband with broad shoulders and thick black hair who looked like Liam...would come home to her each night. A husband.*

She turned away from the window and closed her eyes, thinking of how she had felt when he had kissed her.

Stop it! She pressed her fingertips to her temples. She was attracted to Liam only because he was here, helping her. He was being kind and gentle because he felt sorry for her. She needed to see her feelings for what they were— purely an emotional distraction from the dangerous situation she was in.

Her ears were still ringing and her head throbbed. Willie and Bridget had assured her that she would soon regain her memory. Hysterical amnesia, they called it. They had even offered referrals to specialists who could help her when she returned home.

Home. East Bennington. Excitement welled inside her at the thought of going home. Did she live in a house? An apartment? Although Bridget had done everything to make her feel welcome, Sara could hardly wait to leave. Surely once she was among familiar things, her memory would return.

A burst of hearty male laughter came from downstairs. Liam. Even his laughter made her feel warm and secure. A flush of embarrassment washed over her. What must he have thought when she behaved so foolishly over a silly photo of a man she'd never seen before? Trent Sherburne, Liam had told her, was a politician running for Senate.

So why, at the diner, had she said she knew Sherburne, while now she had no memory of ever meeting him?

Yet if she'd had such an emotional reaction to Sherburne's photograph, she must know him.

Or did *he* know *her?* Maybe Trent Sherburne knew something about her life, her past, her friends. Perhaps she and Liam could arrange to meet him. Liam had said that he was here for a rally, right on Bellwood Island.

She started toward the door, then paused.

What if Trent Sherburne knew something about who had placed the bomb in her car? If she went with Liam, she might be putting his life in danger, if she hadn't yet. She thought of Liam's family, of Bridget and Willie, who she might already have put in danger just by being here.

Somewhere in the corner of her brain lurked the answers. So why couldn't she remember?

SEATED IN ONE OF THE LAWN chairs near the dock, Liam looked up to see a slender blond woman dressed in a police officer's uniform stroll across the grass toward him. Bounder greeted her noisily, barking as he circled her. On her way, the blonde exchanged waves and hellos with three of his sisters, who were seated at the umbrella table, bouncing toddlers and infants on their laps.

"Hi, Liam," Detective Francie Zarella said as she came up to him and gave him a hug. She seated herself in the white Adirondack chair next to him, her curls bouncing around her face in the brisk sea breeze. The gold badge pinned to her chest shone brilliantly in the sun. "I just stopped by to drop off a christening present for little Bridie, and I thought this was a good time to update you on what I found out about that Cadillac with the gold hubs."

He hid his excitement behind a detached expression.

"The car isn't from the island. I dispatched the description to the state police headquarters and to Boston's aerial traffic controller. If that car is on the highway, we'll know it." Her hazel gaze remained fixed on him.

"Thanks, Francie. I owe you one."

"Yeah, I'll keep count." She grinned. "So you're working a case, huh?"

"Nothing I can talk about."

"Mmm, why am I not surprised?" She glanced at the large dial on her black wristwatch. "Wow, I've got to scoot. I'm due back at work soon. When Al called in before noon, I told him you were at your family cottage for the weekend. He said he'd try to drop by later to see you. I think he's going to challenge you to another game of handball. He hasn't forgotten the last time you trounced him at the club."

Liam grinned, remembering that Al had lost all three games. "I guess he's been nursing his revenge all this time."

"Men and their games." Francie chuckled, shading her eyes from the sun as she gazed at him. "Do I take that as a yes, you'll meet him at the club tonight?"

"'Fraid not, Francie." Just then Liam saw Sara step down from the porch and start across the lawn toward them.

"I'll be leaving this evening," he continued, his gaze on Sara. "I'm not sure when I'll be back, but I'll definitely stop in at the station when I do."

Francie followed his gaze and her smile faded when she saw Sara coming toward them. "Why am I not surprised?" she muttered to herself.

WHEN LIAM HAD FINISHED the introductions, Sara tried very hard to hide her nervousness. What was there about the police officer that made her feel so tense? Sara focused on Francie's warmth and charm. Her face was pretty without makeup, her fair skin sporting a heavy dose of freckles. Francie's bright, intelligent eyes were filled with questions as she shook hands with Sara.

Was she here because she had news of the car bombing? Sara decided not to ask, letting Liam deal with the police. After all, he had taken on the job of her protector.

Liam turned to Sara. "I've known Francie and her partner, Detective Al Ranelli, since we were in kindergarten together."

Francie smiled. "Al always wanted Liam to join the force, but this daredevil here—" she gave Liam a friendly poke in the ribs "—went off to see the world after high school and we've barely clapped eyes on him since."

"Having six older sisters does that to a guy," Liam said with a grin.

Francie's hazel gaze lingered on her, and Sara wondered if the detective thought that she was more to Liam than just a friend.

"Well, I better be going," Francie said finally, getting to her feet.

"Thanks for stopping by." Liam ran a hand through his thick black hair. "I'll try to—"

"Stop at the station and say hello next time I'm out," Francie finished for him. She shot him a grin, then turned her attention to Sara. "Nice meeting you."

"Same here." Sara watched the police officer stroll toward the narrow road where her car was parked. She wondered if Francie had a thing for Liam.

How could Francie not be attracted to him? Sara pushed back the unbidden thought. Why should she care? *Besides,* Liam was single, and obviously free to enjoy looking at attractive women if he so desired. Just as long as he kept his libidinous attention away from her.

"You look rested. Did you manage to sleep with all the noise?" Liam asked.

She smiled. "Yes, I feel much better."

"Good. When will you be ready to leave for East Bennington?"

"Whenever you are."

"If we leave now, we'll be there before dark." Liam got up and started toward the cottage. She followed, then veered off to where Bridget was helping little Katie fly a dragon kite. "I'll only be a minute," Sara called back to him. "I want to thank Bridget before I leave."

He fell silent as he watched Sara make her way toward the dunes. He took a whiff of the crisp ocean air, just the thing to clear his thoughts. If she was on the level, then she was being targeted by a killer.

From what he'd seen from the fragments he'd helped the bomb experts retrieve from the parking lot, the explosive charge had been set by a pro. If she was a spy, working for a terrorist group after the Land-Net 17, then he was in serious trouble.

Either way, he couldn't do his job if he couldn't think of her as a client, even a dangerous client. So the sooner he stopped thinking of Sara as a woman he'd like to take to bed, the better.

If only it was that easy.

Chapter Five

Liam clicked on the turn signal and veered the rented Ford onto the expressway ramp for East Bennington. Although he much preferred to drive his Alpha Romeo, the flashy two-seater convertible would be too easy to follow in case they were being tailed. The nondescript four-door sedan he'd rented also held more trunk space for the equipment he'd brought with them.

The three-hour drive from his family cottage on Bellwood Island had given him plenty of time to think about the woman sitting beside him. Sara. What if she was telling the truth? Whenever he took an assignment, he needed to believe in the purpose of the case. Freelancing gave him the opportunity to pick and choose. If he couldn't trust that Sara was telling the truth, he wouldn't be worth a damn to her. Either way, he couldn't live with himself if he failed to protect her.

He peered into the rearview mirror, then the side mirror. How long had that silver van been following them? Had the men in the black Caddy rented another vehicle? Would the car bomber be waiting for them at Sara's house? Liam slanted a glance at Sara as she studied the road map.

She looked up just then. "Take the next exit ramp to your left. According to the map, the road will take us right into East Bennington."

Liam noticed her hands trembled as she refolded the map. She wasn't as calm as she tried to appear.

He took the turn onto the ramp and was relieved to see the silver van continue north along the expressway. Maybe they weren't being followed, after all.

Cool it, O'Shea. You're a hair trigger. Relax.

What must this be like for Sara? In the next few minutes they'd be entering the town where she lived. If only time would stand still and they could forget everything and begin again. What would it be like to spend this beautiful April afternoon together?

Where would you like to go, Sara Elizabeth Regis? Liam thought. *Window shopping along Main Street? Horseback riding along a woodland path? Or to a movie matinee, where we could make out in the back row?*

Who are you, Sara Regis? And why am I so drawn to you when I don't have the slightest idea who you are?

EAST BENNINGTON WAS A typical New England village that revered its colonial homes and ancestral landmarks. Sara was delighted with the historical ambience. The main square with its white church and steeple, and beds of golden daffodils and forsythia hedges, looked like a picture postcard.

"What a charming place," she said as they drove past block after block of older, family-style homes shaded by mature trees. But her joy turned to despair when she realized that these sights should have been familiar to her. Her insides suddenly felt so tight she found it difficult to breathe. What if those men who had blown up her car were waiting here for her?

Determinedly she leaned back and focused on her breathing, but try as she might, she couldn't keep her hands from shaking.

Thank God Liam was with her. Bridget had assured her that she would be safe with him, yet Sara had already sensed that. He seemed to be the kind of man who would follow through and do whatever was necessary. She glanced up at his handsome profile and was rewarded by his reassuring smile.

"One ninety-six...your house should be on your side of the street," he said, glancing at the two- and three-story Victorian and Cape Cod style homes.

As the house numbers increased, she almost forgot to breathe. One hundred twenty-two, twenty-four... Her heart hammered in her chest.

"This is it," Liam said, pointing to a beige-and-brown two-story Cape. The For Sale sign on the front lawn gave Sara a start of surprise. She felt disappointed, too. The house looked as strange and unfamiliar as her room at the Sand Dune Motel had.

The brick bungalow across the street and the white Victorian with the picket fence directly beside the driveway didn't look familiar, either. She scanned the area, looking for anything she could recognize. Nothing.

"Could there be some mistake...?"

She let the words fade when he shook his head. "No mistake. This is your house."

Her house. *Dear God, please let me remember something.*

After Liam parked the sedan in the driveway and shut off the motor, she glanced at the open porch, with its green-

and-white striped awning over the door. "I—I don't have a house key on my car key ring. Maybe I keep a key hidden somewhere."

His mouth quirked. "No problem."

"What do you mean?"

He unhooked his seat belt and unfolded himself from the car. "Stay here while I check this out."

She watched as he climbed onto the porch and fiddled with the door, opening the lock in less than a minute, and stepping inside. About ten minutes later, he appeared again, coming over to open the car door for her. "Everything's okay," he said, his gaze searching the neighboring houses.

The wooden boards creaked as they made their way across the long porch toward the door. Up close, she noticed the house was on the verge of needing major repairs. The white trim had been painted recently, but the asphalt driveway was crumbling in places. Gregory Urquhart had said Sara lived with her grandmother until she'd died several months ago. Maybe this had been her grandmother's home. Maybe Sara was selling to buy something more to her liking. The idea gave her hope.

"How did you open the door?" she asked as he turned the knob.

Liam produced the tiny gadget from his pocket. "A handy toy no burglar should be without," he said, grinning as he pushed open the door.

Her insides fluttered as she stepped over the wooden threshold and peered into the kitchen. For an instant, all she could do was stare.

"CAN'T YOU DO ANYTHING right?"

"Wh-who is this?"

"Who the hell do you think? And don't say names over an open line, you idiot."

Ziggy sat up straighter in bed, careful not to wake the blond woman lying beside him. "Hey, boss, I tried to call you earlier. I'd called the bank and…what you promised ain't there."

"And it won't be until you finish the job. Where is she?"

"She's history. I told you."

"Yeah? Well, I just heard she checked out of the motel with some guy."

Ziggy glanced at the sleeping woman, then cupped his hand around the phone mouthpiece. "She checked out, all right," he whispered. "When she turns the key of her car, bingo! She's gone from this world."

"Oh yeah? Her car blew up, but no one was in it."

Ziggy sat up straighter, fully awake. "That's impossible."

"Like hell it is. She had an electric ignition starter, you idiot. Now listen! She's only half your problem. Where's the friggin' package?"

"I told you. It wasn't in the motel room or her car. She must have buried it along the dunes somewhere."

"She was in too big a hurry, or don't you remember?" The person on the other end of the line swore. "I want that package. Now find it."

Too much was happening too fast. Ziggy shook his head. "Where else should we look?"

"Her house, dummy. Go to Massachusetts and look for it there."

"But, boss, what about the woman?"

"Let me worry about her. You've got her address in East Bennington. Go there and get the package. And who knows? Maybe you'll get lucky and find the woman there, too."

Ziggy stared at the phone as the connection was cut. The silence was deafening. He slammed the receiver down, gathered his clothes and looked for his shoes.

Less than ten minutes later, he lumbered along the hotel corridor to the next room. His heart was still racing when he pounded on his brother's door. He kept banging on the wood panel until he heard the safety chain slide off the hook, and Vinny pulled open the door. The clamor of Elmer Fudd and Bugs Bunny filled the air.

"Shut off that damn TV," Ziggy ordered, barreling into the room. "We're in trouble."

"What do you mean, pushing your way in here and telling—"

Ziggy grabbed Vinny by his T-shirt and almost lifted him from the ground. "The boss just called. The woman used an electric starter on the car. The goddamn bomb blew up an empty car, you stupid—"

Vinny let loose a sharp jab at his brother's windpipe, the jolt making Ziggy's eyes bulge with surprise. Then Vinny pushed him back against the wall. "It's not my fault, you idiot. The woman was your responsibility. I did my work." He punctuated his words with another shove. "If something's screwed up, it's your fault." Then he moved to the coffee table and picked up an open bottle of beer. "What if the boss is lying? What if he's saying the broad wasn't in the car just to stall giving us our money?"

Ziggy gave a snort of disgust. "Thinkin' never was your strong suit, bro." The idea that the boss might renege on the money had never crossed Ziggy's mind, but he'd be damned if he'd let Vinny know that. "That's stupid," he said finally. "One word from us and the big boys in Vegas move in on him. Word travels fast. He can't put out a contract and not come through with the dough. If he does, he'll be wasted."

Ziggy glanced at his gold watch. "Come on, pack your things and get ready to roll. The boss wants us to go to the chick's place in Massachusetts. He thinks the package is there."

Vinny jerked his head around. "Drive all the way to East Bennington without the rest of our dough?" Anger darkened his cheeks with a ruddy plush. "I hope you told him what he could do with that idea."

"Yeah, well, here's what I think. I say we call that motel clerk and ask him what happened to the bitch and her car. If he says no one was injured in the bomb blast, then we'll know the boss is on the level."

Vinny drained the last of his beer, his scowl fixed on his brother. "I don't give a damn what you think," he said, his voice low and ominous. "I want my money. You hired me, not the boss. I've done my job. You owe me." He strode toward the TV and picked up the remote control. "And as far as I'm concerned, you go hunt for the package by yourself." He turned his back on Ziggy as he changed channels with a flick of his thumb. "You know where I'll be. Just remember, I want my money, and now."

Ziggy watched his brother sink into an oversize stuffed chair in the corner and stare as cartoons sprang to life on the television monitor. No sense trying to convince Vinny with logic. Money was the only thing that Vin respected. Besides, what Vinny said was true. It was Ziggy's neck in the noose. The boss had hired him, not his brother. The redhead could identify him, and so could the clerk at the Sand Dune Motel. It was Ziggy who had made all the telephone arrangements and who could be fingered when the cops started asking questions. But he didn't like working solo. He needed Vinny. They were a team.

Like a lightning bolt out of the sky, a possible solution occurred to him. "Vinny, I got an idea."

The young man's chuckle was drowned out by Bugs Bunny's laughter.

He wiped his mouth with his hand. "You owe me money, and I want it."

Ziggy spun around. "What choice do you have? Get your stuff and meet me in the car in five. If you want to see your money, you'll be there." He thrust his hand in his pocket and pulled out his car keys as he made his way toward the door.

"Why the hell should I?" Vinny snapped.

"'Cause if you don't, I'll put out a contract on you. When word gets out, the moon won't be far enough away for you to hide there."

His brother stared at him. "What are you saying?"

"I'm saying you either come with me to the chick's house and help me find that package or you're a dead man. When we find it, we'll double our asking price to the boss."

Vinny sat up straight, thinking. "Yeah, an' the extra money will be my bonus."

A bitter taste came to Ziggy's mouth. He hated to be squeezed by his own brother, but the cut could be decided later. Now, he had to find that package and the woman. And if he had to lie to his little brother to get the job done, well, that was just the price of doin' business.

Chapter Six

Liam gazed into the last bedroom overlooking the tree-lined street. Ruffled lace hung at the windows. Sprigs of pink roses trimmed the wallpapered walls, and what looked like a hand-crocheted spread covered the double bed. The decor was simple, yet had a natural grace that reminded him of Sara.

He stepped into the room and couldn't help wondering yet again who Sara was. He was more surprised with what wasn't in this room than what was. No framed photographs of lovers, or photos of any kind. No stuffed animals, books, posters or the dried floral bouquets that had littered his sisters' rooms as they grew up. All he saw were functional items of a woman who lived simply and honestly. Yet he sensed that Sara was so much more.

His gaze dropped to the four-poster bed, and he could imagine her lying there, warm and naked, waiting for him. He would brush her hair, taking long smooth strokes while she watched him in the mirror. He would apply lotion to her skin until it was as smooth as silk, dabbing scented oil on places that would make her pale cheeks blush crimson.

He swore to himself. *What's wrong with you, O'Shea? If there's one thing her bedroom says it's that she's not*

someone to have a fling. The Saras of this world want a
gold ring on their finger, not some wild roll in the hay with
a guy who'll be gone in the morning.

He drew in a deep breath and ran a hand over the knotted muscles of his neck while trying to brush the wanton thoughts from his mind. He was here to do a job.

"Sara," he called, not recognizing his own hoarse voice. "I think the last room on the left side of the hall is yours." He moved back into the hallway and waited for her.

When she stepped from the middle bedroom into the corridor, she carried what he guessed was a photo album. For the past two hours since they had arrived at her home, she had silently wandered through the house, more like a stranger looking warily to buy the place than the owner.

Yet what had he expected? What must it be like to lose your past? It would be like losing the very fabric of your being. Your life, erased. He could only imagine the devastation a person would feel.

As she stepped toward him, her fingers trailed along the walnut banister, as if touching the well-worn wood might somehow conjure up a memory.

"I feel like a trespasser," she said again, just as she had when she'd walked into the living room and studied the framed photographs crowding the white fireplace mantel.

Personally, Liam was surprised to find the house so depressing. From the heavy, overstuffed furniture to the dark walnut wainscoting and maroon flocked wallpaper, nothing about the place matched the Sara he knew.

But you don't know her, O'Shea.

True, he didn't know her. He wanted to believe she was an overprotected, unattached schoolteacher who had lived with and cared for her ailing grandmother. Although Liam enjoyed indulging his fantasies, the sooner his partner called with the background report on her, the sooner he could help Sara regain her memory.

She laid the album down on the hall table, then came to his side. "I'll finish going through the album later." She gazed up at him. Shadows of fatigue circled her eyes. He felt a jab of compassion for the hell she must be going through.

He wanted to hold her, convince her that everything was going to be all right. Instead, he raked back his hair, feeling completely out of his element.

When she moved past him on her way into the bedroom, the ends of her long hair brushed his bare arm. He wasn't prepared for the reaction of pure sexual arousal that jolted every one of his nerve endings. No woman before had ever affected him like this. Damn, maybe he should call Clete and switch places with him. What excuse could Liam give her if he were to suggest that Clete act as her bodyguard while Liam worked backup?

Every operative knew how stupid it was to become involved with a client. Sara was in danger. He didn't need to compound the risk by losing his objectivity. He needed to give this situation some serious thought.

"This must be my room," she said as she pulled a long strand of red hair from a hairbrush that lay on top of the dresser. She opened the top right-hand drawer and peeked inside. "Nothing looks familiar." Her voice held a whisper of regret. "The terrible truth is I don't like this house. I don't like the life I must have led. I had hoped—" She stopped abruptly and blinked, as though suddenly embarrassed. "I'm sorry. I guess I am tired." She closed the drawer and glanced around the room. "I wish I could find something that made me believe I live here."

"Maybe you'll remember after you've had a chance to rest. Why don't you lie down? I'll hunt around some more downstairs."

She gave a little shrug. "I'm tired, but I'm too keyed up to rest. I'd rather keep looking." She tugged open another drawer.

"Did you find anything that might help us?"

"Not really. The back bedroom overlooking the garden must have been my grandmother's. A pair of bifocals and a tube of arthritis liniment were still on the bedstand." Sara's mouth lifted in a mirthless smile. "The photos on the mantel are quite old. It was as though my grandmother lived in the past." Her eyebrows furrowed with curiosity. "I didn't see any photos of people of my parents' generation. Very strange." She hesitated, then added, "I wonder why my grandmother kept this big old house?"

Liam wanted to take her in his arms, tell her not to worry. His gaze fixed on the bed…her bed. No, he'd better not touch her. Not with these feelings surging through him. "You'll feel better after you've rested." Damn, he sounded as trite and cheery as a get-well greeting card.

She slammed the drawer shut and went to the telephone on the bedside table. "I think it's time to call my brother."

He rushed to stop her. Until Clete finished the background check on all her family members, both alive and deceased, Liam couldn't have her alerting anyone else that she had amnesia. It was bad enough that she had told Gregory Urquhart, but that couldn't be helped.

Still, Liam didn't want to add to Sara's fears that a family member might be connected to the fact that someone wanted her dead. "If your brother heard from you in your condition," he said gently, "he'd worry. Why not wait a few days and see if your memory comes back?"

Her expression became pensive as she took a seat on the edge of the bed. "I hadn't thought of that." She glanced up at Liam. "What if I call him and say I was thinking of him and just wanted to talk?"

Her suggestion melted his heart. But he knew it wasn't a good idea. He also knew Sara had a strong will. If she wanted to call her brother, she would. He couldn't be her watchdog 24/7. He needed to show her the danger she was in without frightening her. "I can understand why you'd like to talk to Jeremy," he said gently, "but until we know who rigged your car with a bomb and why, we need to be cautious."

"You can't possibly think Jeremy was involved?"

"Until we know who did, we need to be careful."

She shot him a skeptical look. "Acting paranoid won't help the situation." She stood and moved to the dresser, her fingers worrying the top of a perfume bottle. "I'm sorry, Liam. You're right. I won't call. But…" She gave him a look that said the matter wasn't settled.

He was relieved that she seemed willing to drop the subject for now, at least. He noticed her hands trembled as she twisted the gold knob from the bottle, then closed her eyes and sniffed the perfume.

Sara shook her head. "I hoped it would remind me of something." She shrugged. "I don't find the scent particularly appealing." She put down the bottle, her shoulders sagging. "Liam, I'd like to be alone for a while."

He didn't want to leave her, yet could understand her need for privacy. "Sure. I thought I'd look around the property. I'll be outside if you need me." She didn't look at him as he left, closing the door behind him.

SARA OPENED THE CLOSET and the pleasant scent of cedar filled her nostrils. A pink, fuzzy bathrobe hung from a hook behind the door. Simple dresses, boxy suit jackets, long tailored skirts, slacks and prim blouses hung neatly along the rod. A schoolteacher's wardrobe, Sara mused with a hint of disappointment.

Sara Regis taught world history and English literature at a girls' private school. What had she expected to find? Feather boas and sequined garter belts?

A twinge of disappointment washed over her. Instead of the warm, loving family she'd hoped to find, her parents and grandmother were dead. Her only sibling—a brother—lived and worked in Venezuela. She was alone, with not even a cat.

At least she had Liam. She closed her eyes, recalling the sensations of his fingers caressing her face as she'd kissed him. Those kisses had left her tingling with desire. Yet while she had yearned for him to kiss her again, she also feared it. He'd only been trying to comfort her. He felt sorry for her, and the last thing she wanted was his pity. Besides, he was her protector, and was only doing his job.

A man who looked like Liam O'Shea probably had female clients falling all over him. More than likely he expected Sara to fall hopelessly for his charms. Well, that was the last thing she wanted. So far, she had no proof of past success with the opposite sex, but she had a sixth sense about a man like Liam O'Shea. He could break her heart if she gave him half a chance.

She forced her thoughts back to the matter at hand and clicked on the closet light. Shoes and handbags lined the top shelf. *Neat and tidy,* she decided, making a face. Another boring trait to add to the list of who Sara Regis was. Yet nothing she uncovered brought so much as a pinprick of memory.

She closed the closet door and turned to the last piece of furniture she'd yet to go through, the fruitwood spinet desk by the window. She pulled out the chair and sat down. Lifting the slanted lid, she wasn't surprised to find the contents neatly organized. An accordion portfolio bulged with financial papers. Bank deposit books, monthly reports from several New York brokerage firms. A glance at the large account balances surprised her. She held her breath as she rechecked the name on the accounts: Sara Elizabeth Regis.

Well, she might be dull as dishwater, but she had managed to acquire substantial savings, both in liquid assets and a diversified portfolio. She was a wealthy woman. She gloried briefly in the discovery. Maybe her brother could provide more light on her financial situation.

She bundled the papers back inside the binder. Later, after a hot bath and dinner, she would go through these things again. Now, she'd needed to keep hunting. Something was bound to jolt her memory.

From the bottom drawer, she removed a box of expensive dove-gray stationery. Hidden beneath the box was a book with a red silk cover. She felt a rush of excitement as she opened it and a number of papers spilled onto her lap. Smiling, she realized the book was the first thing that actually looked messy. Maybe she wasn't a lost cause, after all.

Crammed inside were photos, letters and two postcards postmarked Caracas and Maracaibo, Venezuela. Her fingers trembled as she flipped through the pages. Her breath caught; she'd found her diary!

"ARE YOU LOOKING FOR something, young man?"

Liam glanced toward the voice. A small woman, her white braid neatly crowning her head, squinted at him through the chain link fence that separated Sara's yard from the neighboring garden. In the woman's gloved hands were a garden trowel and sun hat.

Earlier, when he'd first come outside, he had noticed the neighbor's curtains flick and someone peer out at him. He'd been aware of eyes watching him while he'd checked the basement locks and windows along the back of Sara's house.

Considering the cool, raw, overcast weather, Liam couldn't help but smile at the gardening props the woman had chosen to mask her inquisitiveness. He waved as he got to his feet. No doubt the woman had noticed the strange car parked in Sara's driveway. From the suspicious glare behind her bifocals, he decided he was probably lucky she hadn't called the police.

"Hello, ma'am." He gave her his most charming smile, but it did nothing to soften her guard dog scowl.

"I asked you a question, young man."

Liam brushed at the knees of his jeans and sauntered across the dormant patches of grass toward her. "I'm a friend of Sara's. She's inside—"

"I don't see her car."

"She came home in my vehicle." He didn't think it necessary to explain that the car was rented. "We arrived a few hours ago."

Her mind digested the information and her blue eyes sharpened further. "You her new boyfriend?"

Liam softly chuckled. This woman could give lessons on interrogation to the CIA. "Sara and I are just friends."

She lifted a disbelieving white eyebrow, then inspected him from head to foot, as if considering whether he was worthy to be Sara's boyfriend. Or maybe she didn't believe him. Finally she said, "I'd wondered where Sara had gone off to." She studied him warily. "Since her grandmother died, Sara doesn't go off without telling me." She stuck her chin out as though daring him to refute the statement. "Do you work with her at the academy?"

He shook his head. Deciding not to play her game of twenty questions, Liam took the offensive. "You must miss Sara's grandmother," he said, guessing the two women might have been about the same age. "Had you known her for a long time?"

The woman's blue eyes studied him over her bifocals. "You must not have known Mrs. Regis." Her gaze narrowed. "An irritable old bat. I never knew how Sara put up with her." She shook her white head. "Sorry to speak ill of the dead, but that's the truth. That woman never gave anyone a moment's peace."

"I didn't know her," he said, unable to hide his surprise. He stepped forward. "I'm Liam O'Shea."

"You're Irish?" The white brows lifted again. A tiny smile curved her lips. "Maggie O'Reilly." Her eyes twinkled and her smile became a grin. "Pleased to make your acquaintance, Mr. O'Shea."

Liam's own smile was genuine. "Call me Liam. And the pleasure's all mine." He leaned against the fence post and began to ask questions in earnest.

SARA CLOSED THE COVER of her diary and leaned back against the bed bolster. Apparently, she wasn't one to write down her most intimate feelings. The diary held little information about her private life. The pages were filled with class notes, teacher appointments, meetings and notes about her students, her classroom plans. The only exception was the letter from her ex-boyfriend, Daniel.

"…This can't be a big surprise, Sara. You've known how things were between us. Better we end things now. And don't blame Stephanie. These things happen. I hope you understand."

Dear God, even her last love affair had been boring. How strange to see the handwriting of an old lover and not feel a reaction. She folded the single sheet of paper and stuffed the note inside the envelope. The postmark had been dated just before Valentine's Day. Shortly after her grandmother's death.

A sad way to start the year, she realized. She sat up, digesting the information. Hadn't Liam said that one reason for amnesia was that she couldn't face a trauma in her life? Could two losses, so close together, block memory?

Sara shook her head vehemently. No. Not unless she was some wimpy, overly protected houseplant. The idea was ridiculous. Whoever she was, she felt strong and spirited.

She placed the diary back inside the desk drawer, lingering over the postcards from her brother, Jeremy. Even his messages were brief and without emotion.

"Riding up the Teleférico—it's the longest and highest cable car system in the world." The picture was amazing—the cable cars looked like tiny dots suspended over the mile-high city, with towering mountains in the distance.

Another card showed sparkling white beaches and an azure ocean with purple mountains reaching to the sky. "Thanks for the birthday gift. I've been on the rig for two months, so just picked up the mail. Leaving Monday. Will write later."

Leaving Monday for where? To return to work on the oil rig? Had Jeremy written another letter? If so, she hadn't found it. Instead of answering questions, the more she discovered about herself, the more queries she had.

Why hadn't she played up her good features with makeup? The only cosmetics she'd found were moisturizers, cold creams and standard toiletries found in any home.

Why didn't she own pretty, lacy underwear? She felt another pang of disappointment. The utilitarian white bras and panties she'd found were depressing.

What if she'd been running away?

If your memory doesn't return after you've seen your home, maybe you should consider hypnosis.

Liam's words tumbled through her mind. Suddenly she felt too exhausted to think. She closed the cover on the desk, her gaze flitting across the room. This house held nothing of the life she'd hoped to find. The woman who lived here was more girl than woman. Virginal.

Stunned, she realized she'd found no birth control paraphernalia. How long had she and Daniel been together? Could she still be a virgin? Dear God, was she frigid? Was that why Daniel had dropped her? If their relationship had been hot and passionate, there was certainly no sign of it.

Suddenly she thought of Liam.

Several lights appeared in the houses across the street. It would be dark soon. She glanced at the clock: 6:48 p.m. Poor Liam, he must be starving.

Was she a good cook? There was only one way to find out, she decided as she went down the stairs toward the kitchen.

LIAM WAVED GOODBYE to Maggie O'Reilly and headed back toward Sara's house. Her neighbor had proved a welcome source of information, which brightened his mood. Overall, the trip to East Bennington hadn't answered his questions, but Maggie, bless her sharp, prying eyes, had provided a few details about Sara's relationship with her brother and late grandmother that were worth checking. More important, he had no doubt that Sara's nosy neighbor would make use of his private cell phone number if anyone suspicious came around asking questions about Sara.

He had just reached the side of the house when his cell phone rang. "O'Shea," he said, taking a seat on the porch step.

"Liam, it's Clete."

"About time you got back to me. Where are you?"

"Never mind that now. Where are you?"

"East Bennington. We're at Sara's house. Why?"

"Look, Liam, I don't have time to explain. Just get Sara out of that house pronto."

Liam jumped to his feet. "Why? What happened?"

"The state police found a black Cadillac with gold hubcaps in a shopping center parking lot. The car was wiped clean, except for a clear print behind the rearview mirror. I just heard from the crime database. The print belongs to Ariel Ziegler, a contract killer for organized crime out of Vegas. He's got a brother, Vincent, who's served time for illegal explosives, among other things. You've got yourself a pair of hired assassins on your tail."

Contract killers? The words froze in his brain.

"You and Sara get the hell out of there. Someone's taken a contract out on her. And whoever hired the Ziegler brothers won't stop until Sara is dead."

Chapter Seven

"Where will we go?"

"Good question," Liam said to Sara as he hauled the suitcase from the back of the closet. "We'll decide once we're on the road. Just grab what you need, then we're out of here."

Sara dashed to the desk and hurriedly emptied the contents from one of the drawers. "Everything is happening so fast. When will we come back here?" She paused, then whirled to face him. "Maybe this is some horrible mistake."

"There's no mistake, Sara. I'll give you the details once we're on the road." He took the leather accordion file from her hands and tossed it inside the suitcase. "Hand me your clothes from the closet."

"No," she said, glancing at the closet door. "I don't want any of these things."

He looked up, surprised. "Why not?"

"I'll buy something new. Something that I feel is mine." She gave the room another quick glance. "I'm ready. Let's go."

He hefted the case in one hand, then took her arm as they

headed toward the stairway. "Before we go, I want you to say goodbye to your neighbor, Maggie O'Reilly."

She looked up, surprised. "I thought you said it would be safer if no one knew I had amnesia."

"I did, but Maggie said you never leave town without checking in with her first. No need to draw unneeded attention to yourself. Just say a quick goodbye, and tell her you're going away with me for a few days."

Sara frowned. "What if I don't act normally? She'll be suspicious."

"Not if you keep it brief. I'll wait in the car."

Sara drew in a deep breath. "I'll give it my best shot."

When they reached the car, he handed her his business card. "Be sure she knows you're leaving with me by your own volition."

Sara took the card, her expression doubtful. "Okay. I'll only be a minute."

Ten minutes later, she climbed back into the car. Her face was flushed, but she was smiling.

"Well?" Liam said, backing the car out of the driveway.

"Whatever you said to Maggie made a great impression."

"Oh?" he asked innocently.

"She thinks we're going on some romantic getaway." Sara narrowed her eyes. "What would give her that idea?"

Liam kept his gaze on the road. "Maybe she's the romantic type?"

Sara lifted an eyebrow. "Well, she gave me a hug and told me that it's about time I have a bit of happiness." Sara shook her head. "If she only knew."

He gave her a quick glance, in time to catch her smile.

"Thanks for smoothing things over with my neighbor. Maggie said she'd been worried about me. When I left just now, she seemed so happy for me." Sara patted his knee, then folded her hands demurely in her lap. A tingle of excitement raced through him at her mere touch.

Liam wanted to grab her hand, but instead squeezed the steering wheel as he brought his thoughts back in line. "You're safe, and whoever is behind all of this won't be able to find you. That's what's important."

Sara swung her head around, frustration flashing in her green eyes. "But I can't keep running. You said once we were on the road you'd share what your friend told you on the phone."

"Of course. You have the right to know." He related everything, including Clete's opinion that someone wanted Sara dead. Liam merged the rental sedan into the middle lane of traffic bound for Boston. She remained quiet for a moment, thinking.

"Someone wants me dead. So I'm forced out of my house, going who the hell knows where?" Her eyes whipped to his, bright with anger. "I can't keep running all my life!"

Her ire was a good release from the shock and stress she'd been under, Liam decided. She might not be thinking logically, but she was fighting back. Maybe this meant her memory was returning. Brianna had said that if Sara had hysterical amnesia, her true personality would begin to reveal itself when the shock of the traumatized event began to wear off. He could only hope it was true.

She closed her eyes and grimaced. "I'm sorry. I didn't mean to take out my frustration on you." She opened her eyes and gazed at him. "What have I done for someone to take out a contract to have me killed? What kind of people am I mixed up with?"

"Don't worry about that now. You might be completely innocent of—"

Her eyes widened. "Might? You have doubts about me?"

His fingers tightened on the steering wheel. Her question was valid. Did he have doubts about her innocence? "No, Sara." He realized that any idea that she could be involved with subversive activities had faded.

"Then why do these people want to kill me?"

"We're going to find out, Sara. In the meantime, I'll keep you safe."

Her shoulders stiffened. "You can't keep everyone around me safe. We were lucky no one was hurt in the car bombing." She shook her head. "Poor Maggie O'Reilly. My other neighbors." She pressed a hand to her face. "I'm endangering innocent people."

"We don't know that." The next Interstate 495 ramp loomed ahead. "Are you tired? Should we keep on driving or would you like to stop for the night?"

Sara shuddered. "Let's keep going. I feel safer when we're moving."

He understood. "I'll take the interstate. We can grab a bite to eat. Let me know when you want to stop."

She turned toward him. "I'm sorry, Liam. You must be exhausted, too. Let's pull off at the next exit and find a motel. You must be starving."

He wasn't feeling tired, but he was getting a case of the willies. He couldn't seem to shake the uneasy feeling that something bad was waiting to happen.

Knock it off, O'Shea. He shrugged. "Maybe we should find a motel near a shopping center. You'll want to pick up a few things. You didn't bring much with you."

As they approached the next major exit, numerous

restaurants, motel and hotel signs appeared. A neon out-
line of King Henry VIII loomed above the others. A fire-
cracker of a display in changing colored lights beckoned
the weary traveler to the five-star theme park resort. "Hey,
that looks like fun," Liam said.

Sara lifted her head. "A resort? But we're only staying
the night."

"So what? A resort has plenty of people. There's safety
in numbers. After what you've been through, some R and
R might be just the thing to relax you." Her faint smile was
his reward.

Liam switched lanes, then settled back to do some
thinking. One thing he'd learned in his thirty-three years,
especially during his time in Special Forces and
TALON-6, was that when he had one of his premonitions,
he should take heed. His mind went back to that night four
years ago in that humid Colombian jungle. He'd had the
premonition all day before the ambush that had killed
Stewart.

He glanced in the rearview mirror at the stream of cars
behind him. *Whoever you are, you bastard, you're not
hurting Sara. Not as long as she's with me.*

A LARGER-THAN-LIFE STATUE of a smiling Henry VIII, his
arms outstretched in a welcoming pose, stood inside the
Tudor-style lobby of the luxury resort. Sara glanced at the
reception desk and smiled as the uniformed staff rushed by.
Men dressed in breeches, uniformed jackets and stiff ruffs
around their necks hurried about their duties like extras on
a movie set. The woman behind the reservation desk wore
a flowing scarf at the end of her cone hat, her pretty face
framed in a wimple.

Sara gasped and turned to Liam. "Do you know the name for the headpiece that woman is wearing?"

He glanced at her. "No, what?"

"It's a wimple." She smiled at his look of confusion. "Don't you see? I'm remembering. Gregory Urquhart said I'm a history teacher. If I know that garment is a wimple, maybe it's a sign my memory is returning."

Liam beamed. "I told you so! All you needed was to feel safe. Get some solid food in you and some decent rest, and you'll feel like a new person in the morning."

Sara smiled, almost believing him. She glanced around at the tall, mullioned windows, the medieval-style tapestries draped across the stone walls. "If I wanted a perfect place to drop out of the twenty-first century, this would be it."

A few minutes later, they entered an elevator flanked by two full-scale suits of armor. Despite Liam's attempt to put her at ease, she caught him studying each guest who entered the elevator as they made their way to their floor. She knew he was ready for action. Beneath his black leather jacket, she'd glimpsed the shoulder holster that carried his pistol. He might have another strapped to his boot, for all she knew. Someone was trying to kill her, and she couldn't allow amnesia and the effort to try and remember her past to get in the way of what was at stake. The lighthearted feeling she'd had a few moments ago scattered like fairy dust.

Her hand trembled when she opened the hotel room door with the key card. She was glad they had agreed to share a suite with adjoining bedrooms and baths. After that horrible fright of the car bomb, she wasn't sure if she'd ever feel safe again. Having Liam stay in the connecting room might provide the only sense of safety she would experience tonight.

After she'd slid the security chain on the door and they were alone in their suite, Liam checked out the terraced balcony behind the French doors, then the adjoining rooms. A few minutes later, he returned. "Everything looks secure. I'll be right behind that door over there," he said, pointing across the living room. "All you have to do is yell, and I'll be at your side in a heartbeat."

His tone was gentle, and when he touched her face, Sara almost shivered at the sensations his caressing fingers elicited. She pressed her palm against his long-fingered hand. The hand of a protector, a healer, as well as a bodyguard.

Her throat tightened as she forced her attention to the present moment. "Liam, would you mind leaving the door ajar?" She knew she had been pushing down all her emotions about what had happened these past twenty-four hours. She didn't need to add lust to the mix. And if she was going to cry, she didn't want him to hear her. Yet she couldn't bear the thought of being completely alone.

"Of course not. Want to grab a bite to eat downstairs?" he said lightly. "There's at least three different restaurants in this section of the resort alone."

She ran a hand through her hair. "All I want is a hot bath and a soft bed."

"You need to eat something. What about room service?"

"Great. That is, if it's okay with you."

"Sure. While we eat, we can plan our next strategy."

She shrugged. "Frankly, I don't know what to do next."

Liam gave her a look of empathy. "Hey, it's expected. You've been through a lot. You need to rest. Relax." He glanced at the amenities listed in the leather-bound hotel book on the desk. "Maybe you'd like a massage?"

She shot him a fragile look. "Maybe later, after we discuss what our options are."

He handed her the room service menu. "Why don't you order something while I make another phone call?"

"What would you like?" she asked as he crossed the room.

"A steak. Rare. And a salad. Blue cheese dressing." Liam strode to the connecting door, which opened into a living room identical to her own.

He had to get away from her. She was in great danger, yet the way she looked at him with such trust, such sweetness, he thought his heart might break. One more minute and he would have taken her in his arms and kissed her until they were breathless. And that was only for starters.

Annoyed with himself, he picked up his cell phone and strode toward the balcony doors.

AFTER SHE HAD CALLED room service and ordered their food, Sara felt too nervous to sit down. She was still in shock, she realized, as if she had stepped into an unknown world.

She strode to the French doors and threw them open. A cold, damp breeze filled with the smell of sea and salt invaded her senses, and her heels clicked against stone as she stepped onto the balcony. The courtyard below was deserted at this time of night. Splashing fountains dotted the grounds, and illuminated topiary cast deep shadows along the cobbled paths that curved among the well-lit wintry gardens.

Overhead, no moonlight penetrated the thick bank of clouds. She peered around the corner and saw that Liam's balcony doors were open, too. His voice carried on the night air as clearly as if he were standing beside her. He must be enjoying the view while he talked on the phone.

"Sounds like our guy," she heard him say. "Fax me the Ziegler brothers' mug shots. I've got a feeling we'll get a positive ID from the motel clerk at the Sand Dune Motel when he sees their photo."

She couldn't force herself not to eavesdrop. She heard Liam hesitate, as though listening.

"Oh, another thing," he said. "Did you get the report from Sara's prints?"

Her attention sharpened a notch. *Liam ran a check on me?*

"Mmm. Anything else turn up?"

In a few seconds, Liam continued, "We have no proof of that. If she and Kitty were sorority sisters, that doesn't prove Sara remained close with Kitty after she became Mrs. Trent Sherburne."

Sara didn't know why, but she didn't want to hear any more. She stormed back into her suite, locking the French doors behind her.

WHEN LIAM CLOSED his cell phone, he turned back toward the connecting door and found it closed. He knocked, and after a few moments heard the tumbler turn inside the lock. The door swung open.

"Well, I trust I passed?" Her tone was accusing as she folded her arms across her chest.

For a moment, he didn't know what she was talking about. Then he realized she must have overheard his conversation with Clete. He could see the feeling of betrayal in her eyes as she faced him. "Yes, you officially passed. But with me, you passed a long time ago, Sara Regis."

"I'm so glad." She crossed to the other side of the room. He followed the sweet sway of her hips with his eyes until she slumped at the end of an overstuffed sofa. He could easily put his arm around her, take her mind off all of her worries, but now wasn't the time.

"That's what you've hired me to do. It's my job to check on everything and everyone. Including you." He couldn't let it go. "Yes, we ran your prints. It's standard procedure. Especially since you couldn't give us any history on who you were."

"No need to explain. I'm fine with it."

She was anything but fine, and he knew it. But she'd been wound up tighter than a drum ever since the car explosion. If she needed to release tension, he much preferred an angry woman to a crying one.

"Well, what else do you know about me? Have I been in prison? Am I wanted by the police for a crime?" Her green eyes blazed with fire but her voice was even and controlled. "Tell me. Isn't that why I'm paying you?"

He wondered how much she had heard, so he decided to tell her everything. He'd hoped to wait until morning, until she'd had a restful sleep, before hearing the report. But it was more important that she trust him. "No prison record," he said finally. "In fact, you've never had so much as a parking ticket." He raised an eyebrow, waited for some kind of reaction. From the tight set of her mouth, he knew she was still angry. "Sara, this isn't personal."

She shrugged, the motion sending the curtain of red hair shimmering about her shoulders. "I know. You're only doing your job." In the soft lamplight, with her face bare of makeup, she seemed fragile and vulnerable. Yet she couldn't have looked more beautiful.

He took a deep breath and focused. "Clete also ran a deep background check on Kitty and Trent Sherburne. So far, the only connection between you, Kitty and her husband is that you and Kitty had been sorority sisters. You obviously know each other."

"The name doesn't sound familiar."

"Kitty St. John was her maiden name."

Sara shook her head. "Neither name rings a bell, I'm afraid."

"Did you notice a yearbook when you were going through your things? Anything at all from your college days?"

"No, but I might find something in the photo album I brought with me."

"Well, it's a start."

"Anything else?"

Liam hesitated. "One other thing about Trent."

She looked up.

"Kitty met Sherburne in college while she was working as a volunteer on his first run as a senator. Seems Trent is something of a womanizer. Several lawsuits were filed against him while he's been married, but all were settled out of court." Liam knew he was on shaky ground with this, but he had to press to see if she'd have some kind of reaction. "Sometimes high-profile men running for Senate take advantage of their adoring campaign workers, especially impressionable, idealistic women who are attracted to strong charismatic men."

Sara sat up straighter. "I'm not following you."

"His wife wasn't the only coed who found him attractive." Liam waited, studying her blank expression.

After an awkward pause, she asked, "Are you suggesting I was one of his campaign workers? You think that maybe I might have had a crush on him?"

Liam unclenched his jaw. "I'm only being thorough."

"What proof do you have?"

"Nothing, as yet."

"Are you sure this line of reasoning is going to find out who hired that killer to blow up my car?"

There was a knock on the door and a man's voice called out, "Room service."

"I'd like to dine alone," Sara said, getting to her feet.

"You don't have that luxury," Liam stated with authority. "We need to plan our next strategy, and we'll work over dinner." He didn't look at her as he crossed to the door and peered through the eyehole. Her eyes narrowed as she watched him open the door, rush the hotel employee away with a tip, then wheel the cart into the room.

Neither spoke very much through dinner. After they finished their meal, Sara curled up at the end of the white sectional couch. "If you're willing, I'd like to hire you for as long as it takes to find the man who sent the Ziegler brothers after me."

"You mean I'm still on the case after midnight?" He smiled as he glanced at his watch. "Which is in two hours and fourteen minutes, by the way."

Her lips curved sarcastically. "You said we need a strategy."

"Okay, let's recap what we know for sure." His businesslike tone matched hers.

She leaned forward. "From what the motel clerk said, I arrived at the Sand Dune Motel around 4:30 a.m. on a Sunday, appearing tense and in a hurry. I asked him if I'd received any messages. He said I looked as if I were expecting someone."

"The room clerk didn't say that for sure," Liam amended.

"From what we know, it makes sense." When he nodded in agreement, she continued. "My bed wasn't slept in. I'd brought an extra change of clothing. Casual clothes. I left the motel on foot, within ten minutes of arriving. Where could I have gone on foot?"

"At that time of night, there wasn't anyplace open except the hotel lobby," Liam added. "Or another motel room?"

"Do you think I was meeting Trent Sherburne?" Her tone was defensive.

"I'm not implying anything. But it's a good guess that you went looking for someone, at the motel."

"I can see the accusation in your face. Maybe you should get a list of the other motel guests."

"I already have. Trent Sherburne isn't listed, but if he had been there, I doubt he'd have used his real name. Besides, the clerk didn't recognize Sherburne from his photos."

Her eyes slitted to two green jewels. He felt like a clod for implying she was having an affair with Sherburne, but Clete believed that they couldn't ignore the possibility. "We need to be thorough," Liam insisted finally.

"Of course."

She didn't believe him. Right now, he wanted to take two steps and close the distance between them. If he held her, he could show her how he felt, for words were useless.

Sara lifted one elegant shoulder. "Maybe I waited outside for someone. Someone who was picking me up in their car?"

Liam picked up on her train of thought. "Maybe he arrived late?"

"He?" Her cheeks flushed as she leaned forward, her legs curled under her. "If you think Trent Sherburne and I were having an affair, say so." Her eyes glittered.

"Sara, I didn't say that."

"You're always saying we need to look at the facts." Tears sprang to her eyes. "I don't know what I might be mixed up in. I can't remember. You said yourself that whatever horror it is, it's so terrible I'm blocking it."

Liam moved beside her. "Facing facts doesn't mean jumping to conclusions." His voice was calm, logical, exactly the opposite of what he was feeling.

"Hear me out, please, Liam." She put a hand on his shoulder. "We know that the Ziegler brothers rigged the bomb in my car. Maybe I met the Zieglers by accident. Maybe I did something to make them angry. Now I'm going to pay with my life."

"No," Liam said emphatically. "My experience is that contracts are set up ahead of time. The Zieglers are from Las Vegas. My guess is that they were hired by someone and they came east to do the job."

Her eyes widened. "Whoever hired them must know by now that no one was injured in the explosion." Her voice rose with fear. "They're going to keep trying until I'm dead."

Sara was coming to terms with the situation in her own way. Liam knew she needed to verbalize it, understand the danger she was in. But he'd never expected to find this so personal, so painful. He was losing his objectivity with her, and to do so put them both at risk.

"We can't deny that," Liam said, determined to be professional. "But we can't ignore that, whether you remember it or not, you told me this morning, when you saw Trent Sherburne's picture on the side of that van, that he was responsible for someone's death."

"I know you told me, but I can't remember now." Sara shook her head. "Do you think he's the one who hired the Zieglers?"

"Let's put that in the 'maybe' column. We know that Sherburne is known to you and that you had a stressful reaction to his picture. Agreed?"

She pressed her lips together. "Clete claims that Sherburne's wife, Kitty, is my sorority sister. And Kitty is married to a womanizer."

Sara sat up, her face troubled. Suddenly, tears sprang from her eyes. She jumped up from the couch.

Liam got to his feet and caught her arm. "Sara, it's okay to cry. Don't feel you have to run off."

She turned to him and his arms encircled her. She clung to him, her shoulders shaking as she sobbed.

"Shh, sweetheart. Don't think about it. Whatever it is, you're safe. We'll face this together."

She was trembling and he held her tighter. She drew back finally, her eyes bright with fear. "I can't keep running."

"You won't have to run. I'll find someplace to keep you safe. Don't worry, I won't let anything happen to you, Sara." He traced a finger along her high cheekbones, her delicate jaw, those moist, sweet lips.

Her mouth was full and sensuous, and he remembered that her lips were as soft as they looked. Dear God, he was only human.

Her lashes fluttered as he lowered his mouth to hers.

Chapter Eight

His kiss was gentle, warm, hesitant. She held her breath, enticed by the faintly musky smell of his skin. When she didn't pull away, he slanted his head to fit their mouths more perfectly. Her heart fluttered as the kiss deepened. She felt intoxicated by his primal male taste.

He pressed his palm against the curve of her spine and pulled her closer. Her back arched, lifting her breasts. Her head was spinning and, to keep from falling, she felt compelled to slide her fingers through the thick, silky black hair that brushed the back of his collar.

The warnings she'd given herself about becoming involved with a man like Liam dissolved like rain into parched desert sand. When his tongue sought the sensitive area inside her mouth, she felt it was an invitation for more. Shyly, she responded.

The need to touch him surprised her. She both craved and feared these strange feelings he'd liberated within her.

When his hand moved over her breast, she trembled in surprise. She heard Liam groan as his fingers slipped inside the front of her bathrobe, peeling away the strap of her bra to fill his hand with her bare breast. Her fingers tightened in his hair when she felt his rough fingertips gently massage her nipple.

"So soft," he said, his breath warm and damp as his finger and thumb gently rasped over the sensitive nub until it was hard with yearning.

His mouth found hers again, and she moaned, feeling an urgent surge of desire. His arousal was obvious. Sara felt her own body answer with a sweet, willing need.

His head dipped and his lips closed around the sensitive tip. She moaned again and arched against him reflexively.

He stilled, one hand remaining on her breast, and for a moment she almost cried out, on the brink of surrender. He drew back, raking his fingers through the hair falling over his forehead. When her gaze met his, she saw that his blue eyes were dark with regret. She tried to speak, but couldn't. Then he released her.

Shocked at her overwhelming sense of desperation, she pushed away, unsure of her footing. Her heart was still thudding, her breath fast and shallow.

"I shouldn't have done that." His voice was gravelly. "I'm sorry. It won't happen again."

She turned away, her backbone rigid as she drew her bathrobe tightly across her chest. She shivered, her fingers clenched into the thick lapels. Behind her, she heard him cross the room with long strides. The door to his suite swung open, then closed, the sound as hollow as she felt.

Tears sprang to her eyes as she whirled around, hoping that maybe… But she found herself very much alone.

"SLOW DOWN, ZIGGY. The last thing we need is a cop on our tail."

Ziggy glanced into the rearview mirror, then back at his

brother, sitting beside him in the passenger seat. "There ain't no cops on our tail. If you don't like my drivin', you can take the wheel."

Vinny's black eyebrows formed a V as he glared at his sibling. "You told me to follow the map. I only got two hands, you know. I ain't no octopus. So what do you want me to do? Drive or check the route?"

Ziggy swore. "Quit your bitchin'. I'm in a rotten mood."

"So what's new?" Vinny snorted as he peered at the green highway information sign directly above the overpass as their rented black SUV sped underneath it.

"Damn it, Ziggy, slow down. I can't read that fast."

"That's it!" Ziggy slammed his foot on the brake pedal. "I'm pulling over and you're driving."

"Oh, quit your beefin'. You're hungry, that's all."

Ziggy's stomach growled and he glanced at the dashboard clock. "Seven-fifteen. No wonder I'm starvin'."

"I'm hungry, too." Vinny studied the map spread across his lap. "By the look of that highway sign, we'll be in East Bennington in about an hour, providing we're not pulled over for speeding," he said with a note of sarcasm. "Let's find a room for the night and get an early start in the morning."

"That's the first good idea you've had all day." Ziggy glanced at the road map in his brother's lap, then back at the highway. "Any good hotels around here? My neck is still sore from that fleabag we stayed in last night."

Vinny pointed to the array of hotel and restaurant signs posted alongside the interstate. "What's the matter? You blind?" he taunted. "You don't need a navigator. You need a Seeing Eye dog."

Ziggy ignored the sarcasm and pointed to a blinking neon sign towering above the others. "Hey, what's that?"

Vinny glanced up from the map and peered at the over-size caricature of Henry VIII outlined in flashing colored lights. "King Henry the Eighth, Luxury Resort," he read aloud. He turned to Ziggy. "Hey, ain't he the one who had all those wives?"

Ziggy snickered. "Yeah. There was a guy who knew how to handle his broads. The minute they got lippy, off with their heads."

Vinny howled with laughter. "Henry sounds like our kind of guy and our kind of place."

THE NEXT MORNING, Sara closed the women's magazine she was reading and stepped from the bubble bath. The scent of gardenias rose from the thick froth in the oversize tub as she grabbed a thick gold Turkish towel and began to pat herself dry. Her mind was still filled with the article she'd been reading as she glanced at the mirrored wall.

She felt a blush creep up her neck as she studied her nakedness, remembering Liam's kisses. How desired and happy she'd felt for those few glorious moments he'd held her in his arms. She'd kissed him back, not as an inexperienced schoolteacher, but as a passionate woman sure of what she wanted.

But why had he broken off their kiss? Didn't he find her attractive? Wasn't she alluring enough?

Her gaze dropped to the magazine that she'd found on the coffee table this morning. After reading the article "How Passionate Are You?" and taking the enclosed test, her mind again filled with the kiss she and Liam had shared.

Why had her ex-boyfriend dumped her? Had she responded to Daniel as she had to Liam? Her cheeks burned as she thought of how Liam's kisses had almost melted her bones. Yet after seeing the drab life she had led in East Bennington, passion seemed imaginary at best.

Her fingers brushed the one set of clean underwear—the white cotton bra and matching panties—that she'd brought from her bedroom yesterday. She disliked the plain, unattractive style.

Sara gazed at the smoky gray-and-pink marble walls of the dressing room and bath. Was such extravagant luxury making her head spin? Certainly the Sara Regis who lived in that dark old house on Monroe Street never thought twice about wearing frumpy underwear. Could amnesia bring about a personality change? She was beginning to think so.

She considered it as she towel-dried her long hair. Maybe Liam's psychologist friend, the wife of his TALON-6 partner, would know. The idea of becoming more like the woman she wanted to be filled her with excitement.

Fifteen minutes later, Sara was ready to meet Liam downstairs. She glanced at the clock: quarter past seven. She had fifteen minutes to spare. After last night, when he'd broken off their kiss with a hasty apology and marched out of her suite, she felt self-conscious about seeing him.

She glanced around for something to do, then remembered she'd wanted to phone her brother. Now that Liam had received the background report on her, her brother must have been cleared, as well.

She curled up in a chair and reached for the phone. Besides, hearing her brother's voice might bring back more of her memory.

"WHAT CHANGED YOUR MIND about meeting with Brianna and letting her hypnotize you?" Liam asked as he stirred his coffee.

Sara sipped delicately from her water goblet. "A magazine article I read this morning." She gave him a Mona Lisa smile.

"A magazine article?"

Her grin widened. "Let's just say the article made me realize that the sooner I regain my past, the sooner I can start living again." She glanced away, her expression wistful.

Whatever had changed her mind and made her eager to cooperate with the psychologist, Liam was relieved and grateful.

Sara seemed altered this morning. Earlier, when he'd looked up to see her smiling at him as she stepped from the escalator, she'd seemed happy and relaxed. For a few light-headed moments, he'd wished they were a couple, spending a few stolen days together.

But they weren't together, not *that* way. He was on a case, she was his client and they had a strict business relationship. *Or should, no thanks to him.*

What the hell was the matter with him? Over the years, he'd kissed many a beautiful woman, and even though he always allowed his body to respond, he'd never lost control. Until last night with Sara.

He'd spent the whole night thinking about her, dreaming about her and the way she'd responded to him. God, she'd almost brought him to his knees. It had taken every bit of fortitude he had to leave her. If he'd known for a fact that she wasn't a virgin, he might not have. Yet if there was that slight chance, then her first time had to be special. Very special.

Despite the cold showers last night and this morning, his hormones still surged at the thought of her soft, kissable lips and her incredible body. He'd liked the feel of her moving against his hips. Liked it way too much. If he didn't start thinking about something else, he'd have to head back to his room for yet another cold shower.

He watched her take a sip of her orange juice and smile at several members of the staff, dressed in English Tudor livery, as they refilled coffee cups and delivered plates of food. Coming here to a theme park resort with a fairy tale atmosphere was exactly what she needed to forget the danger she was in, if only for a few hours. From what the psychologist, Brianna Kent-Landis, had explained to him, Sara needed to be fully relaxed or she wouldn't be a successful candidate for hypnosis.

Today, he'd awoken with a firm resolution. He wasn't some randy kid, and he'd be damned if he'd act like one. He enjoyed challenging himself, and from now on, Sara Regis was his own special challenge. So what if she was sexy, beautiful and equipped with that natural, vulnerable sweetness that had almost been his undoing? He'd managed to control himself and his attractions to women before. He could do it again.

He wiped his mouth with the linen napkin. "When would you like to leave for New York City?"

"As soon as possible, if that's okay with you."

"Fine. I'll make the arrangements."

"Arrangements?"

"I'll call the psychologist and arrange for her to see you. Then I'll check with the TALON-6 receptionist to see if an apartment is available for us in the TALON-6 building in midtown."

Surprise lit Sara's face. "An apartment in their office building?"

"Not only convenient, but safe. The entire building was built with the latest in high-tech security. All the latest bells and whistles." He smiled at her growing surprise. "You'll love it."

When they finished breakfast, Sara glanced around the restaurant, then back at Liam. "I noticed several floors of boutiques in the arcade as I rode down the escalator just now. Do you think I'd have time to shop for a few things before we leave?"

"Fine. I'll come with you."

"No, no. Don't bother." She smiled, and for a moment she looked almost happy. "Stay and finish your coffee. I'll meet you back in the suite."

Liam stood as she left the table, then sat and watched her thread her way among the tables toward the exit. Every male over ten years old turned to watch her leave. He still found it puzzling that a lovely woman such as Sara wouldn't have dozens of male admirers, yet her home showed no evidence of that.

His thoughts strayed back to Maggie O'Reilly and what Sara's neighbor had told him about Sara's life.

"Never had a good word to say about anybody, that was Sara's grandmother. Especially men. She drove both of her husbands away. Her son, too, for that matter."

Liam couldn't help but wonder what had happened to Sara's grandmother to make her so bitter. He smiled to himself. Apparently Sara hadn't suffered from her grandmother's adverse beliefs about men—if Sara's reaction to his kiss last night was any indication.

He drained his coffee. Maybe when Sara's memory returned, and he caught whoever was trying to kill her, he and Sara could steal off for a getaway weekend. Then maybe he would convince her, once and for all, how very special she was.

"THIS WOULD LOOK LOVELY against your delicate complexion," the salesclerk said in a lilting French accent. She held out a black lace peignoir and matching teddy. Already Sara had purchased several sets of handmade Belgian lace bras and panties in the most incredible colors—or as the salesclerk had called them, *palettes*—of sea-mist green, pearl and whisper-blue.

"I'll take it," Sara said, enjoying the thrill of buying something for herself that was not only extravagant, but totally out of character for a drab, old-maid schoolteacher.

When she stepped from the Lingerie à la Cecille boutique, Sara clutched the strap of her purse tightly, her head swiveling as she gazed in wonder at the glittering stores along the arcade. She didn't know which way to go first. A Patriots Day sale was going on in the next showroom. Across the aisle was a hair salon, featuring a holiday makeover. She hoisted her packages and made a beeline toward the salon.

TWO HOURS LATER, Sara couldn't believe what she saw in the mirror. "Is that really me?" she said under her breath. On shaky legs, she rose from the makeup chair. Her dark red hair, which had been trimmed to shoulder length and styled, shone like garnets. The aloe-scented green mudpack had left her skin tingling, and the makeup artist had highlighted and shadowed the planes and angles of her features, making her look…beautiful.

"Oh, *mademoiselle,* you are *trés belle,*" said Jacques, the hairstylist. "A vision of loveliness."

She blushed, uncomfortable with the attention. Would Liam like her new look? The thought brought warmth to her cheeks.

"Thank you," she said simply, unable to express what was in her heart. She paid her bill, then left a generous tip for the artists who'd worked over her.

She took a moment to get used to her new strappy high heels and the wispy skirt of the silky emerald-green dress she'd purchased and insisted on wearing. As she made her way along the arcade, she tried to swallow the bubble of laughter when she saw the tall, confident woman reflected in the plate-glass shop windows.

Four columns of elevators, disguised as ornately carved arched wooded doors, stood at the end of the mall. She headed toward one. Two men stood in front of the adjoining tobacco shop, openly gaping at her.

She felt immediately uneasy, obviously not being used to such blatant masculine attention. Gathering her packages close to her, she averted her gaze from the men as she scurried past. She broke into a run and squeezed inside the crowded elevator just as the doors whooshed shut.

Why hadn't she asked Liam to stay with her when he'd offered? No, that was ridiculous, she decided, pressing the button for their floor. She was perfectly safe. Perfectly safe.

"IT WAS HER, I tell ya."

"Can't be. What are the odds of her stayin' at the same place we are? Besides, somethin' about her didn't look the same."

"If it wasn't her, it was her twin."

Ziggy glowered at Vinny. "I'm tellin' you, it looked like her but it wasn't, understand? They say everybody's got a twin."

Vinny rolled his eyes. "Jeez. Imagine having two brothers like you."

"Look, smart ass. That chick was not the one we're after. Now let's go. We've got a job to do."

"I say we tail her and make sure."

"How? That tower has twenty-nine floors."

"I'll check her name at the desk."

Ziggy swore. "Damn it, Vinny, do you think she'd stay here under her own name? Last time we saw her, she was runnin' like hell, remember?"

"She's met someone. A guy. The boss told you that she vanished from the motel without her car. Maybe her boyfriend picked her up. Maybe she's staying with him here." His eyes lit up. "Say, we could whack the both of them."

"You're nuts." Ziggy bit off the end of his unlit cigar and spat it on the floor. "You go after her if you want. But you're wastin' your time. I'll be in the bar, checkin' the scores."

LIAM WATCHED SARA DASH from the hairdressers and race across the arcade. He had wanted to give her the freedom of a few hours to herself, but under the circumstances, he knew that letting her out of his sight wasn't safe. There was little chance they were being followed, but with the sophisticated tracking devices available for sale to most anyone with Internet access, Liam couldn't rule out the possibility that somehow, he and Sara were being electronically trailed.

He checked his watch, then climbed aboard the next available elevator. With luck, he'd arrive on their floor at the same time, and she wouldn't know he'd been following close behind.

As the elevator doors whooshed open, Liam's cell phone rang. He stepped on, then answered.

"I must have the wrong number," a man said.

"Who is this?" Liam asked guardedly.

"Jeremy Regis."

Liam realized that for Sara's brother to have his number, she must have called him earlier and given it to him.

Liam glanced around the elevator. If she had called Jeremy on the hotel line, someone could have been listening and picked up her conversation. Liam didn't like the possibility that the man on the other end of the line might be impersonating her brother. "I think you have the right number. Hold on a minute, will you?"

An awkward pause followed. "Who are you?" Jeremy finally asked.

The elevator hummed to a stop at the next floor, and Liam stepped aside for a white-haired couple to squeeze from the back of the cage and slowly make their way into the corridor.

"Maybe you should call back in about an hour," he murmured into the phone, his gaze on the floor indicator. He had eight more stories to go before he reached their suite, and judging from the number of guests in the elevator with him, Sara would likely make it upstairs before he did.

"Has something happened to my sister? Why won't you let me speak to her? And who the hell are you?"

"No, she's fine. Look, I can't talk to you just now." Liam's agitation increased as they stopped again and several more people sauntered into the cage. An uneasy feeling, one he couldn't explain, skittered up his spine.

"Who the hell are you?"

Several more people pushed forward. Liam glanced at the growing line of people waiting to board the elevator and swore to himself. Damn, he shouldn't have gotten on this damn thing. "Sorry, old boy, I'll explain everything later."

Liam hung up, hooked the phone back on his belt. "Hold the door. I'm getting off." He had three more floors to go, but knew he'd make better time by taking the stairs. He had no idea why, but felt an urgency he couldn't explain. He squeezed past several couples and exited the elevator just before the doors whooshed shut.

He stood for a moment, listening. Although the hall was quiet, he felt a charge in the air, as if from an electrical current. The hairs on the back of his neck were standing on end by the time he made it to the stairwell.

Chapter Nine

Sara stood in the doorway of their suite, fumbling with her packages as she drew the key card through the lock, when Liam burst through the heavy metal doors from the stairwell.

Startled, she turned toward him, her glossy hair swishing over her shoulders. Liam almost lost his breath when he saw her. She was radiant in an emerald-green dress that clung to her curves and showcased her great legs. Several pink bags and boxes were strewn at her feet.

"You look…terrific," he said, then chided himself for such a banal line. She was so much more. It wasn't the new clothes or the zingy hairdo. He could see that, ever so slowly, she was becoming more comfortable with herself. It was like watching a flower bud swell, then burst into bloom.

"Were you running?" she asked, pushing open the door. He reached for her packages and followed her inside.

"Exercise," he said, panting. He felt so relieved that she was safe. He didn't know why, but he still felt uneasy as he stacked the bags and packages on the table. "I see you found a few things," he noted with amusement.

"Thanks for the help," she said, scooping up several bags and parcels to carry them to her room.

"Your brother called," Liam said when she returned.

"Oh." She folded an empty bag, her face revealing no emotion. "Well, er, I phoned him this morning before breakfast. He wasn't in so I left a message on his voice mail. I asked him to call me at your number." Despite her poise, she slid him a guilty look. "Did you speak to him?"

"Only to tell him to call you back in an hour."

"I'm glad you did. I wanted to ask him about our father," she said, taking a chair by the window. "From what Maggie O'Reilly said about my grandmother, I'm curious about the family dynamic." She crossed her legs. "I figured Jeremy could answer my questions."

She tugged on the short hem of her dress as the flared skirt framed her shapely legs. "There's so much I don't understand."

"For instance?"

"Why did I stay with our grandmother after our mother died, and why did Jeremy live with our father? What were our parents like?" Sara shook her head, causing her hair to glow in the sunlight coming in the window. "You're so lucky to have a family, Liam. Your sisters, their husbands, your nieces and nephews…" She shrugged. "If I ever have a family…" Her words trailed off and her expression turned sad.

He remembered how naturally Sara had warmed to the idea that he had a large family. Some women were sensitive to their biological clocks ticking. Then he remembered Clete Lawton's hunch that Sara might have been Trent Sherburne's lover. A married politician with senatorial ambitions might not welcome his mistress putting pressure on him to leave his wife during a primary election.

Liam put the thought aside for now. Clete had never met Sara. Once he saw her innocence and vulnerability…

Damn, there was no need to torture himself with Clete's theory.

Bailey, the TALON-6 secretary, had said that she was checking on a new lead from Melody Price, one of the ex-girlfriends who was willing to talk about Trent Sherburne. Maybe she could shed some light on Sherburne's personal life. For the time being, Liam decided not to mention it to Sara.

"I think I'll try to call my brother now." Sara glanced at the clock on the desk. "That is, if we have time before we leave?"

"Sure," he said, relieved to break his train of thought. "I'll finish packing. I'll be in the next room if you need me." He rose, not looking back as he opened the door to his suite.

SARA'S HAND SHOOK with nervousness as the phone rang. When she was about to think her brother wasn't going to answer, a deep male voice growled, "Jeremy Regis."

"J-Jeremy?"

After an expectant pause, he said, "Sara? Is that you?"

A rush of unshed tears squeezed her throat. "Yes," she managed to answer. His voice didn't sound familiar, but what did it matter? This was her brother. Her family. She wasn't alone.

"What's going on? When I got your message on my answering machine, I couldn't believe it. And when I called back, some man answered. He wouldn't let me talk to you. What's going on there?"

"Jeremy, why were you surprised that I called?"

"Shocked was more like it. Don't you remember?"

Something made her hesitate to tell him that she had

amnesia. Instead, she asked, "I'd like to hear your thoughts."

"Ha, that's a switch." His sarcasm surprised her. He paused, as though waiting for her to refute him. When she didn't, he continued, "Look, Sara, I don't know what you want, but the last time we spoke, you said you never wanted to speak to me again. Now, two months later, you call me, on a Monday, knowing perfectly well that I'm not at home during the week. Today I just happened to be in because of a hydraulic valve breakdown. What gives?"

She took a deep breath to clear her head. She'd had no idea they had quarreled, or why. She took a fortifying breath, unsure how to reply. "Do you remember why I was so angry at you?"

"Hell, yes. But I still don't understand your attitude."

She was totally confused, yet didn't want to alarm him further. "Why don't you tell me your side of things?"

She heard his slight gasp of surprise. "Why the switch?"

Several moments past as she scrambled for a response. She didn't want to expand the gap between them, yet still didn't want to reveal that she'd lost her memory. She didn't know why, but thought it best to go with her instincts. Finally she said, "Maybe I've had time to reconsider, Jeremy. I'd really like to hear your thoughts about all this."

She heard him sigh. "We always fight over the same old thing. You were pissed off at me for not coming to Granny's funeral. You said what you always did—that she was family. And I said that my grandmother died the day she found out Mom was pregnant with me and kicked her out. Even after they married, Granny never acknowledged Dad." He paused again, as though waiting for Sara to jump in and upbraid him. Instead, Sara tried to make sense of her brother's words.

"I guess you're still sore," he said, "about what I said next, huh?" The anger she had heard in Jeremy's voice was gone, replaced with a sadness that tugged at her heart-strings. Her conversation with her brother wasn't going at all as she had expected it to. How could she get their relationship back on track? She forced her mind onto his question. "What do you think?" she prompted.

She heard him sigh again. "I didn't mean it, sis."

"What didn't you mean?"

The pause lengthened, and Sara thought that maybe her brother wasn't going to tell her. Finally, he said, "I'd said if you could cut me out of your life that easily, then you were just as callous as the old lady."

Sara closed her eyes at the charge. "I didn't mean that, Jeremy," she said hoarsely. Was she as embittered as her grandmother? Were they two of a kind? She fought for something conciliatory to say. Finally, she asked what was in her heart. "Do you think we can start over, now that she's no longer an issue between us?"

The uncomfortable silence stretched again. "I'd like that, sis," he said softly at last.

She swallowed the tight lump in her throat. "Then I'm glad I called you."

"Me, too."

Now it was Sara's turn to remain quiet. "Do you mind if I call you in another few days?" she asked a few moments later. "Just to talk?"

"Yeah, but let me give you my new number. You can reach me directly at work on the oil rig."

Happily, she scribbled down his phone number, then

said goodbye. Her eyes were moist when she clicked off the phone.

She really had a brother.

"I JUST GOT OFF THE PHONE with Brianna and she suggested that maybe we should stay here one more night." Liam came from his room and found Sara on the balcony. She was curled up in a patio chair, looking relaxed, with the leather-bound album open on her lap. He took a chair beside her. "She thought it was a great idea for you to go someplace safe, relax and take your mind off everything that's happened."

"But I thought you were in a hurry to get to your office in New York?" Sara closed the family album and pulled her hair back from her face. Despite a steady breeze from the sea, the day was warm, the air filled with a salty tang.

"Brianna won't be at her office until tomorrow. I've made an appointment for you at 1400 hours." He grinned when he saw her confusion. "Two in the afternoon," he explained.

She smiled. "Thanks, Liam. I do feel safe here." She looked over her shoulder and stared wistfully at the rolling lawn that stretched to the sea, where sailboats bobbed in the sunlight. A golf course bordered the shore, and visitors strolled about the English topiary gardens below.

"I'll call the hotel desk and tell them we're staying on another night." As he started to leave, he noticed the white tissue knotted in her fingers. Had she been crying? "Did you reach your brother?"

Sara nodded. "I wish I could say that his voice sounded familiar, but…" She sighed. "Apparently he and I quarreled the last time we spoke." Briefly, she told Liam the content of her conversation with Jeremy.

"Siblings often have disagreements. You and Jeremy couldn't be worse than me growing up with six older sisters." He laughed. "I learned to duck before I could sit up."

She grinned and he felt glad that he could make her smile.

"I've been going over these photos and I don't see anyone who might be my brother. I think the picture you found in the bottom of my bag might be of Jeremy."

"The man standing beside the palm tree?"

"Yes. After seeing where I live, I think my grandmother must have forbade displaying any pictures of him. For that matter, of my parents, too." Her expression turned wistful. "I wonder what hold my grandmother had over me?"

"You'll know when your memory comes back. And from what Brianna said, the sooner you relax, the sooner that might happen."

Liam strode to the glass table and picked up the hotel publication. "What do you feel like doing?" He leafed through the pages. "Tonight there's a jazz combo in the cocktail lounge." He realized he knew nothing about what she might like to do for fun, and he looked forward to discovering who she was. He flipped a few more pages. "More shopping along the arcade?"

"I would like to keep busy. It keeps my mind off the Ziegler brothers, or Trent Sherburne, or how I could be mixed up with them."

How could he be so foolish to think that, just because she wasn't talking about them, she wasn't worried? Liam took her hand and pulled her to her feet. "Let me come to your rescue." He smiled when she gave him a wry look.

"What do you have in mind?"

"A surprise." He kissed the palm of her hand. "You trust me, don't you?"

She gave him a lopsided smile. "I have no choice—
you're all I've got."

"Let's hope I'm enough."

When they reached the ground floor a few minutes later,
they were still holding hands. Her slight fingers were warm
and fragile in his grip, and he felt as though he wanted to
go on holding her hand forever. *You're definitely losing
your head, O'Shea,* he warned himself, then dismissed it.
The past twenty-four hours had been hairy, and they
needed a bit of fun to relax. Hell, he wasn't going to lose
his head as he had last night and kiss her again. Yet if his
partner knew how Liam was beginning to think about Sara,
Clete would insist that he take himself off the case.

No sweat. He could handle his emotions. Until more
missing pieces of Sara's past were revealed, Liam didn't
want anyone else taking responsibility for protecting her.
And for now, he wouldn't think about what that meant.

Fifteen minutes later, Liam paused in front of a jewelry
store in the arcade. "Let's go inside and look around," he said.

Sara glanced up in feigned surprise. "Don't tell me
you're going to buy me an engagement ring, get down on
one knee and beg me to marry you," she said with laughter in her voice.

He was delighted that she was finally relaxing enough
to tease. "Didn't my sisters warn you that I'm not the marrying kind?" he retorted.

Just then a pretty blond woman appeared from the back
room. "Can I help you?" she asked as she came forward.

"The earrings in the window," Liam said. "The ones
with the stones that are the same shade as this lady's dress."

The clerk glanced at Sara and smiled. "Oh, I know the
exact ones you mean."

Sara looked up in surprise. "Did I miss something? How could you have noticed earrings? We were walking by the window at a pretty fast clip."

"I confess, I saw them earlier when you were shopping."

"How could you know the color of my dress before you saw me wearing it?" She had no sooner asked the question when the answer came to her. "You were following me."

He grinned. "Guilty as charged."

Her eyes widened, but before she could respond, the clerk returned with the glittering earrings.

"A perfect choice," the blond woman said, holding one up beside Sara's ear. Set in gold, the three sparkling green stones dangled from a delicate gold chain.

Simple, yet elegant, just like Sara. "I'll take them," Liam said.

"You'll do no such thing," Sara argued. "I can't let you." She whirled around and followed the clerk to the cash register. "I won't need them boxed," she said to the woman, whipping out her checkbook. "I'll wear them."

Sara sent Liam a warm smile. "Thanks for thinking of me. They're perfect."

He nodded. *So are you,* he thought to himself.

Sara and the salesclerk moved to the mirror at the other side of the jewelry counter while Liam took a seat on the empty deacon's bench by the doorway. He'd never seen Sara as relaxed as she'd been these past few hours. If only he could keep her this way.

Just then his cell phone rang. His gaze remained on Sara as he answered, "O'Shea here."

"Mr. O'Shea? It's Maggie O'Reilly." She sounded out of breath.

The hair on the back of Liam's neck stood up. "Maggie, is anything wrong?"

"Oh, Mr. O'Shea. I was in my kitchen letting Mitzie inside just before my TV show, *Love Stands Forever,* came on."

"Mitzie?"

"My Persian." Maggie took several deep breaths. "Just then I saw a black SUV pull up in Sara's driveway. At first I thought it was Lorraine Dudley, the real estate agent, showing Sara's house to a potential buyer. Then I remembered that Lorraine drives a blue Subaru.

"These two men got out of the van. They looked like salesmen. Dark suits. Ties. They went up the porch steps and opened Sara's kitchen door. I thought to myself, how did they get a key to Sara's house?

"I figured Lorraine must have given the men a key. But when she didn't show up, I called her at the real estate office. Lorraine said she would never give a key to prospective buyers without being there herself. I remembered that you told me to call you if anything out of the ordinary happened."

"You did the right thing, Maggie. Are the men still there?"

"Hold on. I'll look."

Before Liam had a chance to warn her that these men might be dangerous, he heard Maggie's footfalls crossing the hardwood floor. Moments later, she came back on the line.

"Yes, I can see them through the dining room window. Two men. Both large. One is huskier than the other. Black hair, thick heavy features."

The Ziegler brothers. They might be planting a bomb, which could endanger the entire neighborhood. "Maggie, listen to me. I want you to lock your doors. Then call the police and tell them what you've told me. Call Lorraine and tell her that until she hears from Sara, she shouldn't show her house or go near there, understand?"

"Yes."

"Then call me back when the police arrive, okay, Maggie?"

"You and Sara can count on me."

"Good girl. Thanks, honey."

"Just being a good neighbor," she said, and Liam could hear the pride in her voice. "Oh, and Liam? Did I tell you that I got their license number?"

Chapter Ten

"You've known since this afternoon that the Ziegler brothers broke into my home and you're just getting around to telling me?" Sara's face radiated shock and anger.

After she and Liam had left the jewelry store, they had spent the day wandering through the resort, chatting with guests as they took afternoon tea, admiring the sixteenth-century tapestries in the Catherine Parr and Jane Seymour galleries, and finally, after a leisurely dinner, listening to a jazz trio in a cozy lounge over drinks.

During all that time, Liam O'Shea had been keeping secrets. While he had appeared to be easygoing, he'd known that the Ziegler brothers had broken into her home. She shuddered, wondering if deception was a learned skill or if he came by it naturally.

"I wanted to wait until Clete called back with the police report," Liam said, brushing back a tendril from her face. "I thought you would take the news better if I could also tell you that the Zieglers had been arrested. And they have."

Sara remembered the phone call that had interrupted their romantic dinner. At the time, Liam had said the call was business, and she had believed him.

His hand lingered on her cheekbone, his touch soft and caring. "You were finally relaxed and enjoying yourself. I hated to tell you and spoil our time together. What could you have done except worry?" His apologetic smile was disarming. In the candlelight, his sapphire eyes glittered, looking darker than usual. And so deep she could easily lose herself in them.

Sara felt an incredible urge to step into his arms. She wanted him to hold her, to keep her safe. Instead, she turned away, needing to distance herself from his spellbinding gaze. She closed her eyes, trying desperately to fight the urge to seek comfort in his embrace.

"I can't afford to feel safe," she said moments later. "Regardless of how relaxed I feel, it's an illusion." She met his look with steely determination. "Someone wants me dead, and I must be aware of everything that's going on."

"That's logical to a point, Sara." His voice was soft, yet matched her resolve. "But until your memory returns, you can't be certain who from your past might be trying to harm you. Let me worry about who hired the Ziegler brothers. Your job is to relax so your memory will return."

She knew he was right. "I'm sorry—" She broke off abruptly. "I know you're right." She was tired and feeling too vulnerable. "So what did Clete tell you?"

"After Maggie O'Reilly called me, I phoned Clete, who was en route to your house, and asked him to get down to the police station at East Bennington and find out what was going on. He checked the car license number that Maggie took down and had it run through D.M.V."

"D.M.V.?"

"Department of Motor Vehicles database," he explained. "The report verified what Clete and I guessed. The Ziegler brothers were driving the black SUV leased by a garbage company in New Jersey that's a cover for organized crime."

The breath whooshed out of her. "I'm glad I'm sitting down."

"The good news is that the Ziegler brothers are in custody. They can't hurt you."

"Can they be made to talk? Can we ask them who hired them? Who wants me dead?" She tried to think logically, but without a past, without a memory, she had no idea where to start. "I think I need some air," she murmured, pushing away from the cocktail table. Liam was right beside her as they made their way from the club.

They had passed the cash register and were crossing the bar when they noticed a crowd gathering around a TV mounted from the ceiling.

Liam stopped and glared at the set. Sara followed his gaze to the wide-screen projection monitor. A pretty, dark-haired news announcer was giving a report. "That's Bellwood Island's local TV news anchor," Liam whispered.

"…was reported missing earlier today. Kitty Sherburne is the wife of Trent Sherburne, the senatorial candidate in the upcoming primary election scheduled in a few weeks."

The photo of an attractive blonde in her late twenties filled the screen. "She was last seen Saturday night when she left Boston after attending a local political fund-raiser for her husband's campaign. A spokesman for the family was unavailable for comment."

Liam stared at Sara, who looked horror-stricken. "I know that woman. I remember Kitty."

GOING DIRECTLY TO THEIR suite instead of seeing the hotel doctor was Sara's idea, not Liam's. He still didn't approve, but he was discovering very quickly that Sara could be as stubborn as he was when she wanted to be. He unfolded his long legs from the couch and closed the balcony doors. The night air was chilly and an unseasonable spring frost had been predicted.

Kitty Sherburne was out there somewhere, Liam thought. And if there was a connection between Kitty's disappearance and Sara's amnesia, how would he find it?

Frustrated, he keyed in the home phone number of the CEO of TALON-6 and waited for someone to pick up. "Brianna," he said when a woman answered. "Hi. Just the person I was hoping to talk to."

When he had finished bringing her up to date on what had happened to Sara, he added, "She's in a fragile condition. She says she can remember Sherburne's wife, yet her reaction to the news that Kitty was reported missing was way over the top."

"What do you mean?"

"Well, if I'd heard that one of the guys I'd gone to college with was missing, I'd be concerned, sure. I might even give the family a call, if I'd known him well. But Sara went completely to pieces. It was as if Kitty had been her long lost friend or something."

"Liam," Brianna began softly, "if Sara has hysterical amnesia, she's bound to overreact to things. Remember, the shocking event that terrified her is still in her memory, whether she's aware of it or not. Amnesia means that the patient is unwilling to remember. Unless Sara can gather her courage to face whatever caused her memory loss, she may never recover."

"That can't be true, Brianna." Liam heard the frustration in his voice. "If you could see her, you'd be convinced she's doing everything she can to remember."

"I know, Liam. And part of her wants to recall the past. But from what you've described about her reaction to Kitty Sherburne's disappearance, it sounds as if Sara knows more than her mind can handle right now. This is one of the classic symptoms of hysterical amnesia."

"So what are you suggesting?"

"Without seeing Sara, all I can suggest is that she visit a doctor as soon as possible. If she won't, there's not much you can do."

"I've tried," Liam said, "but she's terrified. I'm lucky she's willing to see you."

After a brief moment, Brianna said, "Go with your instincts, Liam. I'm sure that's what Mike would tell you if he were here. May I speak to her?"

"She's in bed for the night," he said, glancing at the bedroom door, behind which Sara had cried herself to sleep.

"Then don't disturb her. When you arrive in New York tomorrow, go straight to the TALON-6 building. Mike said that the apartment is ready for your arrival. Unless Sara is rested and relaxed, she won't be a good candidate for hypnosis."

"I'll tell her. Thanks, Brianna."

He heard her pause for a moment, then say, "She's more than a client to you, isn't she." The words were more of a statement than a question.

Is it that obvious? Unwilling to admit it, Liam said, "Sara's a special woman."

In the lengthening pause over the line, he could imagine what Brianna was thinking. *Don't get involved, Liam. Keep your professional distance.*

"Take care of yourself, Liam."

After Brianna had hung up, he clasped the phone in his hand longer than necessary before finally putting it away.

Yes, Sara was more than a client. He was drawn to her in a way he didn't understand—despite the fact that his professional side told him she could be involved with organized crime, that she might even know what had happened to Trent Sherburne's missing wife, Kitty. Yet with nothing but raw instinct, he knew she was innocent of any wrongdoing.

He opened the French doors and took several deep breaths of the cold air. A northeasterly wind was moving up the coast. Snow flurries were predicted in the mountain areas tonight. So much for springtime.

He left the door open as he went back to the couch and picked up the phone again. He ignored the cold draft that drifted inside as he tapped in the number for the Bellwood Police Department.

"Let me talk to Police Chief Martin Delderfield," Liam said to the dispatcher.

"Chief Delderfield is on another line. Can someone else help you?"

"Detective Ranelli, please."

"Please wait while I connect you."

Liam's hands clenched into fists as he waited impatiently.

"Ranelli."

"Al, this is Liam."

"Liam!" The sober tone switched instantly to a friendly one. "Francie told me that she'd seen you at the cottage yesterday. Are you still at Bridget's?"

"No. I'm on my way back to New York." Liam wondered if Francie had mentioned the attractive redhead who had also been visiting with him at the cottage. Since Al hadn't mentioned her, maybe Francie had kept the incident to herself. Liam hoped so.

"Say, Al. I'd like a favor. I just heard on TV about the missing persons report on Kitty Sherburne. Can you give me any details?"

"Sure. Her maid called in the report this morning. Maid had the weekend off, and when she arrived back at the house today, she noticed Mrs. Sherburne's bed hadn't been slept in, the mail had piled up, telephone messages hadn't been answered since Saturday morning." He paused for a moment. "Why the interest, Liam?"

"Hmm, you know. I'm nosy, I guess." He knew his friend didn't buy that old cliché, but Al was also professional enough to know not to ask again. "Where was the husband this weekend?"

"On the campaign trail. Sherburne returned home this afternoon. The maid called him immediately when she discovered the wife missing. Thought maybe she'd left unexpectedly to be with her husband. Guess she does that often enough. Anyway, Sherburne came into the station this afternoon, with his lawyer, to talk to the chief."

"Sherburne had his lawyer with him?" Liam asked, surprised.

"Seems the lawyer is a personal friend. He came here to look over the press release before giving a statement to the media. Poor Sherburne. Reporters are having a feeding frenzy over this. Our phones haven't stopped ringing."

Liam could well imagine, especially with a husband who had a colorful reputation as a womanizer. "I'll let you get back to work, buddy," Liam said. "Thanks, Al."

Liam clicked off the phone, his thoughts on the upcoming primary and how the media would play up the womanizing angle. Sherburne was the new boy on the national political circuit, from what TALON-6 had found out about him. With his wife missing, he might not be able to keep the skeletons in his closet hidden for long.

And how did Sara play into this?

Liam felt something tighten in his chest. Somehow, wondering about that didn't leave him with a very good feeling.

"YOU'RE JEALOUS," Kitty said, her dark eyes sparking with anger. "You're saying those things because Trent chose me over you."

"You don't know what you're saying," Sara cried out. She slid an arm around Kitty's shoulder and tried to nudge her back into a chair. Somehow she had to make her friend listen to the truth.

Kitty jerked away, swearing. She stormed to the closet and pulled clothing from the hangers into her arms.

"Get out of my life, Sara. Get out!" Her eyes glittered like hot coals when she threw the garments into the small suitcase on the bed. "I love Trent and he loves me. Nothing you can say or do will ever change that."

Sara struggled with the words, but she had to say them. She couldn't keep them to herself anymore. "You're dead, Kitty," she cried out, anguish overwhelming her. "He killed you. Don't you understand? I told you this would happen."

"Sara! Sara, honey. You're dreaming. Shh." Strong hands grasped her shoulders, and Sara opened her eyes.

"Liam!" Tears streamed down her wet face as she shuddered awake.

"You're dreaming, love," Liam said. "You're safe. You're here with me."

Tremors of panic shook her as she strained to remember the vivid images of the dream. "It was horrible."

"Try not to think about—"

"But I must, Liam." She pulled back to look at him. "The dream held some clue to my past. Even if I'm frightened, I must try to remember."

"Honey, it's not real. It's only a dream." He pulled her to him, and she leaned against his hard chest. He was naked from the waist up. He felt so warm, so solid, so right.

She glanced at the digital clock: 2:18 a.m. "I'm sorry." She raked a hand through her hair. "I didn't mean to wake you."

He grabbed her robe from the chair beside the bed and draped it across her shoulders. "Want to tell me about it?"

"It was Kitty. We were arguing." Sara squeezed her eyes shut, trying to recall the fading images. "It was so real. She was angry. Her face was red, pinched with rage. I—I feel that what I dreamed really happened. But when?"

"Sara, dreams always seem real when they're happening. But in the morning—"

"No." She shook her head, a faint trace of the dream returning. "We were in a bedroom. A motel room. I remember. Kitty was packing, going to meet Trent." A sudden, overpowering feeling of horror gripped Sara. "Oh, dear God, I'm involved with her husband." She stared up at Liam's surprised face. "Clete was right. I'd confronted Kitty about her husband, and in my dream, Kitty was screaming that she and Trent loved each other, and I should stop interfering in their lives."

Tears sprang to Sara's eyes as she gazed up at Liam. Although his face was controlled and expressionless, she sensed his disappointment in her.

"You're telling me that you're in love with Trent Sherburne?" His voice was dangerously calm, collected.

She swallowed a whimper. "I—I must be." She shrugged, glancing away from Liam's questioning gaze. "Didn't you say that I may be repressing something horrible? Something I can't face?" She forced herself to meet his eyes. "Please don't look at me like that, Liam. Help me to face whatever the truth is." She took in a deep breath. "Don't you see? Regardless how horrible and shameful the truth might be, I must face whatever I've done."

Liam stared at her. "You had a nightmare. For God's sake, Sara. Dreams aren't real."

"Dreams spring from the subconscious mind. Whatever I'm blocking, my unconscious knows the truth. You said yourself that Dr. Kent-Landis asked if I'd had nightmares."

Before Liam could protest, Sara clenched her fingers on his shoulders. "Don't you see? I must have been waiting for Kitty at the Sand Dune Motel. I'd arranged to meet her to tell her about my affair with her husband. Of course she was furious. In my dream, she said she never wanted to see me again." Sara's throat moved convulsively. "That's exactly how a wife would react to another woman threatening her marriage. When Kitty left, I must have followed her to her car."

"Her car wasn't at the hotel. The police didn't report that it was missing."

"M-maybe I picked Kitty up from the charity event and drove her to the motel?" Hot tears leaked from her eyes and down her cheeks. "The guilt, Liam. What other reason could there be for this awful, oppressive guilt I feel?" Her shoulders shook as she sobbed, and remorse clawed at her like a creature alive in her chest. "Oh, Liam. I think Kitty is dead, and I'm the one who murdered her."

Chapter Eleven

The next morning, Liam and Sara took a cab from J.F.K. Airport into New York City and arrived at the TALON-6 building a little before noon. While Sara was getting settled in the spacious apartment directly below the agency's corporate offices, Liam took the opportunity to check his messages. He was eager to hear any inside information that Clete might have picked up late last night from the East Bennington Police Department.

Bailey, the agency's secretary, was making copies at her desk. "Liam," she said, half turning as he breezed into the office. "Brianna called and asked you and your client to meet her at Clancy's at noon."

Clancy's was a bar and restaurant off Second Avenue, yet the business operated more as an employment office and private club for its owners—a group of ex-Special Forces and freelancers who hired on for specific assignments. Clancy's was also one of the safest places in town. A stranger wandering in off the street would stick out like a proverbial sore thumb.

Bailey turned back to the copier machine. "Clete called earlier. He wants you to phone him, too."

"Thanks, Bailey." Liam bolted for his office to call his

partner. He was determined not to get into another wrangle with Clete over whether Sara was involved with Trent Sherburne. Especially after worrying over that very thing for most of the night.

What if Sara was right? What if her nightmare was a repeat of what had happened during those hours before she'd lost her memory? Damn, he didn't know what to believe. For all he knew, Kitty Sherburne might have returned to her home this morning with a logical reason for her disappearance.

Yeah, and maybe pigs could fly.

Don't ask for trouble, O'Shea. This case was difficult enough without his own fears muddying the water.

"SO IF NO BOMB WAS FOUND at Sara's home," Liam asked into the phone, "what were the Ziegler brothers doing there?"

"The police don't know," Clete replied. "The Zieglers aren't talking. They're waiting for their lawyers to arrive this morning with bail."

"Bail?" Liam felt his temper snap. With those two on the loose, Sara was in just as much danger as before. "What about the latent fingerprints being found on the car and the bomb that exploded?"

"Latent prints aren't enough for a conviction unless there's other evidence such as a credible eyewitness. A lot depends on what the judge rules as admissible evidence. I'm afraid there's not enough for a conviction."

"Damn, I guess we should have expected that. Anything in the police report that can help us?"

"Not really. From the looks of the contents of Sara's home, maybe they only wanted to scare her. Kitchen cupboards stood open, drawers were turned upside down. They trashed most of the first floor. The police arrived before the brothers did much damage to the upstairs."

Liam's fists itched as he thought about what he'd like to do to those two. Then an idea struck him. "I wonder if they were looking for something?"

"It's as good a guess as any," Clete said.

Liam let out a breath in frustration. "That's about what this case has come down to. A damn guessing game."

"Patience has never been your strong suit." Then, as if to change the subject, Clete asked, "How's Sara taking all this?"

Liam didn't want to tell his partner about Sara's nightmare, so he evaded the question. "I think I'll hold off telling her that the Ziegler brothers will be out on bail soon."

"Why? Shouldn't she should know for her own protection?"

Liam felt that Sara would probably agree with Clete. "I know how upset she is by all of this. I'm trying to keep her calm before she starts her treatment with Brianna today."

"Liam, I don't have to remind you that it's against TALON-6 policy to keep pertinent case information from the client."

"Knock it off, Clete. Don't spout that crap to me."

"Sounds like someone should remind you of your responsibilities."

"Hey, I go back with TALON-6 just as far as you do, Clete. I helped draft our mission statement, remember?"

"Then you should know you're not following procedure." His tone was deceptively calm.

"Lay off, Clete. Brianna said that if Sara doesn't feel safe when she undergoes hypnosis, we'll be wasting our time. I don't think Sara needs to know those two thugs will be back out on bail."

"Liam, I'm going to take the late shuttle back to New York tonight. I'll meet with you in the morning and we can discuss this further."

"Nothing to discuss, partner. Sara is my case and I say what my client will know and when."

"Legally you can't keep any information from her, Liam. We can be sued—"

Liam swore. "Sued? Since when did you turn into a three-piece suit? I can remember when all we cared about were results, chum. And it wasn't that long ago, either."

"This isn't Special Ops, Liam. You're protecting a civilian. Her home was ransacked by the same two men who had wired a bomb to her car. Those are the facts. If you choose to ignore those facts, you're not acting responsibly. Period. Now either you tell Sara those men will soon be released on bail or I will. The ball's in your court."

"Don't give me orders, Clete. I'll tell her, but only when I think she's ready to hear it." Liam clicked off the phone. He looked up to find Sara staring at him.

How long had she been standing there? He glanced away, trying to remember what he'd said that she might have overheard. It was bad enough that she'd seen his temper, but he was truly afraid that knowing those men had ransacked her home might be the breaking point.

She sank into the chair beside his desk. Her lower lip trembled as she glared at him. "Tell me everything," she said simply.

He inwardly groaned. "Sara, do you trust me?"

Her eyelids lowered, concealing her thoughts. "That's a complicated subject. There's trust and then there's this thing building between us. I'm not so sure I trust whatever those feelings are."

It would have been so easy to say he didn't know what she was talking about. But when she looked up again and he gazed into those clear green eyes, he couldn't be anything but truthful. "You feel it, too?"

Her mouth quirked. "I might have amnesia, but I'm not comatose."

He couldn't quite hide his smile as he got up and came to put his arms around her. She wrapped hers around his neck and kissed him hard. Kissed him with an urgency that nearly drove him crazy. Using all his willpower, he finally managed to pull back and take her delicate hands in his. "Sara, there's something I have to tell you." His gaze fell to her lips. He could smell the fragrance of her hair. "I need you to believe that I can keep you safe, sweetheart."

"You know I believe that."

He didn't know if he could get the words out. "There's a chance that the Ziegler brothers will be released, for a time anyway, on bail." He saw her flinch. "Even if they're released, you're safe with me." He squeezed her trembling fingers. "Do you believe me?"

Her voice was calm, her gaze steady as she gave him a smile that sent his pulse racing. "Of course."

He sighed, feeling suddenly buoyant. "I'll never let you regret that, honey." Liam leaned closer, his gaze fixed on hers. "Now, what are we going to do about those other feelings we share?"

She was inches away, gazing at him with her heart in her eyes. "I don't know. What do you suggest?" she offered demurely.

He wanted to reach out and touch her again. But if he did, he'd be a goner.

Somewhere in his soul he knew that if he ever took Sara

to bed, she'd never be just a one-night stand with him. For one crazy moment, he wanted this woman forever in his life. The impossibility of that came crashing down on him.

He was a selfish bastard for thinking any woman could permanently share his insane life. Damn, hadn't he seen that when he'd told his best friend's wife and daughter that Stewart was never coming home? Liam had stayed with Liz and Bailey while neighbors and friends came to hold their vigil. Did he want Sara and their future children to endure that?

"If you were smart, you'd ignore getting involved with a guy like me," he said. His words caused her to pull back. She dropped her lashes quickly to hide the hurt.

He felt like an ass, but it was better to set her straight than to pretend he was anything more than he could be. "Let's go. I'll give you the full report of what Clete told me in the cab."

Liam got to his feet and grabbed his jacket from behind his chair, glancing at his watch. "Come on, Sara. We're going to be late for our meeting with Brianna."

DR. BRIANNA KENT-LANDIS was already waiting for them at a back table when Sara and Liam arrived at Clancy's Bar. The blond psychologist, who bore a striking resemblance to Gwyneth Paltrow, smiled warmly when Liam introduced them.

"I thought meeting over lunch might be more relaxing," Brianna said in a low, husky voice. "Besides, no one makes crab royale like they do at Clancy's."

Sara liked Brianna immediately. "Thanks for agreeing to see me on such short notice. Liam told me how busy you are."

"I hope I can help you," Brianna's gaze warmed with

compassion. "Liam told me that you've refused to go to the hospital?"

Sara shrugged. "Physically, I feel fine."

"Still, I'd like you to be examined by a specialist. We need to rule out—"

"Brianna, is this necessary?" Liam covered Sara's hand with his. "She's been through so much already."

"It is necessary." Brianna's tone brooked no argument. "We need to rule out any physical cause for your amnesia before I see you. To expedite things, I've booked an appointment for you with a leading specialist, Dr. Loeb. He's very kind. You'll like him."

"It's all right," Sara said to Liam. She glanced back at Brianna. "Thank you for booking the appointment. I'll see whoever you suggest."

"Great." Brianna opened the large leather menu. "Now, let's order. I'm starving."

Later, after they'd eaten and the waiter had cleared away their dishes, Brianna suggested to Liam that it would be best if he waited in the lounge. Only after Sara assured him that she was feeling relaxed and safe did he reluctantly leave.

Sara quickly brought the psychologist up to date on everything that she could remember, including her recent nightmare about Kitty Sherburne. When she finished, Brianna hesitated only a few seconds before speaking.

"A nightmare is only a dream, Sara. Nothing more."

"That's what Liam told me. But those images of Kitty came from somewhere."

"You could have imagined them. We'll have a better grasp of the situation when I examine you and see Dr. Loeb's neurological reports." She studied Sara carefully. "But you can't discount that, over the past few days since

Liam found you, you've made real memories. As you've struggled to recall your past, you've been forming new associations about who you are." She smiled kindly. "I can't help but observe how you and Liam look at each other."

Sara felt her cheeks warm. "I'm very fond of Liam. I don't know what I would have done without—"

"That's precisely what I mean."

Sara shook her head, confused. "I don't understand."

Brianna's eyes sharpened. "If your memory is blocked because you're not prepared to face whatever horrible thing is—"

"You mean, if I murdered Kitty Sherburne?" Sara interrupted.

The other woman shrugged. "So far, there's no evidence of foul play concerning Mrs. Sherburne's disappearance. Let's not borrow trouble."

Sara wished she could dismiss the idea as lightly. "I still don't see how Liam has anything to do with me not remembering my past."

"Let me explain. Let's call whatever frightened you the X factor," Brianna said. "Your conscious mind isn't ready to deal with the ramifications of the X factor, so your subconscious mind protects or blocks the event until you are stronger."

Sara nodded. "That makes sense."

"But while your mind grapples with the fear, you meet an attractive man, who is obviously also interested in you." She paused. "While a part of your brain struggles with protecting you, another part is springing to life with the joy of falling in love."

"I'm not in love."

Brianna held up her hand. "Hear me out, Sara. The part

of your brain that wants to protect you is suddenly flooded with these feel-good hormones. In a process that science hasn't come to understand, you find yourself wanting to get on with your life so you can be happy with this new man. Your brain is impatiently pushing you to remember the X factor. But the protective part still wants to bury it."

"You're saying that I'm my own worst enemy."

Brianna gave her a sympathetic smile. "Having feelings for Liam could be adding stress that might prevent you from remembering. Also, your eagerness to regain your memory might be causing you to jump to conclusions about what the X factor might be. The idea that you killed Kitty, for instance."

A rush of relief engulfed Sara. "So you think that maybe my nightmare was just a bad dream?"

Brianna smiled. "Yes, I think it's possible."

"But does that make sense?"

"We're not dealing with what makes sense, Sara. We're dealing with a mind that has been traumatized by something so terrible that it blocked the fear rather than face it."

"So what should I do? Not see Liam anymore?"

Brianna laughed. "Not at all. But you need to stop stressing yourself. You need to relax. Try *not* to remember."

Sara shook her head. "I don't know if I can do that."

"Of course you can." Brianna smiled. "I'll show you some deep-relaxation techniques that you can do between our sessions. You need to unwind, Sara. Once you relax within safe surroundings, you'll be strong enough to face the X factor."

Sara swallowed back the lump in her throat. "You make it sound so simple."

"Yes, it's simple. But I didn't say it will be easy."

Chapter Twelve

Ziggy stretched his long legs and leaned into the soft leather back seat of the Lincoln Continental. "This is the way to travel, eh, bro?" he asked Vinny, who was lounging beside him. "First class all the way." He motioned to the uniformed chauffeur behind the wheel. "Can't say the boss don't have style."

The silver-haired lawyer seated next to the chauffeur glared at the brothers over his Armani wire-framed glasses. Whatever he thought, he kept his comments to himself.

The lawyer's dirty look wasn't lost on Vinny. He scowled back. "The boss let us stew long enough in that hellhole of a jail. What took him so long bailin' us out?" He brushed at a wrinkle on the front lapel of his navy blue suit. "I got half a mind to send him my cleanin' bill."

The lawyer swore. "Half a mind is exactly what you've got, you idiot. Be damn glad the boss posted your bail. Now listen up before I give you your next assignment. The boss isn't very happy with your latest screw-up. Mess up this next job and you'll never work again." He furrowed his gray eyebrows. "Get my drift?"

Vinny returned the glare. "Hey, big shot," he said, leaning forward to jab his finger into the shoulder pad of the lawyer's suit jacket. "Who are you, makin' threats? You're one of the boss's hired hands just like us. And speakin' of which, where's our money?"

A muscle clenched in the lawyer's jaw. "Watch your mouth and be grateful you're out on bail. Another mistake like you pulled at that Regis chick's house will cost you more than what the boss owes you." His lip curled. "Understand?"

Ziggy leaned forward in turn. "It ain't our fault the cops showed up when they did. Hey, the chick must've had a silent alarm or somethin'."

The lawyer eyed him carefully. "What did you expect, breaking into her house in broad daylight?" He turned to glance out the windshield, then fixed his attention back on Ziggy. "You were sent to find the package and failed. As far as the boss is concerned, you didn't complete the job."

"The package ain't there," Vinny chimed in. "Thinkin' the redhead had it was a long shot, anyway. We even checked her mailbox, just in case the Sherburne broad mailed it to her."

The lawyer drummed his fingers on the leather seat. "I checked her mail, too, but that doesn't matter now."

Vinny snorted. "Doesn't matter? Hey, only a few days ago the boss had his shorts in a twist about that damn package. What gives?"

The lawyer's mouth twitched. "I've been telling him all along that there never was a package. He finally agreed with me. The woman must have made up the story. Otherwise, we would have found it by now."

Ziggy's black eyebrows rose. "Holy horse roar. We've been on a merry goose chase all this time for nothin'?"

The lawyer shrugged. "Not exactly. The boss learned a few things since then. You'll see what I mean when I tell you about your next job."

Vinny craned his neck to look as the New York City sky-line came into view. "I gotta buy some warmer clothes. I've been freezin' ever since we left Vegas." He shuddered, then glanced at the fabric of the lawyer's suit. "Say, you should know a good place to pick up some threads. Somethin' elegant, like yours. Custom fitted."

The lawyer muttered something under his breath as he studied the expressway exit signs. "First things first," he said finally. "Take the next turnoff," he told the driver, then grabbed the passenger handgrip as the Lincoln took the curve effortlessly, then merged with the traffic heading toward Manhattan.

Without taking his eyes from the road, the lawyer fished inside his jacket pocket and pulled out two thick, business-size envelopes. "Here are your instructions," he said, handing one to each brother. "The woman is staying at the TALON-6 Agency, a security and surveillance company in midtown Manhattan. Despite the businesslike facade, the building is a steel-and-cement fortress. Her boyfriend, Liam O'Shea, is ex-Special Forces and probably carrying. Be careful. He never lets her out of his sight."

"That redhead's a hottie," Ziggy said with a laugh. "I wouldn't let her out of my sight, neither."

"Get serious." The look the lawyer sent him was chilly enough to frost his glasses. "The TALON-6 building is equipped with state-of-the-art security systems. I've included the blueprints and the latest schematics on the place in your packets. Study them carefully."

"How'd you get a copy of the TALON-6 layout if the place is supposed to be top-secret?" Ziggy asked the lawyer. Then he elbowed his brother. "Hey, maybe they got a traitor at TALON-6?" he said with a laugh.

"Don't be stupid," the lawyer shot back. "Every building in the city, including TALON-6, must meet the city's building codes. Every business is required to file blueprints with the Department of Records at City Hall."

He motioned to the driver to turn left at the next intersection, then looked back at the brothers. "You'll also find confirmation numbers for your hotel reservations and a key to a locker at Grand Central. In it, you'll find further instructions and the equipment you'll need to carry them out. You'll also find a cell phone programmed with an 800 number. Use that phone only to call that number." He studied them for a moment. "Any questions?"

"How much money do we get for this extra job?" Vinny asked impatiently.

The lawyer ignored the question, and Vinny was momentarily distracted as the Lincoln pulled alongside the curb in front of a brick warehouse.

"You get out here," the lawyer ordered. "You'll find a cab waiting for you at the end of the block. You'll ride to your hotel from there." His steely gray eyes focused on Vinny. "The next time I see you, I'll have the rest of your money. The boss isn't a welsher." His lips twitched slightly. "That is, if you've finished the job. And the woman."

Vinny ripped open the flap of the envelope. His gaze widened when he saw the thick wad of money inside. He riffled the bills, and his mouth lifted with satisfaction. "Not to worry, chief. Tell the boss we'll get the chick this time, and she'll go out with a bang."

FOR THE REST of the afternoon, Liam sifted through the latest reports on the Ziegler brothers that Clete had faxed to him that afternoon. According to the criminal records from

Attica Prison, Ariel and Vincent Ziegler had been soldiers for organized crime since their late teen years. Despite being questioned for hours by the East Bennington police, both brothers had remained mum, and were finally released on bail a little more than four hours ago.

"Damn it." Liam threw down the report and glared out the window. Thank God Brianna had agreed to meet with Sara in the TALON-6 conference room for their first session. With the building's state-of-the-art security, Sara would be a virtual prisoner, but she'd be safe. She would also be just down the hall from his office, which gave him an added sense of relief.

Relief, hell. This was the most frustrating case he'd ever worked. What judge in his right mind would allow bail for two hit men, caught red-handed? Whoever wanted Sara dead had very powerful friends.

God, how could he live with himself if something were to happen to her? Liam wondered. Just as quickly, he pushed back the thought. He glanced nervously at his watch again. Sara and Brianna would be in session for several more hours.

He glanced at the mountain of files and computer printouts that littered his desk. Thank God. He needed to keep working.

He'd picked up the report on the Ziegler brothers again when a sharp rap sounded at the door. Not looking up, he called out, "Come in."

Instead of Bailey, whom he'd expected, Clete strode in, carrying two cups of Liam's favorite coffee and a briefcase clutched under one arm.

"Hey, I wasn't expecting you until tomorrow morning." Liam swung around in his chair, taking the proffered beverage. He couldn't help wondering if the coffee was a peace offering, considering how abrupt their earlier telephone conversations had been. He took a sip. "Umm, Colombian black roast. Thanks."

"The way you guzzle coffee, I figured your teeth would fall out if you kept drinking that brew from the vending machine."

Liam grinned as Clete put his briefcase down and perched on the edge of the desk.

"Say," Liam began. "I want to apologize for hanging up on you." He hated to be in the wrong, but when he was, he promptly admitted it. "Sara overheard our conversation, so I told her about the Zieglers." He grinned. "She reacted far better than I thought she would."

Clete shrugged. "Apology accepted. I'm glad she took it well, which proves my point. Don't keep the truth from a client."

Liam didn't agree, but dropped it for more important things. "What's the latest on the Kitty Sherburne investigation? Not much is coming in over the wire."

"Off the record, the police don't suspect foul play. On the afternoon of the day she disappeared, Kitty made a stop at her safety deposit box. Her secretary confirmed that Kitty's passport was kept there. She cashed in stocks and bonds, and withdrew cash from several bank accounts, then wired the proceeds to a bank in Caracas."

Liam stared at him in surprise. "Venezuela? Sara's brother has an apartment in Caracas. I wonder if there's a connection?"

"I thought that would pique your interest." Clete crossed his arms, his features sober again. "When Kitty attended the charity fund-raiser the day she disappeared, she arrived early enough for a photo op and interview with the local media. Yet no one remembers seeing her during dinner. The police are still trying to determine who saw her last."

"Do they think she left with someone at the event?"

"If she did, they took her car. Her BMW is still missing."

Liam wanted to believe that Sara wasn't involved. However, he couldn't ignore the fact that Sara's brother also lived in Caracas. "Have the police checked the airlines?"

"Airports, bus and train stations. But if Kitty wanted to disappear, she'd use an alias. My hunch is that she took off for parts unknown." Clete made a face. "The lady left her husband just weeks before his first primary, knowing that her disappearance would unleash gossip about his dallying. Tales of his philandering would fill the tabloids at every news stand and supermarket." He shook his head. "The perfect revenge."

Liam strode to the window and gazed at the view of concrete-and-glass skyscrapers. If Kitty was alive and well in Caracas, then Sara wasn't a murderer. But what if Kitty had found out that Trent was leaving her for Sara? Sara's nightmare fit that scenario to a T.

What if Sara regains her memory only to find that she's in love with Sherburne?

Liam squelched the depressing thought. "So let's look at what we have." He thrust his fists into his pockets. "Kitty liquidated her assets and wired the money to a bank in Caracas. Sara's brother has an apartment there. We don't know if Kitty left the country, so until that's confirmed, she's still a missing person."

"Kitty's husband claims he has no idea where she is," Clete added. "He also claims there's no marital trouble between them." He pulled out a sheaf of papers, held together by a paperclip. "You can read his notes yourself, but I'll give you the highlights." He slid the papers toward Liam's end of the desk. "Despite having a wife, the randy Trent Sherburne has always played the field. He likes broads, all kinds. Waitresses, flight attendants, an art professor—those are just a few of the conquests he's left in his wake."

Liam shrugged as he opened the file and studied the first page. "Says here that on the weekend his wife disappeared, Trent was on a campaign swing throughout the state." His finger traced down to the last paragraph. "Sherburne didn't return until Monday, when he was notified of his wife's disappearance."

Clete nodded. "Yeah, and so far, his story checks out."

Liam knew that he should level with Clete and tell him about Sara's fear that she'd been with Kitty at the Sand Dune Motel early Sunday morning. But what good would it do? Clete already believed Sara was involved with Trent. For the time being, Liam decided to keep Sara out of this. "Anything else on the Sherburnes?" he asked.

Clete opened his briefcase and removed a brown envelope. "Just this," he said, handing it to Liam. "You're not going to like it, but it's important that you hear this."

Liam opened the envelope and peeked inside. "A cassette tape? What's this about?"

"My interview with Melody Price." Clete fixed his attention directly on Liam as he spoke. "Melody is one of Sherburne's campaign groupies from his early days on the political scene."

Liam frowned. "What has this to do with Kitty Sherburne's disappearance?"

"You'll see." Clete stood and pulled a folder from the

open briefcase, slapping it down on Liam's desk. "Melody used to work as a political volunteer with Sara when they were both freshmen at Boston U."

"Get to the point, Clete. I'm in no mood for a history lesson."

"Seems that Melody had to drop out of college when she became pregnant with Trent's baby. I met the little boy. Melody told me that she and her son are living very comfortably, thanks to a well-heeled benefactor." He studied Liam's face as he spoke. "Care to guess who Daddy Big Bucks might be?"

Liam clenched his jaw and remained silent.

Clete shrugged. "Melody wasn't that talkative, but it doesn't matter. I've pulled some strings and I'm looking into Melody's bank account. I'll find out his name."

"What the hell has this got to do with Sara?"

Clete raised a brow. "Oh, did I forget to tell you?" He pulled from his breast pocket a photo of Trent Sherburne with his arm around two attractive, smiling young women. "Melody wants this picture returned to her. She said it reminds her of her happy college days."

Liam studied the photo. His gut twisted when he recognized Sara as the other smiling coed standing beside Trent Sherburne. The shot had been taken at Sherburne's campaign headquarters, if the flags, red, white and blue balloons and political posters along the walls were any indication. "The picture could be nothing more than a souvenir from an ambitious politician, rewarding two of his loyal, hardworking volunteers," he said.

Clete snorted. "For crissakes, take off your blinders, Liam."

Liam slammed his hand down on the desktop. "I don't

see what this proves. We knew that Sara and Kitty were sorority sisters."

"What if Sara was more than a campaign volunteer with Sherburne?" Clete asked. "If you weren't already emotionally involved with her, you'd see this as clearly as I do."

"I can handle it."

"Melody said all the women had crushes on Sherburne. Can you be sure you'll keep your cool if we find out that Sara and Sherburne were lovers? Or are still lovers?"

Liam picked up the photograph and waved it at Clete. "This picture proves that Sara knew Melody and worked with her on Trent Sherburne's campaign. That's all it proves."

Clete yanked the photo from his clenched fingers. "I think there's more to it and so do you."

"Damn it, Clete." Liam took a deep breath. "I know you're diligent in your research. I know it's your job to think of every angle. But you're wrong about Sara. And if you think I'm losing my objectivity about this case, then you're wrong on that score, too."

Clete remained steadfast. "How are you going to feel if Sara killed Kitty because she wanted to be the next Mrs. Trent Sherburne?"

"That's enough!" Liam pointed to the door. "Get out of my office."

Clete pushed himself away from the desk and moved toward the doorway. "I'm leaving," he said on his way out, "but you can't get rid of the facts quite so easily."

Chapter Thirteen

The following afternoon, Sara jumped up from the leather couch in the conference room and began pacing in front of the windows. "This isn't getting us anywhere, Brianna."

Brianna Kent-Landis couldn't agree more. For the past three hours, she had tried every technique known since Freud, but Sara had blocked, however unwittingly, every attempt to be hypnotized. She was either too traumatized or consciously didn't want to regain her memory. "Maybe we should take a break?"

"What good would it do?" Sara twisted her hands together in frustration. "We've been at this all day. The harder I try to relax, the more my stomach tightens into knots." Tears stung her eyes. "I'm a complete failure at this. I don't know how I'm going to tell Liam."

The desperate, haunted look she'd seen on his face the day before came to Brianna's mind. He'd been waiting outside the conference room after their session. Privately, he had told her about Clete's theory that Kitty Sherburne might have staged her own disappearance in order to sink her husband's political campaign, to get back at him for his philandering. Was Sara the other woman? And was it Kitty who had taken out the contract to have Sara killed?

Sara knew. And until she was willing to unblock her memory, Liam was at a loss to help her.

Brianna crossed her legs and studied the lovely young woman. *How can I reach you, Sara?* Suddenly, an idea came to mind.

"Let's pursue that question." Brianna perched a notepad on her knee. "What if you never regain your memory? What would your life be like?"

Sara sat up, startled. "You're kidding, right?"

"No, I'm serious." Brianna fixed her with her gaze. "What would you do?"

Sara sank down onto the couch again and pursed her lips. "Well, I—I'd—" She hugged herself. "If someone is trying to kill me, I can't return to my old life." She looked up at Brianna, her green eyes round with fear. "I'll have to go away. Hide."

Brianna leaned forward, encouraged. "Okay. Where will you hide?"

"I—I could live with my brother. In Venezuela." She sighed with relief, then a staggering look of fear darkened her eyes again. "If organized crime is after me, they'll…" Her shoulders sagged. "They'll eventually find me, and being with Jeremy would endanger him." Sara glanced up, her eyes wide. "There's nowhere I can go."

Brianna hoped this diversion might help Sara understand the futility of blocking whatever she knew. Instead of facing the truth, she was very near to unraveling. "If you have nowhere to hide, Sara, what are you going to do?"

Her bottom lip trembled. "I don't know."

Brianna pressed on. "Then what *won't* you do?"

Sara blinked, all the more confused. "What do you mean?"

"I mean, what would you absolutely refuse to do?" Brianna uncrossed her legs and leaned toward her. "For instance, I remember when a stalker was after me once. Only I was in denial. I thought I could handle him by myself. It was my aunt who made me realize that I was only fooling myself by discounting the danger I was in. Although my denial gave me a false sense of power over my stalker, it wasn't realistic." Her mouth twisted with the memory. "Thank God for Aunt Nora."

Brianna gazed at Sara's intent face. "We all handle fear differently. Later, when the stalker abducted me and I was fighting for my life, I was blinded by terror, just as you are. Yet when I thought I was going to die, something within me kicked in. I didn't know what I was going to do, but I knew what I wouldn't do. I'd be damned if I'd let the bastard win. That burning desire to keep him from killing me gave me the strength to survive. That's what I'm asking of you, Sara. Your back is to the wall. You don't even know who your enemy is, but you have choices. So tell me, what do you refuse to do?"

The light of understanding finally broke across Sara's face and a slow smile lifted the corners of her mouth. "I'm tired of running, Brianna. That isn't getting me anywhere. I refuse to run anymore. I'm going to stay here, keep working with you—that is, if you're willing to put up with me until I regain my memory."

"That's my girl."

Sara smiled, her green eyes brightening with tears. "Thank you, Brianna. I'm ready to try again."

Brianna glanced at her watch. "Okay, but first let's take a short break. When we come back, I want to try a different approach. Didn't you mention that you brought a photo album with you from your home?"

"How about a cup of coffee?"

Liam sprang from his desk chair when he saw Brianna poke her head inside his office door.

"Sure." He followed her down the hall. When he reached her side, he noticed the shadows around her eyes and realized how trying these sessions were for her, as well as for Sara. "I don't want to break your doctor-client confidentiality," he said finally, "but how's it going?"

Brianna gave him an empathetic look. "Sara might have something to tell you later. Right now, she needs a short break and I offered to get the coffee."

Liam frowned, hoping not to show his disappointment.

"Don't worry, Liam." Brianna's eyes were kind. "I have an idea. Remember the family album that Sara brought from home?"

"Sure. Why?"

"Would you mind bringing it to me? I'd like to go over the photographs with her. If she's in a deep state of relaxation, she might remember something she may have missed earlier."

"I'll be right back."

Brianna watched Liam hurry toward the elevator, and she couldn't help wondering about him. How many scores of women had Liam O'Shea dated since she'd known him? Love 'em and Leave 'em Liam—that was the nickname his Special Forces buddies had given him. But whether Liam knew it or not, he'd finally met his match. He wasn't going to find it so easy to love and leave the gentle Sara Regis.

Brianna smiled to herself as she slid a crisp bill into the

vending machine, then pressed the button for black coffee. She could hardly wait to see what was going to happen when another one of the invincible ex-military men of TALON-6 realized that he'd been felled by one of Cupid's arrows.

ZIGGY ANSWERED the cell phone on the second ring. "Yeah?"

"Just checking to see if you have any questions with the plan."

"Nah. We've looked everythin' over. Piece of cake."

The deep voice on the other end of the line hesitated. "If you've looked over those blueprints, you know the building is impregnable."

"No problemo." Ziggy felt a deep pride in his brother. When it came to blowing up things, Vinny was a regular Einstein.

"What type of…mousetrap will you use?"

"Wha…? Mousetrap? What the hell are you talkin' 'bout?"

The man gave a deep sigh. "Never mind. When will you be ready?"

Ziggy was still thinking about mousetraps, but finally said, "Oh, I get it." He switched the phone to his other ear. "The mousetrap will be finished tomorrow afternoon."

"Too late. I want it delivered today."

Ziggy swore. "Hey, these delicate things take time. Vinny's checkin' out the carrying device now."

"Carrying device?"

"Yeah. You know." Ziggy chuckled. "The means of getting the mousetrap to the mouse."

"Tell your brother he's got until five this afternoon." Then the line went dead.

BRIANNA AND SARA SPENT most of the afternoon sorting the photos from the album into a time line of family members.

"I feel like a detective," Sara said, excited at their progress. Clothing and hairstyles, plus details from automobiles, helped with chronology, but the pictures still hadn't triggered Sara's memory.

"Let's try something else," Brianna said finally. "I'll show you a photo, and I want you to tell me whatever comes to mind. Remember to relax and breathe deeply." She handed Sara the first photo—of a girl of about eight with her family of Barbie dolls. A Christmas tree surrounded with brightly wrapped presents stood in the background. "Tell me, Sara, who do you think took this picture?"

Sara held the photo in one hand. "The girl's brother."

"Why do you think that?"

"I don't know for sure, but I'd guess he's visiting her for the holidays." Sara glanced at Brianna. "It's Christmas, and from all those presents under the tree," she said with a laugh, "the little girl made out like a princess."

"She was a good little girl, then?"

"Oh, yes." Sara stared at the photograph. "She never made any trouble."

"What do you think might have happened if she had 'made trouble'?"

Sara's smile faded. "She'd be put in a foster home?"

Brianna remained silent, hoping for more. Finally she said, "Why do you think that?"

"The girl has no parents."

"Then who bought all of those Christmas presents? Don't you think the little girl is loved?"

A cry broke from Sara's lips and she sat up. "The presents were from my father." Her green eyes shone with awareness. "Brianna, I remember. This photo was taken after my mother died in an automobile accident. My brother had just flown in to spend the holiday with me, and it was Jeremy who unpacked the gifts and arranged them under the tree." She studied the photo closer. "This was taken a few days before Christmas, while my grandmother was at church. When she returned, she was furious. She made a terrible scene, and threw away every gift my father had sent." Sara's face drained of color and Brianna noticed how her hand shook. "My brother did take this picture, Brianna. He was fourteen, and when he stood up for me against my grandmother, she called our father and Jeremy was put on the next flight back to California."

Brianna swallowed the lump in her throat and waited for Sara to collect herself. "Do you know why you didn't go with Jeremy to live with your father after your mother died?"

"My grandmother said she needed me." Sara mumbled the words as though she finally realized this for the first time. "I was afraid that if I ever left her, she would die…"

"Which was what your grandmother wanted you to believe," Brianna murmured.

"I CAN'T WAIT TO TELL Liam," Sara said as she left the conference room with Brianna. They had finished their session around four o'clock, and Sara hurried ahead to find him.

His office door was ajar. He must have recognized her footfalls because he was halfway out the door when she rounded the corner. The smile he gave her made her heart sing.

"We've made a breakthrough," she said, wanting to shout the news. "My brother, my grandmother, growing up in East Bennington—I remember it!" She tried to contain her excitement when she noticed Bailey seated within earshot behind the reception desk.

Liam pulled Sara into his arms and swung her around. "That's wonderful, honey."

Suddenly Sara realized that he had misunderstood and thought she'd regained all of her past. "I still can't remember recent things. I don't know why I went to the Cape or why I checked in at the Sand Dune Motel. But Brianna said that remembering my childhood was a major step." She thought she saw a flash of disappointment in Liam's eyes, but he recovered quickly.

Bailey came over and congratulated Sara. "That's great news."

"Did Brianna say how soon you'd remember…more recent events?" Liam asked.

She hadn't imagined his disappointment. "Liam, I'm doing the best I can." She drew away. "I thought you'd be happy."

"I am happy. That's wonderful news. In fact, let's celebrate. Let's have dinner at Clancy's." Liam slid his arm around her again, and this time Sara didn't pull away.

The phone rang and Bailey gave Sara a thumbs-up as she moved toward the reception desk.

Sara pulled her hair back from her face. "I'm sorry. I guess I'm more tired than I thought."

He cupped her chin. "These sessions have been grueling for you." He hesitated, concern darkening his face. "Would you rather stay in tonight? Maybe have something delivered?"

Before she could answer, a man's deep voice called, "Did I just hear some good news?" Brianna's husband, Mike Landis, stepped out of the corner office. In three long strides, he joined them by the reception counter, his easy grin fixed on Sara. "I don't think I've had the pleasure."

As Liam introduced them, Sara shook Mike's strong, firm hand. "Your wife is incredible," she told him. "I know I'm on the verge of remembering everything."

Just then Brianna appeared from the conference room. She smiled at the small group gathered around the front desk, her eyes brightening with a special glow as they settled on her husband. Sara wondered if people could tell how she felt about Liam by the way she looked at him.

"I was asking Sara if she felt like going to Clancy's for dinner," Liam announced. "Anyone care to join us around eight o'clock? I'll call for reservations." He glanced back at Sara. "That is, if you're feeling up to it?"

"I'd rather stay here. I thought I might work out in the athletic room upstairs. Maybe take a swim. Then I plan to spend the evening sifting through the photographs again. Who knows? I might remember more."

Mike glanced at his watch. "I've got a few hours of work yet to do." He glanced at his wife. "I could take the work home, or if you'd rather, we could stay over in the city tonight."

Brianna slid her hand along his jacket sleeve. "I had hoped to get home early." She turned toward Sara. "Remember to catch up on your rest. Call me later if you'd like to talk."

"Okay," Mike said to his wife. "I'll be right with you, honey. I want to pick up a few things from my desk to take home with me."

Brianna nodded. "I'll wait right here." She winked at Sara. "If I go on ahead, he'll get caught up in his work and stay here until midnight."

Bailey laughed. A buzzer on the security panel beeped and she turned her attention back to the computer monitor, then she punched a few keys. The video monitor positioned on the wall above her desk clicked on, showing a view of the downstairs lobby. A deliveryman wearing a brown hat and uniform stood holding a small parcel.

Bailey glanced up at Liam and Mike. "An express delivery messenger. Are either of you expecting a package?"

Chapter Fourteen

Mike glanced back at Bailey and shook his head. "Not me. I'm not expecting any package. Maybe Clete sent us backup copy from the Kitty Sherburne investigation."

Liam studied the deliveryman on the video screen. The box he held was wrapped in brown paper held together by clear plastic tape. "Funny, Clete didn't mention mailing hard copy when he was here last night."

"Yeah, that's right." Mike rubbed his chin. "Bailey, scan the package through a delay-and-secure five-seven-red alert."

Sara looked at Liam. "What's that?"

"Each TALON-6 security procedure is identified by number and color. Basically, it's a set of instructions," he explained. Sara watched, fascinated, as Bailey clicked the audio button on the instrument panel and put on her headset.

"Do you see the door to the left of the TALON-6 nameplate?" Bailey asked the messenger.

"Where?" The uniformed man stared into the video camera.

"Right in front of you," Bailey explained. "See that knob on the metal door? Beside the brass nameplate on the wall?"

"Oh, yeah." The messenger pulled the door open. "Now what?"

"Place the package inside, on the shelf," Bailey instructed, "then close the door and latch it securely."

Sara stood beside Liam as everyone watched the monitor. When the man did as he was told, Bailey punched several more keys on the instrument panel. A white cardboard box, not much larger than a shoe box, appeared on the video screen. She clicked another key, telescoping the address label into view.

"It's addressed to Sara, in care of TALON-6," Bailey said in surprise. She glanced up at Liam and Sara, then gazed back at the video screen. "The return address label says the package is from Maggie O'Reilly."

"That's strange," Sara said. "I didn't give Maggie this address." She glanced at Liam. "Did you?"

A muscle in Liam's jaw jerked. "No. I don't believe the package is from Maggie," he said, his voice dangerously low. "Bailey, x-ray the package. Let's have a look at what's inside."

Bailey's fingers splayed over the keyboard as she typed. The monitor hummed and blinked. When the static cleared, the contents of the box appeared on the screen.

Liam swore. Sara grabbed Liam's arm and gasped at the deadly image on the screen. She was so astonished that she froze in place. She didn't have to be a bomb demolition expert to recognize what the clock wired to the small detonator, meant.

"Call the bomb squad," Liam ordered, and he clutched Sara's arm. "Mike, take over, will you? I'm escorting Sara to the apartment."

Mike grabbed a free line and punched numbers into the phone. "Stay with her, Liam. I'll keep you up to date." He turned to Bailey. "Print those pictures. Clete might be able to tell if this is the same type of incendiary device as the bomb he found in Sara's car. And print out a photo of the delivery man. Although I doubt whoever sent the bomb would be careless enough to leave a trail, we need to check it out."

"What about the rest of you?" Sara said. "I won't be the only one running to safety." She glanced back at Liam. "We have to warn the other people in the building."

"Don't worry, honey," Liam said gently. "The chamber the deliveryman put the bomb into is especially designed for high explosive devices. Don't forget the TALON-6 building is also a safe house. This structure is equipped with the state-of-the-art equipment to protect visiting dignitaries, heads of state, foreign ministers. Even the president has stayed here while in the city."

Sara's gaze fixed on the image of the bomb on the video monitor. "Don't we need to evacuate the building?"

"No. The chamber is surrounded with six feet of reinforced concrete," Mike said. "The interior wall contains three feet of lead, which has an amazing absorption capability. Even if the bomb went off, it would blast into a specially fortified chamber below ground."

Liam squeezed her hand. "Don't worry, Sara. Everyone in the building will be safe."

"I might add that this isn't our first bomb experience," Mike said, "nor will it be the last."

Bailey turned away from the screen to glance back at Sara. "TALON-6 is one of the top electronic surveillance and security specialists in the world." She looked at Liam with pride. "And electronic surveillance is Liam's specialty. Clete is our bomb expert," she added. "I've watched training videos of him defusing some of the

most unstable, crude homemade devices ever imagined."
Bailey shook her head. "My heart is in my mouth just
watching, and he's as cool as if he were strolling in Central Park."

Liam jerked his head toward Mike. "Landis here is no
slouch, either. He's our resident genius inventor, keeping
TALON-6 on the cutting edge of technology. One of these
days, if he doesn't show up for work, I'll know the CIA
has spirited him away from us."

"While we're shoveling the hogwash," said Mike, "let's
not forget to brag about Russell. He's our wire expert,
overseeing the latest security installations and bringing the
team into the big time. Russ recently installed window devices that cause the glass to vibrate, deflecting any chance
that our conversations can be overheard by outside, para-
bolic microphones."

"Russ has been in Saudi Arabia for the past year, com-
pleting a satellite security network to monitor their oil
wells," Liam interjected.

"Let's not forget Jake," Mike added. "For the past four
months, he's been designing a top-security system for one
of the potentate's sons in Bahrain. The son recently married, and Jake is installing our latest radar devices at the
new royal palace."

"Wow," Sara said with awe. "I'm impressed."

Mike's smile faded. "We're telling you this so you won't
worry. No one can enter the building or ride on the elevator without passing hidden surveillance and security cam-
eras that, within seconds, match their retinas with hundreds
of databases around the world. You're in good hands, Sara."
He glanced at Liam. "Now, why don't you and Sara get out
of here? We'll wait for the bomb squad to arrive."

Liam took Sara's hand. "That's a good idea. Come on, Sara."

"No," she said, her eyes trusting and calm. "I'd like to stay. Really, I'm fine. I'm tired of running."

Brianna smiled. "Then you *should* stay." She glanced at the men. "While we're waiting, let's call Clancy's Bar and order something sent over. We can eat in the conference room."

Liam moved toward Mike. "Can I have a few words with you?"

"Sure." Landis's blue eyes narrowed when he saw the serious look on Liam's face. "Let's use my office."

When they were alone behind closed doors, Liam dropped into the desk chair beside Mike's computer. "I'd like to know how the hell anyone knew Sara was here!" His hands clenched into fists.

"I wondered that myself. Whoever's behind this might be using surveillance of their own." Mike drummed his fingers on the desktop. "How many people knew you and Sara were coming here?"

"No one. Not even my sisters knew where we were going." Liam rubbed his hand along the rough stubble on his chin. "We've made inquiries about Sara, Sherburne and his wife. Inquiries using various databases."

"So? That's standard operating procedure."

Liam propped his fingertips together and leaned forward. "I'd hate to think that any of our government contacts might be on the take, but can we logically rule out the possibility?"

"If you believe that, then we can't rule out the police, either." Mike met his gaze straight on. "The East Bennington PD has our cell phone number, along with the attorney general's office."

"They can't trace my calls," said Liam. "I only use digitally encrypted phones." He shrugged. "No, that's not it." Then an idea came to mind. "Clete has been snooping around. I wonder if his questions alerted someone who might have passed that information along to whoever hired the Ziegler brothers. Could any of the cops be on the crime boss's payroll?"

"That's a possibility," Mike said. "This case is involving some powerful people."

"Yeah, and Clete covered the Ziegler brothers' hearing. He interviewed the Sand Dune Motel staff. He's been investigating Kitty Sherburne's disappearance, and he talked to Melody Price, one of Sherburne's old girlfriends. Whoever took out that contract on Sara might have checked up on Clete, which led them straight to TALON-6."

Mike leaned back in his chair. "What makes me mad as hell is that whoever sent the bomb knows TALON-6 is one of the best security and surveillance agencies in the world. This just proves how brazen they are. It's as though they're thumbing their noses at us."

Liam looked at him. "Are you thinking that maybe Sara isn't the real target, but that whoever is behind this is testing TALON-6 security?"

Mike shrugged. "I don't know. I'm just thinking."

Liam pressed his lips together. "Well, we're damn sure going to find out."

THE NEW YORK CITY Bomb Squad unit didn't leave the TALON-6 building until after midnight. But the bomb technicians had safely defused the explosive device soon after arriving on the scene.

Sara refused to return to the apartment until she knew

everyone was safe. Despite the tense situation, she had shown amazing courage and compassion for everyone. Liam was very proud of her.

As they stepped off the elevator, they didn't speak until they reached the apartment door. "Liam," Sara said at last, "we need to talk." Her words hung between them as he keyed the password into the wall pad.

He gave her a charming smile. "Can't it wait until morning?"

"No. I saw you and Mike duck behind closed doors. I know you were discussing this. Liam, how can I forget that the bomb was addressed to me? I'm endangering everyone who gets near me."

He pushed the door open and stepped back to let her enter. "Let me worry about that, sweetheart," he said once they were inside. He locked the door, then put his hands on her shoulders and began to knead the tight muscles around her neck.

"Mmm, that feels good." She closed her eyes. But when he began to massage her shoulders, he felt her body suddenly stiffen, and she spun around to face him. "What kind of animal would use Maggie's name to send a bomb?"

Liam dropped his hands to his sides. "More than likely the Ziegler brothers figured that a neighbor—a neighbor home during the day—had called the police on them."

"But how would they know her name?"

"Their lawyer could find out from the police report. Or the mastermind behind all of this could. Don't worry, I've already asked Clete to see that the police are keeping a close eye on Maggie's home."

Sara let out a whoosh of air. "Dear God, wherever I go, I put innocent people at risk. Whoever is doing this could easily follow us and send another bomb while we're having dinner at Clancy's Bar. Or while we're getting into a cab. Or anyplace."

He could see her pulse beating in the column of her throat, and he couldn't resist pulling her to him. She didn't resist when he slipped his arms around her, and when she pressed against him he could feel the stiff tension in her body.

"Liam, what horrible thing must I have done to make them try so hard to kill me?" She buried her face in his chest, and he kissed her shining hair and held her closer. Her fragrance—woman and perfume—intoxicated his senses like a potent drug as he inhaled her sweet scent.

He had queries of his own, but he pushed them away. For now, it didn't matter. It didn't matter what she had done.

He had vowed to protect her, to keep her safe. But despite how hard he tried, he couldn't banish one nagging question: after her memory returned, would she be in love with Trent Sherburne?

"Oh, Sara," he whispered with a pang of emotion. For once this was over and the men who threatened her were finally behind bars, what then?

He felt her shudder, and gently pushed her back to delve the mystery of her eyes. He could see a thin ring of amber between the inky black of her pupils and the clear green of her irises. He held her face in both hands. "Whatever happens, we'll meet it together."

She slid her palm up his chest, her fingers into his hair. "Liam, when I saw that bomb, saw how close it came—"

"I know." His voice was gravelly, intense. "It's over. I won't let them hurt you."

She stood on tiptoe to kiss him, her lips parting with desire and something more. Her fingers slipped inside his shirt. "Liam, I want you to make love with me."

He could feel the shape of her body as she moved seductively against him. A swift and powerful wave of desire seared through him. "Yes, I want that, too," he said, the words dissolving as his mouth opened over hers. As their kiss deepened, his hands rose to skim over her breasts. Beneath his fingers, he felt her nipples cinch tighter as he teased them, fondled them.

Her hands roved over his shoulders, creating incredible shivers of delight. She tasted like springtime, so fresh, so guileless, so innocent.

Liam came to a halt, his mind forcing him back to reality. He hadn't planned for this avalanche of feelings, yet he was the experienced one here. A short while ago Sara had looked death square in the face, and her libidinous reaction was a normal one to danger. He sure as hell couldn't take advantage of her. Not like this.

With a strength he didn't know he possessed, he released her. "Honey, this isn't a good idea," he said finally, his voice husky. "It's been a long day." Without looking at her, he stepped aside and hurried toward his room and a cold shower.

EVERYTHING INSIDE HER went still as Sara watched Liam leave. Not a good idea? Why not? She wanted to go after him, but closed her eyes, unable to bear another rejection. She knew he wanted her. She'd seen the heated desire in his eyes, felt the hunger in his kisses. Then why?

She hurried to her room, fighting back the sting of tears. She should have remembered that they had a business arrangement. After all, she was the one who had insisted he do his job without sharing her bed. He was only behaving as he thought she expected.

An hour later, despite her best efforts to rid her mind of Liam, she was still failing miserably. As she finished towel-drying her hair and then rubbed moisturizer over her body, she couldn't help remembering his heated touch on her skin and the way it had made her feel. Slipping on her peach-colored robe, she returned to her bedroom. As she pulled back the sheets, she wondered if he was sleeping peacefully in the next room, or tossing and turning with fitful dreams.

Liam. How frustrating this case must be for him. What was going to happen between them when it was over? What was happening between them now?

The question aroused another flurry of excitement inside her. She knew what she wanted to have happen. Her heart skipped a beat just thinking of him sleeping so near. Why shouldn't they comfort each other in the time they had together? She knew he didn't want any commitment. She could handle that, too.

Yes, she still wanted to make love with him. She wanted to show him what she felt, wanted nothing more than to welcome him into her, to love him with every part of herself. It frightened her to think how happy this made her. Her life was in danger and she had no business desiring a liaison with her bodyguard.

No, she wasn't being honest. She wanted more from him. She wanted a relationship with him, regardless of how silly or foolish that might be. But what if they didn't have tomorrow? What if now was all they had together?

Liam found her desirable. She'd seen the molten desire in his eyes just before he'd turned and left her standing in the hallway. Then why had he left her?

From what Brianna had intimated, Liam loved women, but loved danger more. He always found himself with a large following of accommodating females. Yet didn't he yearn for something else? A home? A warm and loving family? Children?

Damn, she was in enough trouble without complicating the situation with these frustrating thoughts about her protector.

Sara, reach out for what you want, just once in your life.

She trembled at the idea. Yes, she'd escaped death several times, thanks to Liam. She was tired of hiding. She wouldn't hide from her deepest yearnings, either. A shiver of expectation sliced through her. Why not?

Because schoolteacher Sara Regis, who had lived a prim, sheltered life with her grandmother, wouldn't be so open with a man. Judging by the daily appointment diaries found in her home, Sara's social life consisted of weekly travel lectures at the school library and chaperoning high school dances.

At any moment, her memory might return, and she'd be back to that dull-as-dishwater life. Very soon the clock would strike midnight and, like Cinderella, she'd be trapped in her old world of unfulfilled dreams.

Well, the clock hadn't yet struck midnight. For all she knew, tonight might be all she had. Why not let Liam know that she wanted him? No strings. Just this once. Why not live her dream?

LIAM BOLTED UPRIGHT in bed, instantly awake. *Sara.* He could sense her presence even before he had heard her soft footsteps outside his door, as he had that afternoon when she had come down the corridor. He'd known she was there long before he'd heard her. Somehow, they were connected in a way he didn't entirely understand, and he didn't know what to make of it.

He raked his fingers through his hair and grabbed his jeans, which were draped over a chair. He'd barely shrugged into them when the doorknob turned. He finished zipping his pants as she stepped into the dark room. Had something frightened her?

"Sara," he whispered when she came into his arms. She was warm, soft in his embrace. He breathed in the intoxicating scent of her as he felt her heart beating against his bare chest. He slid his hand along the silk that covered her back and hips, then pulled away to look at her. In the moonlight beaming into the room, he saw her face as their eyes locked. Desire and a brief flicker of something else, uncertainty or wariness, shone in hers.

"Why are you here?" His voice was husky. Damn, what a foolish question. His mind swirled with what he should say if she answered him as he desired.

"I'm here because I want you." Her whispered words went straight to his heart.

He dropped his arms at his sides. "Honey, no—"

"Don't you want me?" Her small hands splayed against his chest and he knew she could feel his heart pounding.

"That's not a question I have the right to answer," he said hoarsely. "You know I want you."

Her arms wrapped around his neck as she closed the distance between them. "We both want this." She brushed her breasts against his hairy chest. He couldn't help himself; his fingers closed on silk and tender flesh. He liked the feeling of her moving against his hips. He liked it way too much. She moaned, melting against him.

He released her, fighting to hold on to some thread of sanity. "Sara, we have a business arrangement. I can't take you to bed. Don't you understand?"

She stepped back and untied the belt of her robe. "No, it's you who don't understand." Her voice was a husky whisper. Her robe fell open and she pressed against him. He was rock-hard and straining inside his jeans. "What I have in mind has nothing to do with business."

Chapter Fifteen

Liam's eyes flickered. "What if you wake up tomorrow and remember you're in love with someone else?" His words were like a jolt of ice water in her veins.

I'm not in love with Trent Sherburne, despite what your partner believes, she wanted to shout at him. Instead, she rose on her toes and brushed her lips against his rigid mouth. "Because I would know," she whispered softly. She caught Liam's hand and pressed it to her naked breast. "I would know here, deep in my heart."

The heat from his blue eyes seared her. Then, in less than a heartbeat, his mouth clamped hard and sure over hers, while his fingers caressed her breast tenderly, lovingly. When she thought she would die of pleasure, he drew his head back and studied her face.

In the moonlight from the window, his skin looked bronzed. She spread her hands across the springy black hair that covered his broad chest. The corded muscles in his arms and torso stood out as her fingers combed across them, coming to rest on his hard nipples. She wondered if he felt as she did when he touched her there. "I think you're beautiful, too," she said, turning her head and pressing her lips to lick one taut nub.

She heard him suck in a quick breath. She lifted her head to meet his gaze, and frustration and desire swirled in his eyes.

She heard another sharp intake of breath as he boosted her up against the wall. Reacting instinctively, she wrapped her legs around his waist.

"God, you're so beautiful." He dipped his dark head and buried his face between her breasts. She bit her lower lip to stifle a moan as yearning for him raged through her.

She wouldn't think of what might happen tomorrow. All that mattered was this night—this precious night with this incredible man who had shown her such caring, devotion and tenderness. This night and the delicious anticipation of the wonder of their joining. Regardless of what happened, she would always have tonight.

Eyes closed, she arched back. Her fingers gripped his hair as his mouth closed roughly around her breast and his tongue rasped over the firm nub again and again. He made a sound low in his throat, waiting until she cried out in sudden urgency before drawing the puckered tip into his mouth and sucking.

Her fingers clamped onto his shoulders as she relished the moment. "I want you," she murmured with a sigh of surrender.

"Sara, are you sure?" His eyes gleamed beneath heavy eyelids.

She paused to look at him. In the powerful intensity of his gaze, Sara felt something pass between them that went way beyond words. Never had she been more sure that if she didn't grab this chance, take this leap, she would regret the missed opportunity for the rest of her life. She gave him his answer in the only way she knew—with a kiss.

He groaned low and long as his tongue met hers and delved into the sweet interior of her mouth. Each touch created a new memory for her. It wasn't important that she recall her past. This incredible experience of openness and trust between them was all that mattered. She arched again, unlocking her legs from around his waist, and stood on tiptoe against him, glorying in their desire for each other.

She could feel him straining in his jeans, and shyly found the clasp at his waistband. With a pop, the snap was freed, and she heard his moan as her fingers groped for the pull tab of his zipper.

"I'll do that," he murmured, then sealed her mouth with his as he swept an arm under her knees and picked her up. He carried her to the bed, peeled back the satin spread and set her down against the pillows.

"You should be surrounded by candlelight, fresh flowers, a bed scattered with fragrant rose petals," he said as he gazed down at her, his voice husky with longing.

"We have moonlight and each other," she whispered, impatient for his touch again. The sexy smile he gave her brought a heady yearning that would only be satisfied when he was beside her.

"You're so incredibly smooth," he exclaimed, cupping and lifting her breasts. Her head spun as his thumbs rubbed her nipples, which were already aching for more.

She was barely able to speak when he paused, then pulled down his jeans and stepped out of them. She thought she would die of wanting as she watched him open the drawer of the bedside table and fish for something inside. In the shadowed darkness, she saw a glint of foil. Then with a swift, practiced motion, he was sheathed with protection and at her side again.

He positioned himself between her raised thighs, and his senses soared as he gazed down at her. She didn't flinch as he took a long moment to glory in the sight of her. "You take my breath away," he said finally, eyeing the satiny curves of her body—her creamy breasts, her tiny waist, those long, incredible, shapely legs. He dipped his head and touched one nipple with his tongue.

She writhed beneath him.

He rubbed his open mouth over the rosy tip, then gently used his teeth on her. She moaned in pleasure. "Please, darling. Hurry," she said, the words an anguished plea.

"I want this to be perfect for you. We have all night," he answered, closing his mouth again over one tight, sensitive nipple.

Her eyes shut and she reached for him. Her fingers clenched on his shoulders and she lifted herself so her lips tugged on his earlobe. "Please," she repeated insistently. "Now."

His heart hammered when he found her wet and ready. He covered her mouth with his, and she ached with pleasure when he entered her by slow degrees, gently at first, then more demanding as she kept pace with him. Finally, savoring each moment, he filled her. She went very still, her lovely eyes wide with need. He felt her tremble at the slow, sweet invasion, then they both began to move in the ancient rhythm.

Despite his intentions to go slowly, her passion wasn't subdued and meek, as he'd imagined. She was hot and wild beneath him. Blood roared in his ears as she cried out in sheer pleasure.

Touching, kissing, caressing as the waves of desire built to a grinding frenzy, he cradled her in the curve of his body. Driving, arching, pumping, he felt her tighten, then she cried out, her hips flexing again and again as shuddering sensations rippled through her.

Liam drove into her hard and deep. He'd never experienced pleasure so profound or so exquisite. "Sara. My sweet, sweet Sara," he said, collapsing, panting, on top of her.

SMILING, SARA OPENED her eyes and faced the morning in the afterglow of a night of love. She stretched languidly, then glanced at the tangled sheets and rumpled pillow beside her. Liam had already left, she realized with a stab of disappointment.

She sat up, brushing the hair from her face as she glanced at the clock. Seven twenty-one. Hoping he might be coming back to bed, she snuggled down under the warm comforters, listening for any sign of him.

On the bedside table, a fragrant bouquet of violets glistened in a crystal bowl. She sat up, stunned. When had he called in the order for flowers to be delivered—in the middle of the night? She shook her head in amazement. That man could do anything, she realized, smiling to herself.

The drapes, which had been left open to allow the moon's glow to illuminate their nakedness, now were closed. Her peach silk robe was carelessly strewn across the back of the boudoir chair, the only evidence of last night's passion.

The most important fragments of her past were still missing, she realized suddenly. She had no right to feel so deliciously happy. Not until she learned the truth about who was trying to kill her.

She pressed her lips together and frowned as she thought of the angry words she'd overheard between Liam and Clete outside Liam's office yesterday. Although Liam had not wanted to talk about it with her, Sara guessed that Clete believed his partner was getting too personally involved with her.

As of last night, she and Liam were definitely personally involved with each other. Could he keep his professional objectivity now that they were lovers?

She slipped into her robe and padded to the bathroom, a shadow of guilt tagging her. How could she ignore her own responsibilities? Last night, she'd practically thrown herself at him. Now, in the bright light of day, she realized that impulsive action might endanger Liam's safety. Besides, becoming lovers with him would definitely cause his partner to think so. Would Clete have grounds to remove Liam from her case?

But Clete also thought she had been having an affair with Trent Sherburne, and that she'd arranged to meet Kitty at the Sand Dune Motel the night her old friend had disappeared. A chill coursed over Sara and she drew her robe tighter around herself. But until she could remember the details of that early morning when Kitty had disappeared, or why she'd driven to a strange motel on Cape Cod in the wee hours of the morning, how could she prove that Clete was wrong?

You're doing it again, she chided herself. She'd promised that she would only think about today. Who knew when this precious time with Liam would be over?

She picked up her hairbrush, glancing at her reflection in the mirror. Clete was wrong about his hunch that she'd been in love with Trent Sherburne. She didn't know how she knew, only that she did.

WHEN SHE'D FINISHED dressing, Sara strode into the living room to find Liam in front of the wall of television monitors, glowering at the various shots of the exterior of the TALON-6 building, including three fire escapes, the back parking lot, four street corners and the roof.

His furrowed brow smoothed when he saw her, a dazzling smile replacing his earlier frown. His affectionate look melted away any remaining doubts she'd had about going to his bed last night.

He crossed to her in three long strides, and she sighed as she leaned into his strong embrace. The mixed scents of his aftershave and balsam-scented soap made her heady, and when she slid her arms around his neck he growled in her ear, a sound that was pure male.

"The flowers were lovely. Thank you."

"Not as lovely as you are," he exclaimed, his hand caressing her back. "It took all my willpower not to wake you this morning." His voice was a hoarse whisper. "I felt guilty enough for keeping you awake most of the night."

"All night," she amended with a teasing smile. "And I wouldn't have had it any other way." He dropped his head, and their lips locked in a deepening kiss. With a groan, he pulled himself away. "The bacon…"

She laughed as he dashed for the kitchen, then she paused to treasure the moment. Sharing breakfast with the man she loved… A good man, who was caring, unselfish, loving… She refused to think of anything except this moment. They had each other, and for now, that was enough.

When she entered the kitchen, the delicious aromas of bacon sizzling and coffee perking made her mouth water. She smiled contentedly as she strode up behind him and leaned against his back.

"Can I help?" she offered, sliding her arms around his waist.

He twisted around to kiss her on the lips.

She took the fork from his hand. "If I help with breakfast, maybe we can finish with enough time left over to…" She looked up at him shyly. "You know."

He nuzzled her neck. "Mmm. To hell with breakfast." He turned off the burner and removed the frying pan from the stove. "We'll call in an order of bagels when we get to the office." He tugged her to him, then pushed her back against the counter. "I'm not hungry for food, anyway. Are you?"

Surprisingly, she wasn't hungry anymore. In fact, she didn't care if she ever ate again. His grin widened as he lifted her, and she wrapped her legs around him as he strode back into the bedroom.

Sara giggled, feeling cherished, protected and loved. Whatever happened, their being together last night was a good thing. If Clete found evidence that she was guilty, she'd face her crime. But until that time, she wouldn't turn away from this chance of happiness.

AN HOUR LATER, Liam had just returned from walking Sara to the conference room for her session with Brianna when he noticed Clete step from the elevator and stride toward his office.

"Have you heard?" his partner asked as the elevator door closed. "Kitty Sherburne's body was found late last night, buried not far from the Sand Dune Motel." His gray eyes were sharp and assessing. "We need to talk."

Liam stood, stunned. "Let's use my office."

When Liam was seated behind his desk, he asked, "Why didn't you call me?"

"I was already at the Bellwood Police Department when the call came in," Clete said, closing the door and sitting on the corner of the desk. "I figured you couldn't do anything until this morning. The victim had been shot in the head with a 9 mm Glock. Unofficially, the medical examiner said he thought the time of death was last Saturday night or early Sunday. I asked your cop friend, Al Ranelli, to fax me a copy of the M.E.'s report when it comes in."

Liam leaned back and studied his partner. "Kitty's body turning up blows your angry-wife theory all to hell, doesn't it?"

"Not necessarily. It adds an interesting wrinkle, I think."

Liam frowned. "What the hell does that mean?"

"We know that Kitty cashed in her savings and left town with her passport. I can't prove it, but we need to assume that she was leaving her husband."

"Why do we need to assume that?"

Clete leaned toward him. "Face it, Liam. Kitty's murder means that Sara will very soon be hauled in for questioning. The police detectives are going to piece together probable cause. They've already interviewed the Sand Dune Motel clerk, checked over their registration records for Friday and Saturday nights and, any minute, I expect Bellwood's finest will be issuing an arrest warrant for Sara, charging her with Kitty Sherburne's murder."

"That's bull! Sara has no motive. Besides, you're forgetting that the Zieglers planted a bomb in her car. What are you proposing? That Sara had them rig the device to allay any suspicion?"

"Why not? She conveniently had an automatic car starter."

"Yeah, it's possible. And when I first met Sara, that thought crossed my mind, too. But seeing her, watching her through all of this—"

Clete raised his hand. "Save me the hearts and flowers speech. The police will see it my way."

Liam tried to hold on to his temper. If Clete had let slip to the police or anyone that Sara was staying in TALON-6, he didn't think he'd ever forgive him. "Let's take a walk." He couldn't hide the anger in his voice.

"Good idea," Clete said, accepting the challenge. He whirled around and matched Liam's strides toward the elevator.

Liam punched the down button, then glanced at Clete with lethal calm. "Let's take the stairs."

Outside on the street, he discovered the morning was gray, and a chilly gust of wind met them. Liam turned up the collar of his leather jacket as he and Clete strode silently down Fifty-seventh Street. They didn't speak until blocks later, when they wended their way through the throngs of pedestrians strolling through the park. The only signs of spring were beds of yellow daffodils and red parrot tulips shivering in the chilly breeze.

"Did you tell anyone that Sara is staying at the office?" Liam asked as they cut around a corner and headed down a secluded path to avoid the wind.

"No, but your buddies, Officers Al Ranelli and Francie Zarella, asked where you were, and I told them you were working on a case at TALON-6 and you'd sent me in your place." Clete glanced at him, his face reddened from the wind. "Al wasn't the most friendly guy I've ever met," he added, "but his partner, Francie, more than made up for it. She sends her love, by the way."

Liam could hardly blame Al if he thought Clete had been coming on as a big city investigator out to trespass on Al's turf. He asked, "Did you talk to the M.E. privately?"

"No," Clete said. "The examiner had closed off the crime scene until his people finished with their investigation. Probably won't finish before this afternoon."

"Did Al or Francie give you anything that was helpful?"

"No, but I got a lead on Trent Sherburne," Clete said, sidestepping a flock of pigeons pecking away on the sidewalk. "Apparently Sherburne has high-powered friends. With the primary only weeks away, the last thing he wants is a sticky murder investigation hanging over his head. The grieving husband was unavailable for comment. Did I tell you the FBI was also called in on the investigation? They were getting ready to take over the case by the time I got there. I checked with the agent in charge, who gave me the usual run-around until I made a few calls myself to friends in high places." He sneezed. "I think I'm coming down with a cold, damn it." He pulled out a white hand-kerchief from his breast pocket and wiped his nose.

Liam was too caught up with his thoughts to offer any sympathy. "So what else did you get?"

"Only promises, I'm afraid. Our friend Wendy at the FBI will be sending us copies of their results, including the autopsy report, as soon as they're available."

"Thanks," Liam said, hunching his shoulders. "Anything else?"

"Yeah. Did Sara ever mention that her cell phone was missing?" Clete asked.

Liam felt a heightened sense of unease. "No," he answered carefully. "I thought it strange she didn't have one. Why?"

"She owns one. It was found on the beach, not far from Kitty Sherburne's body."

Despite the cold, raw wind, Liam was starting to sweat. He wished he hadn't let Clete see how much this worried him. A personal article so close to the crime scene would be considered evidence, casting suspicion on the owner. "Did you find that out from the FBI?"

"No. The lobster fishermen who spotted Kitty Sherburne's body from their boat found it when they went ashore to investigate." Clete stopped walking and stood beside a vacant park bench. He glanced around to be sure no one was within hearing distance. "I want you to resign from this case, Liam. Sara can stay with Brianna and Mike while I carry out the investigation."

"Why should I?"

"You know why." Clete poked a finger into Liam's chest. "You've lost perspective. You're no longer functioning as a professional."

"What the hell gives you the right—"

"You know I'm right, O'Shea. As a member of this team, you've sworn to uphold your objectivity."

"Bull!" Liam grunted. "What makes you think I'm not objective? Or have you gone squealing to Mike again?"

"You're in love with Sara. I dare you to deny it!"

"That's absurd. Besides, my personal life is none of TALON-6's business."

"It sure as hell is TALON-6 business." Clete took a calming breath. "You were a member of TALON-6 when you took Sara as a client. And you are using TALON-6 assets on this case."

Liam's fists clenched at his sides. "I heard you. You said what you wanted to say. Now shut the hell up. I don't need you to tell me what to do where Sara's concerned."

He'd turned and started down the path when Clete grabbed his arm. "Not so fast, Liam. You *are* officially off the case."

He swore. "The hell I am."

"Liam—" Just then Clete's cell phone rang. Angrily, he pulled it from his belt holder. "What?" he yelled into the phone.

Liam turned away, gulping the cold morning air. He felt too angry to trust his voice. If Mike and Clete decided he was off the case, there was little he could do. He knew his partners had agonized long and hard before coming to their decision.

Damn, was he unprofessional when it came to Sara?

"Liam, wait up," Clete called to him.

He glanced over his shoulder. Clete was gripping his cell phone to his ear. His fair skin was ruddy in the cold, and dark circles around his eyes gave testimony that he hadn't slept. His nose was red, too, and Liam realized Clete had probably caught a bug from not getting enough rest and from working late hours on Sara's case. He was grateful for the dedicated backup, but decided he didn't deserve his ill humor.

Clete swore as he hung up the phone and clicked it back onto his belt. "We better get back to the office. That was Bailey. She just heard from your pal Al Ranelli. The police found the gun that killed Kitty Sherburne. It was stashed inside the toilet tank of one of the Sand Dune Motel units. Room 26, to be exact. Al said it was the unit where Sara Regis was staying the night Kitty Sherburne was murdered."

Chapter Sixteen

Liam wove in and out of fast-moving traffic along the Long Island Expressway, hedging Sara's questions about why they'd left the TALON-6 building in such a hurry.

Finally, she drew an exasperated breath. "Liam, why are we leaving the city? What's going on? First you rush me out of my session with Brianna just when I'm making major breakthroughs. Then you practically push me into the van, race out of the parking garage without letting me say goodbye to Brianna and Bailey—"

"Do you trust me, Sara?"

"Wh-why, yes. Of course I trust you. But I won't be kept in the dark." She glared back at the long cardboard boxes that rattled in the rear of the fifteen-passenger van in which they were riding. "And what's in those cartons?" she asked.

"Electronic surveillance equipment."

Her green eyes widened. "From TALON-6?"

He nodded. "There's enough equipment to make any-place we're going safe enough to protect you."

"Protect me from whom?" She raised her eyebrows, then jumped at the most obvious conclusion. "The Ziegler brothers." Her startled gaze told him she was waiting for him to confirm it.

"I'll protect you, Sara. Please, don't worry. No one's going to hurt you." Liam glanced into the rearview mirror, then back at the highway. "First we need to find a place to hide."

She blinked in bafflement. "Why? You said yourself that the TALON-6 building is one of the safest in the city." Then a look of understanding suddenly crossed her face. "Something's happened. Have the Ziegler brothers sent another bomb?"

Liam pressed his lips together and stared through the windshield. Damn, he didn't want to evade the truth, but by now, the authorities would be ready to serve Sara with an arrest warrant, charging her with Kitty Sherburne's murder. An all-points bulletin would be issued. If Sara knew about Kitty's murder and that she was the police's number one suspect, all the progress she'd made from Brianna's sessions would go up in smoke.

He didn't trust just calling the police. Liam needed to reach Bellwood Island to talk to his buddy Al and convince him that Liam had already checked out the motel unit the morning he'd met Sara. Once the detective knew this, he'd see that the murder charges against her were dropped. Liam would explain that he'd been leery of her amnesia story, and his cynicism had fueled a complete search of her room. He'd looked in the first place underworld thugs stored their goods—wrapped in plastic and taped inside the flush tank. Liam knew for a fact that when he and Sara had left, her motel room had been clean of any weapons. If the police had found the 9 mm Glock that had killed Kitty Sherburne inside the toilet tank of unit 26, then someone else had put it there.

Sara was innocent and he had to prove it. She was being framed, but by whom? The Ziegler brothers? They had the opportunity, and the desk clerk could substantiate that Ariel Ziegler had been in the motel lobby after the fact.

Once Liam explained this to Al and the charges against Sara were dropped, the Ziegler brothers might be found again. It wasn't impossible to hope they would plea-bargain and give testimony against whoever was bankrolling the contract against Sara.

"Liam! I'm not a child. If the Ziegler brothers made another attempt on my life, I demand to know."

"I'm asking you to trust me, honey. I'll explain everything as soon as I get out of this traffic." He signaled with the blinker and steered the van into the fast lane.

"How can I trust you if you won't level with me?" She switched on the radio, tuning in a news channel. Liam switched it off again. "I said I'd explain, but first I need to concentrate on what we're going to do. We'll find a safe place once we're out of the city, and we'll talk then."

"Promise?"

He took in a deep breath, his eyes fixed on the road. "Yes, I promise."

SARA KNEW THAT LIAM WOULD do anything to protect her. Maybe too much. She knew that Clete believed Liam had lost his perspective over this case. Had Liam argued again with Clete? She glanced at Liam's profile. Jaw clenched, he was deep in thought. His fingers gripped the wheel as though he were capsized at sea and holding on to the only piece of driftwood he could find.

This wasn't the time to try to convince him. She didn't have the facts; he did. Yes, she trusted him. After all, he had proved how much he cared for her.

They spoke little, each deep in thought as they drove

north from the city. It was almost two in the afternoon by the time they'd crossed the Massachusetts state line.

"Hungry?" He pointed to an interstate restaurant and service station that loomed in the distance.

"Yes, and I need to go to the bathroom."

Sara hadn't realized how tired and thirsty she was until she left the women's room and joined him at an empty booth at the rear of the restaurant.

After the waitress had taken their orders and they'd settled back in their chairs, Liam took her hand. "I'm sorry I had to interrupt your session with Brianna," he said, his gaze on her fingers entwined with his.

"I've regained almost all of my memory." Sara glanced at his tanned, square hand, rubbing her fingertip against his flat thumbnail. Such strong hands, she thought. "What's disappointing is that I remember my college days except for knowing Kitty and Trent Sherburne. Or what happened the weekend before I met you." When Liam didn't comment, she went on.

"I remember the automobile accident that killed my mother. I was sent to live with my grandmother, while my brother remained with our dad in California. Since then, Jeremy and I have been virtual strangers." Tears stung her eyes as she remembered the bitter, unhappy woman who'd raised her. "While I was growing up, my grandmother made regular excuses to keep me from my court appointed visits with my father."

"Was your dad driving the car when your mother died?" Liam asked softly.

She looked up. "Why, yes. How did you know?"

Liam shrugged. "Do you think she blamed him for your mom's death?"

Sara nodded. "I remember as a child feeling angry that my dad had kept Jeremy, yet he never fought my grandmother when she insisted I come to live with her."

"Maybe your dad felt he didn't deserve to have you. He had taken away your grandmother's daughter. Maybe he was afraid he didn't have the skills to raise a daughter."

"I never thought of that," she said, falling silent until the waitress appeared with their food. When they'd finished their meal, Liam said, "I wish some of those memories you regained had been happy ones."

Sara gave him a humorless grin. "I wish my grandmother could have found some resolution with Jeremy before it was too late."

"Did Brianna say when she thought you'd remember the rest?"

Sara picked up a fork and speared a torn piece of lettuce. "She said I might regain total memory at any time."

"Yes, and she also told you that it won't happen if you feel unsafe." Liam stirred his coffee. "I promise to do everything to keep you safe, honey."

"I'm tired of making small talk, of pretending nothing's wrong. Something is terribly wrong, isn't it?" She struggled for calm and took a deep breath.

He began to speak, then waited until a burly truck driver ambled past their booth toward the cashier. "I'm only reminding you," Liam said, his voice barely above a whisper, "that you're big game, sweetheart. The hunters are after you. We still don't know who's bankrolling the Ziegler brothers or why you're so important to them. Until we do, you're not leaving my side."

"Tell me why you rushed me out of the TALON-6 building. Running away isn't an option, Liam. I'm tired of running. I want you to take me back to New York."

"Sara, be serious."

She rummaged through her bag, then clenched a handful of bills and threw them on the table. "I'm serious, O'Shea!" She slid from the booth and bolted toward the door.

He tore after her. When he caught up with her in the parking lot, he whirled her around to face him. "Where do you think you're going?"

"I told you. I'm going back to New York. With or without you." He could see her breath in the cold air as she spoke.

"Sara, listen." She heard the pleading in his voice and turned to look at him.

"I know a place at the Cape that we can stay. An old school buddy of mine owns it. He uses the shack in the summer when he works his lobster boat. It's not fancy, but it's clean. No one will notice us there. He lets me stay there when I need to get away from the city. It's remote, and in a few hours, I can hook up enough gadgets to keep an army from sneaking up on us."

She shivered. "You still haven't told me why we can't go back to the city."

"I need to talk to Detective Ranelli on Bellwood Island as soon as possible. When you're safe at the cabin, I'll tell you everything. Then if you want to go back to New York, we'll go."

"Why can't you tell me now?"

His dark blue eyes deepened with feeling. "Please trust me. Please."

Her hand trembled as she pushed her hair from her face. "You know I do."

His arms encircled her and drew her close.

In his warm and comforting embrace, Sara had no doubt she trusted Liam. But if he couldn't confide in her, how well did he trust *her?*

CLETE THREW HIS JACKET around the back of the computer chair and dragged it in front of the console. "Why the hell didn't you tell me that Liam ran off with Sara?"

"I paged you," Bailey said, pouring tea from a brown glazed teapot. The aroma of chamomile wafted through the reception area. "It's not my fault if you don't answer your pager."

Clete scowled at Mike and Brianna, each perched on wooden bar stools. Cups of steaming tea sat in front of them. Though neither said anything, their expressions were clearly questioning.

"Okay, so it's my fault," Clete said. "I left my pager in my suitcase." He grimaced. "Sorry, Bailey. I don't mean to sound like a bear, but I'm so damn angry at Liam I could strangle him."

Brianna put her cup down with a clink. "You can hardly blame Liam. Look at it from his point of view. On one level, he feels that the bad guys are winning. After all, the Ziegler brothers are out on bail, free to send bombs to the woman he loves." She sighed. "But most important, Liam blames himself for not being able to protect Sara from the murder charges. He believes she's innocent, yet all he's been able to do for her is keep her hidden."

Mike glanced at Clete. "Brianna's right. You know Liam. He's an action kind of guy. He's frustrated and he wants results."

Clete swung around in his chair. "Which proves my point. Liam isn't himself. He's stressed from lack of sleep and isn't willing to face facts. The Bellwood PD found the murder weapon in Sara's motel unit. Her cell phone was discovered along the dunes, not far from the murder victim's body. I know he claims he searched her motel room and didn't find any weapons. Who do you think a jury will believe?"

Brianna caught her husband's look, then settled her gaze back on Clete. "Liam isn't aware he's in love with Sara. He wants to believe she's innocent. Why not help him prove she is?"

Mike folded his arms. "Brianna, I know she means a lot to Liam, but legally, TALON-6 can't help Liam once Sara is charged with Kitty Sherburne's murder. Already an APB is out on Sara. If they stop off at a hotel or a restaurant, she could be identified and arrested on the spot."

Clete nodded. "And once an arrest warrant is served, TALON-6 must step out of this. We could be charged with aiding and abetting."

Bailey took a sip of her tea. "That means we'll have to report the van Liam is driving as stolen." Her face looked grim.

Clete glanced up. "What van?"

Mike took in a deep breath. "Liam *borrowed* the white van, plus some surveillance equipment, when he left with Sara."

"Borrowed surveillance equipment?" Clete whistled. "So he's planning on hiding out until when?" He swore. "We need to stop him for his own good, as well as Sara's."

Mike glanced at his watch. "He'll call in soon."

"Want to bet?" Clete swore again. "I told you. I warned him about losing his perspective. He'll legally endanger TALON-6. Mike, we've got to report the van stolen immediately."

Bailey moved to the window, her back to them. "Liam is usually very logical."

"He can be a hunch player, too," Clete interjected.

Brianna met his gaze. "Sara is innocent until proven guilty."

"You're all correct," Mike said, getting up and leaning against the counter. "But TALON-6 can't become involved in legal entanglements. Liam knew he was acting alone when he left the city with Sara. That's why he didn't tell us. I'll give him four more hours. Then we'll report the van and the equipment stolen."

Bailey crossed her arms and frowned out at the rain droplets beginning to hit the window. A storm was moving up the coast, and the darkening sky looked threatening. "Four hours isn't very long."

Mike frowned back at her. "Bailey, this doesn't mean that we don't believe in Liam."

Brianna spoke up. "That's true, Bailey. But we can't forget about Sara." All eyes turned to her. "Liam isn't alone out there. Sara's a strong woman. I have a hunch that despite her memory problems, she has a solid sense of right and wrong. If they find themselves in a tight spot, Sara will do the right thing."

Chapter Seventeen

"Watch where you walk," Liam warned as he shone the flashlight along the rough wooden planks that led from the driveway to the wooden steps of the fishing cabin. All Sara could see in the darkness were piles of lobster traps, fishing nets, brightly colored buoys and who knew what else littering the path.

She held on to the rickety railing as she warily made her way to the upper deck of the building, the floorboards creaking loudly as she approached the door. Liam went ahead, opening it with a key he found beneath the faded welcome mat.

Once inside, Sara was pleasantly surprised. From what she'd seen of the cabin in the splash of light from the van's headlamps as they drove up the bumpy driveway, the gray shingled building looked like an old fishing shack. Inside, it was much more. The place was immaculate, with knotty-pine walls left natural. The scent of pine was refreshing. Red burlap curtains covered the windows, and framed Winslow Homer prints hung on the walls.

"The light is on your left," Liam muttered as he carried in their gear. Sara put down the plastic sacks of groceries they had bought at the last town they'd passed through before arriving on Bellwood Island. With the sudden rainstorm, she couldn't see how near the cabin was from the ocean, but she could smell the salt and hear the tide rushing in.

"Maybe we shouldn't turn on a light," she said, wary of arousing suspicion from fishermen along the shore.

"The lights can't be seen from the sea or the road." Liam turned on a small lamp, which illuminated the corner with a warm, cozy glow. "The windows are shuttered and fastened securely."

"You're certain your friend won't mind that we use his cabin?" she asked.

"I'm sure," Liam said, checking the window latches. He strode to the stone fireplace in the corner and picked up some dried sticks from the kindling basket. "A few years ago, TALON-6 installed a security system for his business," he explained, arranging the kindling on the hearth. "He said anytime I wanted to use his cabin, to go ahead."

She moved to the round wooden table by a window and took a seat. She felt incredibly tired. Her shoulders and muscles ached, more from tension than anything else, and she knew Liam must be weary, as well.

Within minutes, a bright flame was feeding on the dried sticks. Wood snapped and popped as the fire licked the fresh log Liam had laid across the andirons. She couldn't help being impressed. Regardless of where they were, Liam had a simple knack for getting the job done. Not only did she love him, she admired him and trusted him with her life. So why was she so bothered that he was keeping something from her when he only wanted to protect her?

Maybe it was all those years of hearing her grandmother say that men couldn't be trusted. *They'll say they love you, then when they get what they want, they'll leave you for the next fresh conquest.*

Sara was startled as her grandmother's words played in her head. The memory was as real as if it had a life of its own.

No, whatever was troubling her was between Liam and herself. Liam didn't completely trust *her* with what he knew. He was somehow afraid that if she learned the truth, she might do something. Something that he wouldn't want her to do. But what?

She rose and unhooked a bottle of water from a six-pack container. "Want one?"

He shook his head as he picked up a plastic bag of canned goods and began putting them inside the wooden cabinet beneath the counter.

"Let me help you," she said, kneeling beside him. Outside, the rain had begun in earnest, drumming a melodic rhythm on the tin roof. The scent of burning wood drifted throughout the cabin. As they worked side by side, Sara found herself fighting off a nostalgic longing to forget their troubles and think only of Liam and this romantic hideaway, if only for a few hours.

But this wasn't a romantic interlude. She was in hiding, waiting until tomorrow, when Liam would return from the police station and explain everything to her. Tomorrow. *After I speak to Al, we can return to New York.*

Something wasn't right. Detective Al Ranelli was Liam's good friend. So why couldn't Liam just call him?

Liam put the last can on the shelf, then leaned over and kissed her quickly. "I need to bring in some wood for the night," he said as he got up.

He opened the door and a rush of chilly, damp air blew into the cabin. Outside, she heard his footsteps creak across the wooden deck and fade with the wind. She looked around the empty cabin. In the corner, on the floor, was a telephone.

She was beside the phone before she could think who she should call. TALON-6. She would talk to Brianna or Bailey. Ask them if they had heard any news. When she put the receiver to her ear, her hopes nose-dived when she heard the dead silence.

Disconnected. Of course, what did she expect? She stomped toward the fireplace to warm her hands. Then she remembered Liam's cell phone usually hooked to his belt.

You trust me, don't you, Sara?

Yes, she trusted Liam. But whatever the danger, he had no right to keep her from the facts. They were in this together. If he wouldn't tell her, then she'd find out for herself.

The sound of footsteps outside the door jerked Sara's attention back to the door. Liam entered, arms full of split wood. Beneath his shirt, she could see his biceps bulge with the weight as he strode to the wood box and emptied his armload. The grin he gave her went straight to her heart. She returned it, then averted her gaze back to the fire.

She had no time for sentimentality. Later, when Liam went outside to string the surveillance net, she would call TALON-6 and find out what was going on.

Somehow, she knew that he would consider it an act of betrayal. What if he never forgave her?

She couldn't think about that now.

SARA PUSHED UP the sleeves of her sweater, then dipped her hands into the hot, sudsy water. As she washed the few dishes from their meal, she couldn't keep her eyes off the far counter where, a little while ago, Liam had laid his gun and leather holster. Beside them were his cell phone, bill-fold and keys.

"How long will it take you to put up the surveillance net?" she asked, feigning a casual tone that she didn't feel.

Liam stepped from the closet, wearing the yellow rain slicker and hood he'd found earlier. "An hour at the most." He came over to her. "Why? Going to miss me?" He shot her a charming grin.

Her smile was automatic. "Of course," she said, her gaze on the water glass in her sudsy hands. Since she and Liam had become intimate, she'd felt so connected to him that she was afraid he could somehow sense what she was about to do. She remembered that she had tucked Bri-anna's business card, with her telephone and pager num-bers, inside her bag the first time she'd met the psychologist, at Clancy's Bar.

Soon she would know what Liam was hiding from her. Yet one look in his eyes and she might lose her nerve.

"I'll fill the wood box before I go," he said, sliding his arms around her. "I wouldn't want you to get cold while I'm out there," he whispered in her ear.

She leaned into him, her hands pressed against his shoulders, and laid her head against his solid chest. Her eyelids closed, and she breathed in his delicious masculine scent. Oh, if only they could stay here like this.

She felt the touch of his lips on her forehead, and she was half tempted not to make that call. Why ruin these pre-cious hours together? Why couldn't she trust him and wait until he returned tomorrow after talking to his friend, De-tective Ranelli?

Heaven help her, when he held her like this, she couldn't think straight. All she wanted was Liam.

But a tiny voice in the back of her brain nagged her into letting go. Somehow, she feared that whatever Liam was hiding from her concerned what Brianna had called the X factor—the hideous fear that Sara had yet to face before her complete memory would return. Yes, she had to go through with the call to Brianna. Just as soon as Liam left.

"I don't want to leave you." His voice was hoarse and low. "But the sooner I go, the sooner I'll be back." His lips found her mouth, and she didn't realize she'd been holding her breath until she returned his kiss.

When Liam left the cabin, she stood there for what seemed like a lifetime. Finally, she moved toward the phone and clicked it on. The instrument felt cold in her hands as she punched in Brianna's home number.

AFTER LIAM HAD INSTALLED the last grid sensor around the defense perimeter of the cabin, he hunted about for something with which to test the electronic alarm net. He picked up a heavy branch from a fallen maple tree and bounced it across the ground toward where the sensors were located. Immediately, the tiny security monitor on his wrist beeped. *Thank God,* he thought with a sigh of relief. It was almost 8:00 p.m. Between the rain and the early darkness from the storm, setting up the net had been twice as difficult as he'd thought. Tomorrow morning, he wanted to get an early start to meet Al at home before he left for the police station. Liam wouldn't have any time in the morning to correct an adjustment on the surveillance net if it was needed. The sooner Liam gave his statement, the sooner Al could begin the paperwork necessary to dismiss charges against Sara. So far, his luck was holding.

Luck? Who was he kidding? The woman he loved was

wanted for murder, and he had little time before the authorities found them. It wasn't the police he was worried about, although he knew that Sara's description would be on every police bulletin by now. His buddies at TALON-6 would be on his tail, and no doubt Mike and Clete would eventually find them. Yet he knew his partners would give him all the time they legally could before they came searching for them.

Liam understood their reasoning. He'd do the same thing if the tables were turned. He knew he was breaking the law, but he felt Sara was too fragile in her present state to put up with being charged for a crime she didn't commit. Protecting her was the one thing he could do.

WHEN SARA CLICKED OFF the cell phone from her conversation with Brianna, she was stunned. No wonder Liam had rushed her out of the city, desperate to save her from jail. Kitty Sherburne was dead. Murdered. Shot with a handgun that had been found in Sara's motel room.

"Your cell phone was found near the murder scene," Brianna had said. Sara shook her head. She felt as though she was in a daze.

Despite the evidence against her, she knew she hadn't killed Kitty. She was innocent; deep down, she knew she couldn't have killed anyone. And Liam believed her. Somehow, with the man she loved by her side, they would prove her innocence.

But first she had to protect Liam from himself. He had risked everything to save her, even his career, his friends, his future. She couldn't let him be arrested for aiding and abetting a criminal, even if she was innocent.

She knew what she had to do. Tomorrow morning, when

Liam left for the police station to talk to his friend, she would call Al first and give herself up. Then there could be no chance for Liam to be connected with her. The evidence might link them, but as long as Sara reached the police department first, Liam would be safe.

Somehow, she knew this would all work out.

The door opened and Sara turned to see Liam enter the cabin, the wind howling behind him. His face, dark with the shadow of his beard, brightened with the flash of white teeth when he gave her a heart-stopping smile.

Liam. I love you so, her heart sang as she realized what he had sacrificed for her. She fought back the sting of tears as she flew into his embrace.

Struggling for calm, she took a deep breath. "It felt like you were gone forever," she said into the hollow of his neck.

"Mmm." He nudged her back against the wall, pressing himself against her as her fingers undid the clasps at his neck, his hands tracing up and down her curves. "I take it you missed me?" he teased.

"Let me show you how much," she said, peeling away his rain slicker. The garment dropped to the floor in a yellow heap as their fingers moved feverishly over each other's clothing.

"This might take all night," she murmured into his ear as he swept her up and carried her toward the bed.

"WHO WAS ON THE PHONE?" Mike Landis murmured to his wife as she drifted back into his study. His gaze remained on the architectural blueprints sprawled across his desktop.

"A client."

Her pithy answer caused him to glance up. Her greenish gaze remained on the notes he had penciled in the margins of the drafting sketch, but he noticed her mouth twitch.

"Kinda late, isn't it?" he asked, more than curious now. "An emergency?"

Brianna didn't answer. Instead, she brushed his cheek with a kiss, then put her arms around his neck as she leaned over his shoulder. "No," she said finally, her mouth curling into a grin.

Mike pulled his wife into his lap. "I know that look, Dr. Kent-Landis." He smiled when he saw her lips curl into a smile. "You want me to beg you, don't you?"

She laughed. "I can't tell you due to doctor-client privilege." Her eyes danced when she met his. "But I know you're terribly worried about Liam, so…"

Mike's eyebrows lifted as he studied his wife's relaxed expression. "Ah, you want me to guess?" he said, finally catching on that she was trying to tell him something without breaching a professional confidence.

She nodded. "I'll give you a hint. It concerns two people who are very dear to us."

Mike sensed that Sara Regis had very much been on his wife's mind ever since Liam and Sara had left the office that afternoon. Sara had called Brianna, and whatever transpired between them, he didn't need to know. The important thing was that Sara and Liam were safe.

"I think I'll call Clete," Mike said, reaching for the phone, "and tell him not to worry about Liam and Sara."

Brianna smiled. "Don't forget to call Bailey, too."

THE NEXT MORNING, Sara had just finished zipping up her jeans and was brushing her hair when Liam stepped inside the cabin. The smile she gave him tugged at his heart.

Reaching out, he swept wispy strands of dark red hair from her cheek. "I hoped you'd still be in bed." He nipped her earlobe gently between his teeth, and was rewarded by her soft moan of pleasure.

When she turned toward him, he slid his hands beneath her sweater and was delighted to discover she wasn't wearing a bra. "I came in to leave you a note. I was going to head straight to the police department, but one look at you and I don't know if I'll be able to tear myself away."

She clung to him with an urgency that surprised him. For a moment, he thought she might be afraid he wasn't coming back, but then brushed the crazy thought away. He bent his head to kiss her, knowing full well how precious each moment they shared was.

Liam couldn't imagine what he would do if he ever lost her. Not after he'd found the one woman with whom he wanted to share the rest of his life.

Leaving her in their bed this morning had been the hardest thing he'd ever done. He'd awoken with her lovely face pressed into the crook of his arm as she slept, her thick lashes fanning her cheeks. Her hair, spilling across his chest, had reminded him of a sweet meadow.

If only he could freeze the precious hours they had together, he thought as their kiss deepened. His hands caressed her breasts, and her nipples responded instantly, tightening into buds.

He groaned. "I promise I'll hurry back as soon as I can."

Her lips trembled into a smile. "How long do you think you'll be?"

His face grew serious. "An hour at the most. That is, if I catch Al before he leaves for the station." Liam also wanted to read Al's report about the gun found at the motel. Obviously the Ziegler brothers must have gone back to the motel to plant the gun in Sara's unit, and Liam hoped something in Al's report might shed more evidence as to that possibility.

Thank God Sara hadn't asked him any more questions. Maybe she trusted him, after all. He gave her a reassuring smile. "Don't worry, I'll be back before you know it, then we can leave for the city." He cupped her chin. "I love you, Sara."

She winced and swallowed hard.

He kissed her again, and when he moved away, he pulled a small device from his jacket pocket. "This is the alarm for the security net. I've already set it. If anyone comes across the property line, this buzzer will ring to let you know." He laid the mobile device on the kitchen table. "We're isolated here, especially with the early morning fog. When the sun burns off the mist, it's possible that some of the lobstermen might pick up their stored traps or lines. If so, just ignore them. They won't come inside. More than likely they'll load up their traps or nets and be off as soon as they can."

Liam pressed the tiny switch on the side of the device. "If the alarm sounds, shut it off so as not to alert whoever comes," he told her. Then he handed her his cell phone. "If someone shows up, call me at the police station. I've keyed in the number."

She glanced at the phone, marveling at the irony.

"Remember, don't make any noise. Sounds travel far by the water."

"Liam, I know what to do. Don't worry about me."

"One more thing," Liam said. "The sensor will activate when I drive off the property." He switched off the alarm. "Turn this knob back on after I leave, okay?" He pressed the activator device into her palm.

"Okay." Tears glittered in the corners of her eyes when she glanced up at him. "I love you, Liam."

He gazed at her for a few breathless moments before he turned and dashed for the van.

Her heart clenched as she stood at the door and watched him start the motor. Plumes of white exhaust spiraled in the cold air. When Liam had left, instead of turning the activator knob on, she placed the device on the table and picked up the cell phone. She pressed the speed dial of the number of the Bellwood Police Department.

Sara heard the number ring and a man's voice answered, "Bellwood Police Department Dispatch. Officer Timothy Greeley."

Dear God, please don't let me lose courage now.

Chapter Eighteen

"Sorry ma'am. Detective Ranelli hasn't come in yet. Would you like to speak to his partner?"

Sara's breath caught. She had to speak to Al before Liam reached him. "No, I need to speak to Ranelli himself. This is urgent. It's about the Kitty Sherburne murder. Will you page him for me?"

"Right away, miss. May I have your name, please?"

"I—I'd rather not give it." Her chest felt so tight she didn't think she could breathe. "I'll hold," she managed to say, "while you page him for me."

Sara felt a tug of relief when the officer agreed. While she waited for Al to call in, she opened the cabin door and inhaled a deep breath of cold air to help clear her mind. Wisps of early morning fog still hovered over the water, and the cries of seagulls and the sound of surf crashing over rocks on the shore filled the air.

She stepped out on the creaky deck and was taken aback to see fishing gear piled along the deck and steps. Large, menacing gaff hooks leaned against tall stacks of wire lobster traps. Heaps of black fishing nets and colored wooden buoys stretched precariously along the deck.

Last night, she and Liam could have easily tripped over

something and fallen over the railing. Then she remembered how carefully Liam had guided her around the dangers. Just as he had since she'd met him.

Yes, he'd sacrificed everything to keep her safe. Now it was her turn to protect him. She cast one last glance over the toolboxes, ropes and wrenches scattered on the deck before she turned back inside to wait.

Why hadn't Detective Ranelli answered his pager by now? What if Liam had already reached Al's house in town? Her heart raced at the terrifying thought.

No, it wasn't possible. Last night, it had taken Liam and her over twenty minutes to reach the cabin after stopping in town for groceries. Liam couldn't have reached Al yet.

But what if Liam had called Al and arranged to meet him? The van contained all sorts of equipment. Of course Liam would have thought to pack additional cell phones. Her pulse pounded with fear. Damn, why hadn't she thought of that?

She pressed the cell phone so hard to her ear that her head hurt. Tears stung her eyes when she finally heard a click and a baritone voice spoke.

"This is Detective Al Ranelli. May I have your name, please?"

Sara's hand shook as she grasped the phone. "This is Sara Regis. I know you're looking for me. I want to give myself up."

She heard a slight hesitation, then he asked, "Is Liam O'Shea with you?"

Thank God Liam hadn't contacted Al yet. Her luck was holding. "No. I'm alone." She drew in a shaky breath. "Liam knows nothing about this, or anything about what I've done." That wasn't exactly a lie, but she needed to keep

Liam free of any implication that he had aided or abetted her leaving New York City.

Tears spilled from her eyes as she thought of how Liam would feel when he found out that she had been arrested. She forced back the thought. "Please, will you send someone for me? I'm at a vacant fishing cabin on a small peninsula about twenty minutes from town." She looked around, realizing that she had no idea how to give directions to the place. "There's a phone that's disconnected, but if I give you the number, do you think you could trace my location?"

"I think I know where you might be," Al said. "Did Liam take you there?"

She didn't want to admit to anything that might involve him. "I'd rather not answer that."

"Is the cabin up on pilings, and is there a long deck attached? Is there a winding dirt track from the main road, about half a mile long?"

"Yes, I think so."

"Figures. You're at the old Jefferson place. He and Liam were in Special Forces together. Stay where you are, Ms. Regis. I'll come and pick you up myself. I know Liam would want that. I'm on my way."

She heard the phone click off, and stared at it, noticing that her knuckles were white from gripping the instrument.

Oh, Liam, I hope somehow you can forgive me.

SARA FINISHED FOLDING her clothes into the small suitcase, then glanced around the cabin checking for anything she might have left behind. Staying busy would help keep her mind off the giant butterflies in her stomach. Never had twenty minutes seemed like such an eternity.

Finally, she picked up her case and placed it by the door. In the distance, she heard a car motor whine up the road.

Her stomach clenched, and she dashed to the door and poked her head outside. A police cruiser bounced along the rutted driveway and finally jerked to a stop on the other side of the cabin.

Thank God Al hadn't turned on the siren or flashed the blue strobe lights. She was nervous enough. Her heart hammered as she picked up her suitcase and started for the door. She heard the car motor turn off, and from the kitchen window watched as the driver's door opened and a tall, broad shouldered, uniformed policeman step from the cruiser.

He was alone. What had she expected? A SWAT team, guns blazing, surrounding the cabin? She watched him glance along the shore before he walked slowly around to the steps at the side of the cabin.

Detective Al Ranelli was almost as muscular as Liam, with a short, military buzz haircut. Something seemed familiar about the jerky slant of his shoulders when he moved, and the way he slightly favored his right leg when he walked.

Something familiar and frightening.

There was no time now for a panic attack. Sara tried to shake off the terror and feeling of déjà vu. Her mind was playing tricks, that was all. She'd put her hand on the doorknob when she remembered her blue jacket in the coat closet. She ran back and yanked it from the hook, and was reaching for her suitcase when she looked up.

Through the kitchen window, Al Ranelli stared at her.

She froze. Fragments of memory snapped into place. The cruel lines of his face. This same man standing on that foggy morning, arms out straight, pointing a gun at Kitty, who pleaded with him not to kill her....

Sara screamed, just as she had that morning. She froze, heart pounding, as she also had. But what else could she have done? Al Ranelli and two other burly men had already found Kitty, who had been waiting for Sara at the Sand Dune Motel.

All the missing pieces of Sara's college years burst forth in her mind like a bad dream. She and Kitty had been college dorm roommates when Kitty had announced her engagement to Trent Sherburne. Sara wasn't in love with Trent, she realized abruptly; she hated him. He was more than a womanizer.

Trent had almost date-raped Sara when she was a freshman at Boston U, she recalled as another part of her memory kicked in. She'd been ashamed, afraid to speak out against the popular senior from the powerful family, especially after he'd boasted that no one would believe her.

But to keep her friend from marrying the bastard, Sara had confronted Kitty with the truth, even knowing that their friendship might be at stake. Kitty had angrily refused to believe her, ending their friendship, as well as all contact with Melody Price, who had become pregnant with Trent's child.

Years had passed, until one night last week a telephone call had stirred Sara from sleep—from Kitty. Her old friend had pleaded for Sara's help. Kitty had found bank records that proved her husband's senate campaign was being financed by organized crime.

When she had confronted her husband, Trent had pleaded with her to look the other way. "If I don't, I'll be killed," Kitty had related to Sara.

"What do you want me to do?" she had asked.

"The crime boss doesn't know about you," Kitty said, her voice breaking. "You're the only one I can trust. Please, Sara. Please help me get away. I think they're following me."

"Why don't you call the police?" Sara had urged her.

"You don't understand, Sara. They *are* the police."

The past slammed into the present as Sara stared at the cold-blooded killer who had gunned down Kitty Sherburne.

Al Ranelli rested his arms across the door frame as he studied her through the glass. His mouth lifted in a knowing smile. He knew that she recognized him. He pulled out his side arm from the black leather holster and aimed the revolver at her.

"Open up, Sara." His voice was as cold as the morning air.

Sara's mind whirled. She held her suitcase, trying to think of some way to use it as a weapon. There was only one door to the cabin. The windows were shuttered. Even if she could pry one open, lobster traps were heaped outside, blocking the way. There was no escape.

"I can easily break the glass and open the door. You know I will, Sara. Now be a good girl. One… Two—"

"Wait!" Sara's hands shook as she moved toward the door. She was going to die if she didn't think of something.

LIAM GAVE Detective Frances Zarella a big smile. "Hi, Francie. Is Al around? He'd already left for work when I stopped by his house a few minutes ago."

Francie looked up from the computer screen and shook her head. "Somebody called Al earlier. Then he phoned back to say he had a pickup to make before he came in this morning." She smiled. "Have a seat. The coffee's hot. Al should be here any time now."

"Did Al say how long he'd be? It's important I see him."

Francie glanced at her watch. "He knows we're due at the courthouse at nine o'clock. Don't worry, Al's never late." She eyed Liam flirtatiously. "Say, how come you keep getting better looking while I just get older?" She laughed, but when Liam didn't join her, her face sobered.

"What's the matter?" Her tone immediately changed to a professional one.

"I really need to get in touch with Al. Try his pager?"

"Sure. Hold on." She left her desk and hurried toward the dispatch center. Liam drummed his fingers on the counter, then paced back and forth. Damn, what was keeping her?

He glanced at a group of snapshots framed above her computer terminal. A black Persian, towheaded twins who resembled Francie's young nieces and a photo of Al with...

Liam picked up the photo and stared at Trent Sherburne. A cold chill went through him. Al and Trent Sherburne? Just then, Francie came back to her terminal.

"I spoke to Officer Greeley," she said, taking a seat. "He said he took the call for Al this morning. Greeley will be out in a minute. He can tell you more."

"Say, Francie. When was this taken?" Liam held up the photo of Al Ranelli and Trent Sherburne.

She beamed. "Al is Sherburne's number one bodyguard during this year's primary campaign." She looked at the picture with genuine affection. "Al's worked so hard." She glanced back at Liam. "Al's always felt like he was second fiddle to you. But he's been doing private duty with the Sherburne political bigwigs, and he hopes he'll be transferring to Washington when Trent is elected this fall."

A middle-aged, balding police officer strode toward them, carrying a clipboard.

"Tim," Francie said, wheeling to face the older man. "Any clue where Al went?"

Tim glanced at the clipboard. "At 8:03, he received a call-in from a woman who wouldn't give her name. I paged him and when he phoned in, I connected them. That's all I know."

"Any way you can trace the call?" Liam asked.

Tim shook his head. "Nope. But maybe we can phone the woman back. Every call to the police department is automatically recorded on our caller ID." Tim leaned over Francie's terminal and clicked several keys.

"She was using a cell phone." Tim pointed to the highlighted line on the screen. "That's the number."

Liam read it and froze. "Could there be a mistake?"

The cop straightened defensively. "Absolutely not."

Liam was almost out the door when Tim looked at Francie. Scratching his head, he asked, "Was it something I said?"

AL TAPPED THE WINDOWPANE with the handle of his revolver, shattering the glass. He carefully reached inside and unlocked the door, his gaze never leaving Sara's face. The door opened slowly, and Al's shoes crunched on the glass fragments as he stepped inside the cabin.

Reacting on instinct, she dropped the suitcase and reached for an iron skillet on the stove. She backed up, gauging his movements very carefully.

"Be a good girl, Sara. I won't hurt you if you do as I say."

"You killed Kitty. Why should I believe you?" Sara inched backward, hoping he would come after her. Then she could make a beeline for the door. The windows along the front of the cabin were nailed shut. Her only escape was through the kitchen door behind where Al stood.

She was trapped.

"Where did you and Kitty hide the package?" Al asked, almost conversationally. He appeared arrogant and extremely sure of himself. Well, why wouldn't he? He held a gun and all she had was a frying pan.

"Package? What package?"

"Don't play dumb. You know. We overheard Kitty's conversation to you on her cell phone. Sherburne didn't know it, but the boss had his house bugged. We heard all his conversations. So you can imagine how upset the boss was when he heard Kitty found out about who was bankrolling her ol' man's political campaigns." Al grinned, stepping closer. "Your friend Kitty wasn't so smart for a college broad. She warned her husband that if he didn't tell the authorities, she would." Al's lips twisted. "Dumb, dumb idea."

She heard the small click as Al took the safety from his gun and stepped toward her. Sara sensed he was preparing to jump her. She edged back. He laughed, as though enjoying seeing her fear.

Suddenly, Sara remembered what Brianna had told her about when she had faced her stalker. *I'd be damned if I would let that bastard win.* Sara felt her panic lessen as her survival instincts intensified. Maybe if she kept Al talking, he'd make a mistake.

"What's in the package?" she asked him.

"Didn't Kitty get a chance to tell you?" His brows rose. "She said she packed the coded notebooks that traced the political donations from the crime boss and mailed them to you." He laughed again as though really enjoying himself. "She didn't know her car phone was also bugged. That's how we knew you were involved. We heard Kitty call you, asking you to meet her at the Sand Dune Motel."

Of course. Kitty had called Sara from her car phone. She'd been half crying, half hysterical as she related what she had inadvertently found out while looking for her passport. Kitty had finally decided to leave Trent, and planned to mail the package to Sara for safekeeping.

But Sara had come up with another idea. She had called back the next day, while Kitty was at the hotel fund-raiser in Boston. The crime boss would have had no way to overhear that conversation.

Sara had remembered that her brother had a long-time crush on Kitty. Knowing she was in trouble, Jeremy would have done anything to help her. When Sara suggested that Kitty mail the evidence to him in Venezuela, she'd been delighted. Delighted, too, with the idea of flying to Caracas and staying at Jeremy's apartment until the mobsters were behind bars.

Kitty had even registered the Sand Dune Motel room in Sara's name so her husband couldn't find her. Sara was to meet Kitty at the motel, then drive her to Logan International Airport.

But Sara had let her down. She'd taken a wrong turn and arrived too late to help Kitty.

"Where's the package, Sara?" Al was almost close enough to grab her. What was he waiting for? Did he enjoy intimidating her?

As long as he thought she might tell him where the package was, she might stay alive, she realized.

"I'll tell you where it is," she said, studying his reaction. His eyes widened with interest.

"Where?" he said.

She tried to gauge the possibility of making a mad dash past him toward the open door. Would he shoot her or go

after her? He'd go after her. As long as she had information he needed, she might have a chance.

"I'll show you where I hid it," she answered.

He snickered, waving the gun. "You'll tell me. Now."

"I thought you and Liam were friends. Why are you
working for these crooks?" she asked, balancing her weight
on the balls of her feet. She was ready to run, ready to try
to race past him, deflecting his gun hand with the heavy
iron skillet.

His smile took on a smarmy look. "Liam always thought
he was too big for this town. He never was one of us. He
lived in Boston, a big-city kid who showed up each summer, lording it over us."

Sara wouldn't believe such a thing of Liam, and for the
first time, she realized how sick Al Ranelli really was.
Even as a child, he must have shown signs of a twisted
mentality.

"Game's over, Sara. Tell me where the package is, or
I'll—" As he took a step forward, she made a dash for the
door, feeling the rush of wind when he reached out for her.
With all her might, she threw the frying pan at his head,
then heard him grunt.

She'd jumped over the door sill onto the deck when she
felt his hot hand grab her ankle. Jerked to a halt, she spun
around and fell on her butt, gasping in pain. Her shin col-
lided with something hard on the floor.

"Get up," he snarled. "We're going to the car."

Sara shoved her hair back from her face and noticed the
heavy tools where she'd fallen. An open tool tray lay
nearby. As Al reached for her hair, Sara grabbed hold of a
long, heavy wrench, swung it and hit him across the side
of his skull, above his right ear.

His hands flew to his head before he slumped to the deck. Sara was up and running, tearing down the steps toward the police cruiser.

The driver-side door hung open. Too terrified to look back, she dived into the front seat. Pulling the door shut, she pressed the automatic door lock. She was lucky. Al had left the key in the ignition, that arrogant bastard. When she turned it, the motor roared to life. Sara shifted into reverse and pressed her foot on the accelerator. Instead of moving, the car tires sent sand and gravel into the air. Last night's heavy rain had soaked the ground and the rear tires spun helplessly, buried in sand.

Glancing back at the cabin, Sara sucked in a breath. Al had just gotten to his feet and was rubbing his head as he started after her.

Throwing open the car door, she lunged out of the cruiser and took off running. A sharp pain shot through her kneecap, but she ignored it, forcing herself to move forward in a mad dash. Sara felt as if she were reliving the nightmare of seeing Kitty gunned down in front of her. Just as her friend had, she was now running for her life. Darting around shoulder-high sand dunes, tripping over clumps of sea grass, tumbling into cranberry bogs, Sara was numb with fear.

Finally she had to stop and catch her breath. Panting heavily, she looked around frantically, trying to get her bearings. She'd lost sight of the cabin and the road.

When she glanced down at the ground, her heart leaped into her mouth. Her footprints were no longer hidden. After last night's rain, her shoes were leaving distinct footprints that Al could easily follow.

"You can't get away," he yelled. "Get back here, you little bitch, or you're dead."

Sara ducked behind a sand dune just as a shot rang out. She dived headfirst into a hollow, flattening herself on the ground. She could taste sand. Painfully, she raised her head and spat.

Another shot zinged within inches of her head, and her heart slammed into her throat. She rolled as fast as she could to her left, putting more distance between herself and the shooter.

Up ahead were more dunes. Springing to her feet, she took off running again. She had gotten away from Al before, and she had to once more, for Liam. She must warn Liam.

More shots rang out, the bullets thumping to the ground with their impact. Al was close. Very close. He was tracking her. Any minute now he would find her, and then—

"Sara!"

She stopped to listen, pressing her fist to her mouth. Was panic making her hallucinate? Or was that really Liam's voice?

Several shots rang out and she realized they weren't aimed at her. Liam had returned and Al was shooting at him. Biting back her fear, she forced her legs to work once more. She had to reach Liam, to warn him. He would think Al was an ally, not an enemy, and that put him in mortal danger. Maybe if she showed herself, she could distract Al and give Liam a better chance to protect himself.

"Liam, I'm over here," she called out, hoping to gain Al's attention.

"Stay down, Sara!" Liam's voice sounded farther away than she had hoped. Almost immediately, three more rapid tat-tat-tats split the air.

The gunfire was coming from her left. She was somewhere between Liam and Al, if her bearings were correct. Maybe she could make her way toward Liam.

Scrambling across the sand, she veered around the larger of two dunes up ahead. She had to try to reach Liam. She had to do whatever she could to save him.

LIAM ROSE ON HIS ELBOW and leaned forward slightly, taking aim. "I've got you covered, Al. Don't make me blow you away, 'cause that's just what I'd like to do, you son of a bitch."

Slowly, Al dropped his weapon, then raised his hands behind his head in the standard military stance of surrender.

"Come on, pal," Al said. "Things don't have to end like this. Your little lady has a package worth millions. Without me, it's worth nothing. You need me and my connections, buddy. Sara will hand it over if you ask her. Come on, Liam," he whispered. "We can split it three ways. I thought I'd go to Mexico. You know how I hate cold weather." He laughed, the sound hollow in the morning stillness. "We can each go our merry way, and you and Red can live the high life you've always wanted. Now what do you say, pal?"

Liam had to bite back what he wanted to tell Al to do with his offer. Instead, he stepped behind him, his .40 caliber Glock trained on the back of Al's head.

The revolver Al had fired was on the ground by his feet. "Take three steps forward and lie facedown in the sand. Now. Hands on your head."

Just then a slight figure dashed into Liam's peripheral vision. Sara! He wanted to shout for joy. Instead, he kept his eyes fixed on the man lying flat on the ground—the man Liam had thought he knew.

Liam didn't move a muscle, but couldn't help calling out, "Are you okay, honey?"

"I am now." Sara rushed toward where Al's weapon lay in the sand, and picked up the standard issue police revolver. She ran back to Liam, giving him the weapon, then burying her face in his shoulder.

After a moment, she glanced back at Al Ranelli. "I remember everything now. Al's a traitor and there's proof. Kitty had mailed the evidence she'd found—bank deposits to her husband, wired to a secret account in the Bahamas. She sent the proof to my brother's post office box in Caracas. We'd better call Jeremy, or he'll be very surprised when he receives her package."

Liam flashed her a grin. "We'll call him from the police station, where we'll file our reports."

Swallowing hard, she nodded. "Sounds good."

Just then several police sirens wailed in the distance. Liam tucked Al's revolver into his pocket and wrapped his free arm around Sara, kissing her on the head as she clung to him. "That's Francie and backup. It'll be over soon. You're safe now, Sara."

"But what about the Ziegler brothers?"

"Francie told me that they were arrested at Logan Airport on a flight bound for Vegas." He smiled. "With your testimony, they'll sing to try to save their skins, plea-bargaining information that will nail the crime boss and my old friend here." Liam glanced back at Al, who had heard every word.

Even in defeat, Al turned his head and sneered.

"I saw Al shoot Kitty," Sara said to Liam. "The Ziegler brothers were with him." Tears stung her eyes as she remembered the shock and horror of what she had witnessed.

"I was late getting to Kitty. If I hadn't taken a wrong turn, I might have been there in time—"

Liam hugged her so tightly that she could hardly breathe. "No, you couldn't. They would have followed you—" *Followed you and killed you, too.*

Damn, if he lived to be a hundred, he would never forget the icy terror that had knifed through him when he'd seen Al train his weapon on the woman Liam loved.

The woman he loved. He glided his hand up and down her spine. Yes, he loved her. When he'd thought he might lose her, he'd realized what she meant to him.

The police sirens grew louder. "Come on, Al. Get to your feet. You're going for a ride to the station."

SARA BENT DOWN TO LAY the bouquet of spring flowers beside the cemetery urn, then stepped back, her teary gaze resting on the shiny granite gravestone.

Kitty, I'm so sorry I couldn't help you. In the three weeks since she had regained the final pieces of her past, and with the help of Dr. Kent-Landis, Sara knew she bore none of the blame for her friend's death.

A long shadow crossed the grave site, and Sara glanced up, shielding her eyes from the glittering sun. "Liam." Her pulse raced when she saw him. "How did you know I was here?"

He smiled, moving forward and putting his arm around her. "Your neighbor, Maggie, told me you were going to be here." His mouth twitched. "I'm glad to see that you're back to telling Maggie where you'll be when you leave town." He took a step toward a stone bench beneath a flowering crab tree covered with pink blossoms. "Do you mind if I intrude?"

Sara smiled, her heart spilling over with joy at seeing him. "You're not intruding. I needed to come here and say goodbye. I haven't been ready until now. " She blinked back a tear. "Thanks to Brianna, I've learned that we can't be everything to all people."

"Hmm."

She smiled, feeling suddenly awkward. She had been meeting with a local therapist, someone Brianna had recommended, to deal with the other issues concerning her childhood and her grandmother. "What about you?" she asked, glad to change the subject. "I received your message that the Ziegler brothers gave testimony to put away the crime boss, Joe Carbano."

"I would have told you personally if you had returned my calls."

She passed over his comment. "I read in the papers that Trent Sherburne pulled out of the primary."

"Yeah. I think his political career is over," Liam said.

"I was glad to find out that Trent wasn't involved with Kitty's murder," Sara said softly. "From what I saw on television, he seemed completely distraught that his political ambition had caused his wife's death."

She looked at Liam, whose gaze was averted. "It must be hard for you to see Al Ranelli sentenced for first degree murder," she murmured.

He nodded briefly. "It was harder on Francie. She decided she needed a change and resigned from Bellwood. She's working for the Boston PD now. We had lunch last week and she's finding the change to her liking."

Sara smiled. "I'm so glad. She seemed very nice." Her heart was pounding like a piston at Liam's nearness. "Have you taken your next case?" She hoped to keep the subject away from anything personal. "Are you going to the Middle East? Europe? Asia?"

He chuckled. "Actually, Clete was the one who volunteered for an overseas assignment. Mike is trying to finish his new deck, in his spare time. And I'm officially on vacation for two weeks."

So this is goodbye? She didn't have the heart to ask him directly if that's why he'd sought her out. Instead, she took a seat on the bench, her gaze on the pink petals littering the grass. It was her turn to remain silent.

"Sara, I want to see you. You've been avoiding my calls. I need to know why."

She looked up at him. "Liam, I want marriage, home and children. I guess you had already sensed that about me long before I knew it myself." She tried not to let it show how much her admission pained her. "I know how you feel about commitment and I can respect that. But I think it's better if we don't see each other." She tore her gaze from him. She couldn't bear to witness the heartbreak in his intense blue gaze.

"Sara, at least listen to what I have to say. You must know how much you mean to me."

She put her finger to his lips. "Darling Liam. It's because I think so much of you that I need to do this." She stood up and brushed his cheek with her hand. "I'm going to my car now," she said, her own heart breaking. "Please don't follow me."

Liam watched her turn and hurry along the walkway, her red hair flying in the wind.

THE FOLLOWING FRIDAY WAS the last day of Sara's first full week back teaching at Smith Bordman Academy. She rose from her desk and crushed her paper napkin into her lunch bag and tossed the remains of her turkey sandwich into the trash bin outside her office door. When she came near the teachers' lounge, she peeked around the door before going inside. Empty. She breathed a sigh of relief, then sank into her favorite plush chair.

Since she'd returned to teaching, the faculty and students had been treating her as if she were a celebrity. Even her brother had called from Venezuela to say how proud he was of his famous sister. *Famous sister?* Dear God, how she hated the attention. Her only hope for peace was to avoid people until they treated her like who she was— plain, ordinary Sara Regis.

"Oh, there you are, Sara."

She groaned, then forced a smile as she turned to face Gregory Urquhart. "Hi, Greg," she said through clenched teeth.

"I've been looking all over for you." He beamed that familiar smile that told her how very proud he was that "one of theirs" had almost single-handedly helped the police arrest a murderer. "Sara, the dean has arranged a little surprise for you this afternoon."

She groaned again. "Please, Greg. It's not that I'm not appreciative, but I really hate all this fuss, and—"

"That's so like you, Sara. Humble, unassuming—all noble traits that are so important in role models for young women today. That's why the dean has proclaimed this as Sara Regis Weekend."

"Holy—" She flinched as she bit back the oath. "No. Please, Greg. I'll do anything, but please talk him out of it, say—"

He laughed. "It's much too late for that, Sara. We've

been planning this surprise since the story about you hit the papers. Now, come with me." He took her arm and marched her toward the auditorium.

"The auditorium!" She dragged her feet. "Greg, I won't go. I hate to make speeches. Please."

"All you have to do is sit and listen." He practically beamed at her. "Everything has been arranged." Before she could argue, he pulled open the auditorium door, and as she stepped inside, the assembly hall exploded with applause. Students and faculty rose to their feet. Shouts and clapping radiated from the rafters, the bleachers, the orchestra seats as Greg led her down the center aisle toward the stage.

After sweeping the huge room, Sara's gaze settled on the tall, black-haired man standing near the podium. Liam.

Tears unexpectedly sprang to her eyes when she saw him. Damn, she was going to act like an emotional fool. Clenching her teeth, she refused to cry. As the applause roared to a crescendo, she couldn't take her eyes from him.

She bit the inside of her lip, struggling for composure. She had sent him away, yet in her dreams he'd come to her, asked her to marry him. *Don't you know, Liam, that I love you and it kills me to see you looking more handsome than any male has the right to be?*

Dear God, how was she going to get through this?

Gregory Urquhart took the stage and began the introductions. She heard his voice, but seeing Liam had turned her brain to mush, and she couldn't remember one word of what the administrator was saying. All she could think of was Liam. How his mouth tasted, how his lips felt. She pressed her fingers to her throat. It felt raw and her palms were sweating.

Oh, Liam, why did you come here? Sara wondered frantically. Of course. Greg had probably put in phone calls to TALON-6. The newspapers had had a field day playing up the local angle, running headlines such as Schoolteacher Fights Off Bad Cop Tied To Organized Crime. Liam was probably too polite to say no.

Applause broke out again as Greg left the stage and Liam took his place at the podium. His voice was low and incredibly sexy as he started to speak. Sara's gaze drifted across the sea of romantic teenage girls, and she couldn't help smiling at their awestruck faces. Yes, Liam O'Shea could mesmerize a crowd of females from age six to sixty.

"...Sara's daring and bravery..."

She groaned. Damn, not Liam, too? She averted her eyes, only half listening as he listed her virtues. No doubt Gregory Urquhart had twisted Liam's arm to do this. No doubt the academy would use her as their poster girl to drum up support for contributions for the new gymnasium the board hoped to build next year.

"Sara Regis is an icon of courage for every young woman here today...." Oh dear God, when was he going to stop?

"...I give you Sara Regis." Liam held out his hand to her. She glared at Gregory Urquhart, who grinned at her from the front row.

Forcing a smile for the audience, she crossed the stage and stood beside Liam. Applause thundered and she kept her gaze on the cheering students.

"We have to talk," Liam whispered in her ear, his hands clapping wildly.

"After putting me through this, you should have no reason to think I'll ever speak to you again," she said with a smile.

When she had finished delivering a very brief thank-you

speech, she descended the stage stairs on Liam's arm. Instead of taking a seat in the chairs reserved for them beside Gregory, Liam kept walking toward the doors, sweeping Sara along with him. Mrs. Wainright, the music teacher, began to play "Clair de Lune" on the piano, and as Sara and Liam escaped into the hall, she couldn't keep from laughing. "You're incorrigible," she said when they were outside on the lawn.

The sun was shining and the air carried the perfume of the crab apple trees blossoming in the courtyard.

"You know why I'm here," Liam said, pulling her down beside him on a bench.

"Yes, Gregory Urquhart made you an offer you couldn't refuse." She giggled, feeling as nervous and fluttery as one of her students on her first date. It was so wonderful just to look at him again.

He laid his arm on the back of the bench, just behind her shoulders. "Sara, please hear me out."

She eased in a breath. When she didn't try to stop him, he took her hand.

"Sara, all my life my sister Bridget has called me an adrenaline junkie. I never took her seriously until I met you. But you made me think about my life, and when you left me to go back to East Bennington to teach, I realized how empty it was without you."

"Liam, please." She lowered her eyes.

"Look at me, Sara. Let me finish. " He waited until her lashes lifted and she met his gaze.

He cupped her chin. "Without you, my work means nothing. My life is meaningless without you in it. I don't need the adrenaline rush of risk or danger." His eyes darkened with admiration, with adoration and something else.

"When I found you out there with Al in the dunes, and he was shooting at you, I'd never been more frightened. While I've been in the service, I've been shot at, stabbed and beaten up. Most of my bones have been broken fighting bad guys, and I can put up with more pain than most men. But none of that physical stuff could begin to be as agonizing as the thought that I might lose you."

Tears sprang to her eyes and her lips trembled. She knew that talking about his feelings was hard for him. But she also knew that regardless of how he felt now, Liam would always choose his work over a long-term commitment.

"I'm sorry I caused you such anguish," she said finally. "I didn't mean to, but…but I won't settle for a part-time romance, Liam. Even for you."

"Honey, that's what I'm trying to tell you. I've been thinking about setting up my own business, designing custom home and office security systems. I've talked to Mike and he's all for it. We're going to expand the TALON-6 Agency and open an office in Boston. He's asked me to run the new business." Liam beamed when he saw her surprise. "We can live in East Bennington, if you want. Or anywhere. That is, if you'll marry me."

She put a hand to her temple. "Liam, I'm astonished and overwhelmed. Yes, I love you, but we need to get to know each other. We can't rush into anything. Especially marriage."

"I've thought of that," he said, pulling out an envelope with an airline company logo on it. "Your semester is almost over. I thought that we could go away when school gets out. The two of us. I know you've always wanted to travel, and I want to show you the world, my darling.

"We'll start with England, visit the Lake District, leisurely tour the rural areas by motorized barge. Then across Europe to Luxembourg, Rome and—" he kissed the palm of her hand "—if you'll have me, we can be married in Paris."

Tears welled in her eyes and her lips parted. "Liam, I—I'm overwhelmed. I don't know what to say, except that I love you."

She leaned her head back and looked up at him, her heart bursting with happiness to think that he cared so very much for her. "I've already given my notice at the school. With the money my grandmother left me, I'd planned to take a year off from teaching." Her eyes widened. "Are you sure you'll be able to take the summer off?"

"Why not? It will take months to get our plans underway for the new agency. Clete and Mike can handle finding the right building and installing the equipment."

"Nothing would make me happier than seeing the world with you," she said dreamily. She peeked into the envelope and glanced at the airline tickets it held. "We leave in June," she cried excitedly. "That's not much time to get ready."

He pulled her to him, slid his arm around her waist. "All we need is each other." Bending down, he nuzzled her ear.

"Would you be disappointed if we waited until we came home to get married?"

"You're not backing out, are you?"

She blinked away tears of happiness. "Of course not. But what do you think about being married at your family cottage on Bellwood Island? I'll ask Jeremy to give me away, and we'll invite Maggie O'Reilly, and everyone from TALON-6—"

"Your future sisters-in-law will be in heaven," he said, laughing. "Are you sure that's what you want?"

Her heart overflowing, she laughed as she twined her fingers with his. "I've already got what I want."

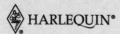
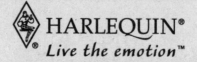

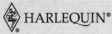

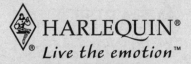

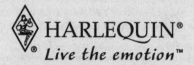

eHARLEQUIN.com

The Ultimate Destination for Women's Fiction

For **FREE online reading,** visit
www.eHarlequin.com now and enjoy:

Online Reads
Read **Daily** and **Weekly** chapters from
our Internet-exclusive stories by your
favorite authors.

Interactive Novels
Cast your vote to help decide how these
stories unfold...then stay tuned!

Quick Reads
For shorter romantic reads, try our
collection of Poems, Toasts, & More!

Online Read Library
Miss one of our online reads?
Come here to catch up!

Reading Groups
Discuss, share and rave with other
community members!

— For great reading online, —
visit www.eHarlequin.com today!

Receive a FREE hardcover book from

H A R L E Q U I N   R O M A N C E ®

in September!

**Harlequin Romance celebrates the launch of
the line's new cover design by offering you
this exclusive offer valid only in September,
only in Harlequin Romance.**

To receive your
FREE HARDCOVER BOOK
written by bestselling author
Emilie Richards, send us four
proofs of purchase from any
September 2004 Harlequin
Romance books. Further details
and proofs of purchase can be
found in all September 2004
Harlequin Romance books.

*Must be postmarked
no later than October 31.*

**Don't forget to be one of the first
to pick up a copy of the new-look
Harlequin Romance novels in September!**

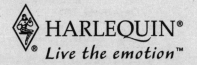

Visit us at www.eHarlequin.com

HRPOP0904

Like a phantom in the night comes
a new promotion from

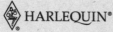
HARLEQUIN®

INTRIGUE®

ECLIPSE

GOTHIC ROMANCE

Beginning in August 2004, we offer you
a classic blend of chilling suspense and
electrifying romance, starting with....

A DANGEROUS INHERITANCE
LEONA KARR

And don't miss a spine-tingling Eclipse tale each month!

September 2004
MIDNIGHT ISLAND SANCTUARY
SUSAN PETERSON

October 2004
THE LEGACY OF CROFT CASTLE
JEAN BARRETT

November 2004
THE MAN FROM FALCON RIDGE
RITA HERRON

December 2004
EDEN'S SHADOW
JENNA RYAN

Available wherever Harlequin books are sold.
www.eHarlequin.com   HIECLIPSE